D0910666

Birthright

Also by Adenike B. Lucas

Vampire Whore

I Love Him, He Loves Me Not

Tales of Intrigue

Adenike B. Lucas

Birthright

ISBN 978-0-9895223-3-5

Printed in the United States of America

*All characters, events, most establishments, and organizations mentioned in this book are a complete work of fiction. Any similarities to any person either living or deceased are both coincidental and unintentional.

Cover Art Provided by:
Navi Robins
graphicdesigns@northshorepublish.net

Content Edited by:
Literati Media Group
LiteratiMediaGroup@gmail.com

Media Content Provided by:
Literati Media Group
LiteratiMediaGroup@gmail.com

With Love
to
My Children
(Unconditionally)

The womb of a woman is a living heart and a spiritual center. It is the gateway between two worlds and the only way to cross into this reality. The womb is a representation of unconditional, enduring, and sacrificial love. Within the womb's spiritual energy, generations of a people are created and given the knowledge of their ancestors.

... For my mother's mother who also carried me.

Birthright

Prologue – 1858

"Y'all takin' too long!"

Peeking out of the thin clothed, make-shift curtain hanging over the window, Bettye saw the ground and sky were covered in a thick blanket of darkness. The night, which usually showcased stars shining brightly, was void of its usual luminance. The hint of the tree-line that served as the property edge where they were going to run, was difficult to see from the window of the worn and weathered cabin known as home.

Bettye anxiously wrung her hands while pacing in front of the window. *I gotta stay patient... my sisters are moving as fast as they can. I'm sure we got enough time to be ready. I ain't seen the signal from the runners yet...* She stopped moving and looked back out the window. The silent lightening lit up the sky. Bettye's eyes widened as the flat land briefly came into view. Using the moment of visibility, she rapidly scanned the landscape for anyone or anything which could serve as a clue that the time had come.

The landscape went dark once again once the lightening finished darting across the sky. She turned her head back to the busy women in the cabin to address them. "How much longer y'all got before you gonna be ready? Time running out."

This was the night. The only night she could prepare the coven of women slaves for their journey up the banks of the James River to meet the rest of the runaways... She peeked out the window once more. No lightning... just the darkest of darkness. Then, she saw it! The start of their journey... The flicker of light at the wood's edge... One flicker... Then one more... That was the signal. Two flickers of candlelight near the wood's edge meant at long last, it was finally time to escape.

Bettye's body tensed with the excitement of flight. She put out the light of her lantern and placed it back on the table, then turned to gather her things. With her hands almost full, she was still able to reach around to grab the last madras clothed bundle of belongings and tie it securely to her back.

"What y'all doing back there that's taking so long!" Bettye whispered harshly emphasizing how dire it was to leave as soon as possible. "We have to go! We got to hurry!"

As the seconds passed narrowing their window of escape, the rumbling of thunder could be heard in the distance. The silent lightening pierced the sky once again making it eminent that a storm was surely on its way.

The group of women were getting close to being late to the meeting spot. If they waited too much longer to leave, they'd have to take their chances without their guide who'd signaled them from the woods. Bettye continued to speak in hushed but forceful tones expressing the urgency of the moment. It was her job to lead them to freedom and she took it seriously. But as much as the group wanted to follow their leader's orders, they couldn't leave just yet.

In the back room of the cramped cabin, the youngest in the group of fleeing women was in the process of giving birth. And even though they timed their escape from their plantation home, Glory Hill, to coincide with the baby's delivery, the child was coming early— too early. And the baby was coming fast. The impending labor put the women in a panic because while their youngest sister, Sunta, was struggling to give birth to her child, she was also at death's door.

Sunta's journey was not supposed to end this way. Being pregnant and escaping from their oppressive master was willed by their ancestors. During the months of planning their leave, they paid tribute to the ones that came before them to assure a blessed voyage. The gifts given to the ancestors allowed the sisters to peer into their future and see that they were all going to walk into their freedom together with the baby in tow. However, the ancestors did not foretell of the events now taking place. It surprised them to see their sister writhing on the ground in pain— ready to bring life into this world, but also about to leave it through death. The ancestors did not speak on what was now the sister's reality, so Bettye and her sisters stood watching wrought with worry as they were now in uncharted territory.

"We can't leave right now Bettye! The babe is coming and Sunta is passing right before our eyes!" Lily said, as she sat at Sunta's belly. She placed one hand on the top of it stroking its crescent soothingly.

Sunta let out a weary moan and without hesitation, Jendi put her bags down, grabbed some loose cloths, and proceeded to dunk them in a bowl full of water. She placed them on Sunta's forehead to cool her off.

"She leaving us Bettye. We can't stop it and dis here baby is coming now." Jendi said as Bettye looked at her little sister writhing on the floor in agony.

Sunta's tears streamed down her face while holding back her screams from every contraction. Sweating profusely, her body glistened in the hot and stuffy cabin. Bettye saw the fear and worry in all their eyes, but she also saw their determination to help Sunta give birth to the only child she'd ever have.

Bettye took compassion on their concern and put her travelling sacks down, refocusing her energy on helping her sister like she'd always done. She kneeled down by her dying, younger sister. Sunta grabbed Bettye's hand to brace herself as another agonizing contraction hit her in the back just as the thunder cracked in the sky. They all jumped from the sounds of the weather. They looked towards the sky in bewilderment and fear, knowing nature was ringing the alarm that their ancestors were coming for either Sunta or the baby.

Sunta slowly opened her eyes in relief, grateful that the pain from the contraction had dulled. She turned her head and looked at Bettye as distress began to cloud her vision and thoughts. Bettye gave her a reassuring wink and a smile, stroked her hair, and then placed a soft kiss on her cheek before whispering, "It's going to be alright. Save your strength to bring this baby into this world."

Bettye rose from her spot beside Sunta and stepped back to be with her other sisters. She grabbed Jendi's hand; giving her the look that it was time to form The Circle. Jendi didn't say a word but knew what she had to do. She grabbed the sister's hand beside hers and the sister beside her grabbed the hand of the sister beside her. Eventually all six pairs of hands were joined together forming The Circle around the dying and the living.

One by one, the tears rolled down Bettye's cheeks as she spoke. "We can't save you little sister 'cause your soul is almost on the other side. But we can save your babe, and he'll be safe with us to grow and to learn just as we were taught."

"It's a boy, Bettye?"

"Yes, Sunta. I saw him crawling around in my dreams the other night with the eyes as blue as the sky. I was going to keep it to myself and let you be surprised, but I think he came to me just for this purpose." Bettye choked on her last words trying to be brave.

"Please tell him I love him." Sunta began crying uncontrollable tears knowing how hard it had to be for Bettye to watch her die. She and all the sisters knew Sunta had grown to be Bettye's heart and soul.

The lightening was no longer silent and finally cracked as the thunder also bellowed making the ground tremble in fear. Sunta felt the room getting cold as she began to hear whispers of her ancestor's voices filling the space in the small cabin.

Bettye looked out the back window to the grand old willow tree sitting by the lake. There, she saw the fog start to gather at its roots and the faint misty glow of a woman's figure slowly began to appear.

"The gateway is open for our sister's soul to walk through," Bettye said solemnly to the others.

"Bettye I'm scared to do this— The Chant. We never tried this on no one! We only seen mama and the others do it once. What if we do this wrong?"

"We can't worry about this now, Mary. We got to do everything we can to save the baby or Sunta… or both!" Bettye rolled her head back as the others reluctantly started a low hum.

"I trust y'all, Mary. It's going to be just fine. Y'all not going to fail me. They not here for him. I can hear their sweet voices singing low in my ear. They coming for me. Just make sure you take my baby with you and I'll wait for him on the other side." Sunta leaned her head back in preparedness and let the women begin the Chant of Forever.

"Ori mo pe o. O ṣeun fun igbesi aye yii. Jẹ ki ẹmi naa duro. Arabinrin baba wa yoo si. Ọkàn rẹ yoo duro.." As Bettye began, another sister repeated the words. Then another, until they all spoke their native tongue with powerful repetition.

As the chant continued, the wind began to pick up, rattling windows on the cabin. Again, the lightning cracked the sky, brightening up the room in flashes as the women began casting their enchantment in succinct rhythm. Their words filled Sunta and allowed her aura to shine through and protect her as she labored. Bettye carefully let go of her sister's hands, breaking the circle, and made her way to the young girl. Mary and Jendi locked hands where Bettye had separated from them, closing the empty space.

Bettye looked between her sister's gaping legs seeing that she'd begun to crown. Sunta let out a horrific scream as she instinctively began to push the baby out of her. Bettye kneeled at her sister's legs as the room full of women took their chant to a low hum.

"Sister, your baby is here. Once I pull him out, you gonna be gone."

"No Bettye. I changed my mind. I can't leave. He needs me… I'm scared."

"Look at me in my eyes Sunta."

Their eyes met before she continued.

"Never mind that talk. You have a job to do right now. This last push is going to take a lot of strength and power from you, so when I say push, you push, and I'll grab him."

The young girl shook her head "no" once again but with a different type of purpose. "Nah-ah. I can't let you take him. I'mma take him out of me by myself. I want to be the first to touch 'em. It'll be the only time I see him… feel him."

"I can see you are determined, and I understand." Bettye took her hands and guided Sunta's to the place where the baby would come.

"Get ready to push gal. Grab him when you feel his head touch your finger-tips."

Sunta shook her head "yes" smiling gratefully as she prepared to deliver her son.

"Now don't you worry none 'bout passing before seeing him. Our circle gonna make sure you stay with us long enough for you to look at him one good time."

Bettye gave her a kiss on the forehead. "We love you Sunta, and we are going to take good care of him." Bettye looked out the window once more at the old willow tree where she could see two more wispy and transparent figures standing stoically and patient. *The ancestors are waiting.*

The sharpest pain she'd ever felt hit Sunta and she arched her back as the sky opened up; pouring out buckets of water. The time had come for her to finally deliver her baby. Sunta braced her body and let out a scream that she could no longer hold. She pushed as hard as she could, allowing her baby to slowly slide from her birth canal. She felt her son leave her body and slide into her hands positioned between her legs. Once she felt his head on her finger tips, she gripped him and pulled him all the way out.

"He's here! He's finally here!" Out of breath, Sunta whispered her words of love, joy, and promise into his ear as she pulled him close for his first and final embrace.

Knowing Sunta was too weak to force the afterbirth out, Bettye pushed down on Sunta's stomach until it was delivered.

Unfortunately, as the placenta finally made its way out, the ending of Sunta's life began.

"Sister you are bleeding everywhere!" Bettye said as the circle of women began to disband. The loving sisters sniffled, and tears fell as the women knew it was the final time they would see her.

"It's almost time for you to meet the angels." Bettye said meekly.

She and the others had never seen life and death in the same moment. They were startled at all the blood and fluid seeping out of one person.

Sunta held her son close to her knowing it was only for a brief moment. Neither the pain of birth, blood loss, death, nor the fear of getting caught escaping was bigger than the moment of being with her first born child. It all didn't matter to her.

"He's so beautiful..." Her voice trailed as she began to slip into unconsciousness.

As suddenly as the rain came, it abruptly stopped; leaving the steam from the hot summer night to rise from the ground as the sound of thunder continued to roll in the distance.

"Bettye... gotta hurry. They'll be leaving for sure soon... we ain't got that much time left..." Alice said.

"Y'all gather your things and let's go." Bettye looked out the window at the old tree, but the ancestors were not there as they were before.

Mary tugged at Bettye's arm. "Come on, Sis. We gotta go. Sunta will be alright. We got to leave now or it's never." Mary kneeled down and kissed Sunta on the forehead. "We are going to take good care of him for you."

She wiped the tears from her face she struggled not to shed as she quickly left the cabin. With a heavy heart, Bettye nodded in agreement with Mary. Keeping a watchful eye for any hunters, she watched the sisters leave the cabin one-by-one.

Being the last to leave, Bettye looked down at Sunta one last time. Sunta's eyes slowly fluttered open and she looked up at Bettye from the splintered and dusty wooden floor.

"We gotta go babe. The worst is over now." Bettye smiled at Sunta; proud of her for the hard work she'd done delivering her babe. She reached in the basin Alice had prepared with warm water and pulled out the knife. Bettye cut the umbilical cord disconnecting the last tie that bound Sunta with her son. She then bent over and took the baby from the dying mother's arms and wrapped him in the old sheet filled with Sunta's natural fragrance from her pallet.

Near the brink of death, she breathlessly spoke. "He so beautiful... I named him... Elijah."

"That's a beautiful name, sis. You just rest now and wait for yo time." Bettye stood from the floor to leave the little cabin one more time.

"Look at his eyes Bettye... You was right... they so blue..." Then Sunta closed hers once more, as the last of her soul left her body. Closing the cabin's door tight, Bettye caught a glimpse of Sunta's spirit slowly running towards the old great willow tree.

Chapter 1
The Present

Medallion saw Waymen as he entered Jasper's, their favorite dining spot. *Eight on the dot. As usual, he's never late,* Medallion thought to herself as she saw him greet the Maître D'. She eyed him coolly as he was escorted to the secluded table-for-two tucked away in the corner of the dining room.

Jasper's, an urban upscale restaurant that doubled as a night club, was the only place in town playing live fusion Jazz every night of the week; making it the place to be for trendy urbanites. The dining area of Jasper's gave the place a cozy, romantic feeling and the most scenic area in the dining room was a quaint 2-person table in front of the beautiful multicolored, stone fireplace. Medallion loved sitting at that table as it was the room's focal point. All eyes naturally ended up on the fireplace which meant all eyes were on her as well, and she liked it that way..

Tonight, however, was a bit different. Unlike all the other times they visited "Jasper's", the evening would be about her. This time she was setting the stage for Waymen to be the star. Tonight was his night. There was no reason to show off for anyone by sitting at the table in front of the fireplace. Medallion knew she had to humble herself and beg at his heels of mercy for once. She needed him to know she was serious this time. She was ready to change and be the obliging wife he wanted her to be. She'd played around with his heart and emotions for much too long, and tonight she was ready to turn it all around.

"Hello Waymen." She stood to meet her husband and greet him with a warm supple kiss, but Waymen intentionally shifted his face to miss the ritual lip lock greeting by hastily sitting down in the seat across from her.

"Hello Medda."

Waymen didn't look at her even though he desperately wanted to. He couldn't risk seeing his wife's gorgeous face and becoming undone by her beautifully rounded eyes. One flutter of her long lashes would have made his heart skip a beat causing him to lose the stern decorum he wanted to convey. His only weapon against her was to not let her get too close emotionally or physically. He was madly in love with Medallion and she knew it, and past encounters like this proved his weapons to survive her tender traps left him looking like the biggest fool.

Waymen picked up his menu and placed it in front of him pretending to peruse the evening specials. He graciously took that moment to regroup and regain his composure before the conversation began.

"Have you ordered yet?" He said with as little emotion as he could.

Medallion was a bit taken by Waymen's greeting. This attitude was new for him. He'd never been so dismissive. She fumbled to pick up her menu and follow his lead; as she didn't know what to do next. The welcoming kiss she wanted to plant on his lips was her opening to soften him up, but he wasn't having it.

"No, I haven't decided yet. I was waiting for you to get here… Maybe we can share a meal?" Medallion looked from her menu to gauge his response. Unfortunately, he continued to stay barricaded behind his. *What's wrong with him? Why isn't he biting tonight?* Medallion was close to dismay trying to figure out how to get him hooked on what she was about to tell him.

"No, I don't think we should share a meal tonight." Waymen signaled the waiter who came over right away.

"Good evening sir, may I take your order?" The waiter pulled a pen and pad out of his starch white apron in preparation.

"Yes, I'll take the Chef's Choice with a cognac, and for my wife, she'll have the salmon with the harvest salad and a glass of ice water." He closed the menu and handed it to the waiter as Medallion looked on with amazement. Waymen had never ordered for her… in fact, he'd never ordered for himself. She was always the one who ordered for the both of them. *So, I guess it's going to be harder than I thought…* She gave the waiter a closed-lipped smile as she handed him her menu. As she did, she felt Waymen finally looking her way. *Alright… I guess I'm on. Here goes nothing…*

"It's good to see you Waymen. It's been a long time. You look well." She smiled at him, but he didn't return the courtesy.

"Thanks." Waymen wanted to pour his heart out and tell Medallion how much he missed her and whatever she had to say, was moot. He just wanted her to be his again. But he just said, 'thanks' and "So why are we here?" He looked at his watch impatiently— not really needing to be anywhere else but trying to insinuate his time was precious and she was wasting it. He was trying his best to keep the upper hand in hopes she was buying into his act.

"Well… Waymen… I know I messed up bad this last time. I keep playing these games with you and I can tell you are tired of them, but Waymen… I'm sorry. I'm sorry I hurt you again. I'm sorry I've put our marriage in danger, and I'm sorry that this wasn't the first time. Waymen, I want you to come home. I know now I can't live without you. It's over between Rodney and me. Can you find it in your heart to take me back?"

Waymen began to sweat. He wasn't expecting her to roll out the red carpet of apologies. He realized how serious she was this time… the corner booth instead of the table in front of the fireplace… the sincere apology… maybe she was ready to be the wife he needed. Still, he wasn't going to give in that easy. He still needed more assurance that this time was true.

The waiter came back with a basket full of a variety of bread and an order of drinks for the table. Waymen took a sip of his cognac and placed it on the table before he responded.

"Medallion, you went too far this time. Everyone saw you with him. You two were out in the open with your affair, carrying on in public like it was normal behavior. I'm out with my fellas, and I see you and him at the pool hall. You bent over the damn pool table and him so-called helping you with your shot!"

The image of his wife flirtatiously handling the pool stick as she let her fingers suggestively slide up and down its shaft popped into Waymen's head when the name "Rodney" was uttered from her lips. His blood was on fire inside of him as he looked at his seemingly remorseful wife sitting across the table.

The night he saw them together at the pool hall, the world around him had stopped. He didn't know how to react. Initially he wanted to crumple up and run the other way, but his friends were there seeing exactly what he was seeing. He couldn't run. He had to handle the situation or face looking like a punk in front of the crew. He would have been the laughing stalk amongst their ranks forever if he skulked away.

"Waymen, I know! It was wrong of me to have even been there with him. I knew it was a chance that you would come there with your fellas. I mean… it's not like I didn't know that's the pool hall you go to. It was a lack of judgment on my part. And then… to have Rodney incite a brawl between you, him, and all of your friends was all my doing. I take full blame for it all."

"As you should!" Waymen retorted.

He glared at her as he spoke. After three unbearable months, the wound she inflicted on his heart was still open, and just as much as he was in love with her, he was that much angrier at what she'd done to him. But through it all he still wanted her… His prize… His golden Medallion. He loved her that much.

Their dinner arrived at the table before Waymen could continue. He wanted to rub her nose in his humiliation from that night in the pool hall, but by the way she was tearing up, he thought his tone may have been too harsh. His stance on being unyielding began to soften as they sat in the corner at the table-for-two at "Jasper's". It now felt wrong to continue to hurt the woman he loved like she'd hurt him. The waiter walked away and they ate in silence;

both feeling uncomfortable and not knowing where the other stood with healing their marriage.

Minutes that felt like hours rolled by until Medallion put her fork down and dabbed the corners of her mouth before she said with little fanfare, "Waymen… I'm pregnant."

The fork with a piece of Waymen's steak was headed to his mouth when Medallion blurted out her news. In shock, he dropped his fork against his plate which clanged and clattered loudly; catching the attention of the diners that sat close to their table. Embarrassed by his fumble, Waymen cleared his throat to simmer his brewing excitement before he spoke. "Medda, what are you saying?"

Medallion shifted in her seat trying to find the best words to break the whole story of her baby's conception to her husband.

"Well… I went to the doctor's the other day because I've been sick… you know like throwing up… cramping… exhaustion, and the doctor told me I am pregnant. Waymen… we can't go on fighting like this. My baby… our baby can't be raised between two households."

"What do you mean our baby? Weren't you sleeping with that guy? It's no doubt he's the baby's father." Waymen folded his arms in a huff; turning to look at the wall beside their table in disgust.

"Waymen, I'm about two months pregnant." Medallion paused allowing the math of conception to sink in for him.

"Remember that night when you came to pick up some more of your things? Remember what we did in the kitchen?" Medallion blushed as she thought back to that steamy night in their home.

The night in question, Waymen had come to pick up some files for his job he'd left in their library. She was cooking dinner when he used his key to let himself in. He thought she wasn't home. He stood in the frame of the kitchen door watching her tush wiggle as she whisked the creamy mixture in her bowl. She lifted her foot and scratched the back of the opposite leg with her big toe. An endearing moment for him to watch. It was a rare occasion to see her in the kitchen doing anything other than grabbing snacks, so Waymen watched her mixing and savored the moment. With a sly smile he pulled out his cell phone and turned the surround sound on in the condo which was connected to his phone's Bluetooth. The opening chords of Luther Vandross' classic, "A House is Not A Home" filled the room startling Medallion; almost making her spill the bowl's contents.

"Oh my gosh, Waymen! Are you trying to give me a heart attack?!" She rolled her eyes at his playful ways and put the bowl on the counter in a huff. "What do you want? Why are you here?" Medallion tossed the whisk into the sink. As she walked past Waymen, he grabbed her arm and pulled her into him.

"You first. Tell me why you're here. You are usually at aerobics this time of night."

He allowed his eyes to roam over his wife's bosom as it bubbled over her snuggly fitted black sports bra. He breathed in deep and slowly released the inhaled air as he lustfully reached to grab a hand full of her jiggly breast. He then licked his lips with want as her skin felt meltingly soft in his grasp.

Medallion felt the warmth of his breath as they stood so very close together. It'd been a long time since she'd been so close to him, but she knew where the encounter was headed. "I um... skipped class." She let the tips of her fingers drag down the side of his fitted jeans as she felt his soft lips lightly kiss the part of her neck underneath her ear. "I... didn't feel like driving to the East End for Zumba tonight." Luther continued to belt out his classic ballad. Waymen began to sway them both to the melodic rhythm.

He untied Medallion's messy top bun releasing her hair which cascaded down her back. He put his fingers into her soft loose coils finding his way to her scalp to massage it.

She began to melt into the palm of his hand that felt its way around her head. Her eyes rolled in ecstasy. Waymen's strong but tender grip bending her to his will... He grabbed Medallion around her waist pulling her in closer and then allowed his other hand to drift slowly down her backside. He grabbed a chunk of her ass; squeezing it like a squishy toy.

She felt the stiffness of his arousal. *I miss this...* His girth always fit her just right. She wanted to give in at that very moment but she'd rather see how much he wanted her. She pulled herself away from his advances and returned to the sink to continue cooking as if the moment never happened.

Waymen stood in silence as she left him standing in the middle of the kitchen yearning for her body. "Are you serious?"

"As a heart attack. You can't just come back in here and start pulling on me like we happily married. Like we are not in the middle of a huge fight. Like you didn't move out months ago 'cause— like you said— 'You tired of me and my shit'. You can't act like you didn't hurt my feelings."

She poured her mixture into a pan and heated the oven. Waymen walked over to her and kissed the top of her shoulder.

"Baby, you know I was wrong for that. For better or for worse. That's what we said right?"

Luther's ballad, "Superstar" belted out the first line of his epic plea reiterating Waymen's point. He fused their lips together and inserted his tongue into her mouth just as Luther serenaded, "Baby, baby, baby, baby, oh, baby, I love you, I really do..."

A tingle went down Medallion's spine triggering the attention of her nipples. This time she pressed into her husband, her tongue interacting with his. She kissed him long before she pulled away.

With desperation, she allowed her heart to speak her mind. "Waymen... I've missed you so much. I've been in our home all alone. No call. No text."

"I'm sorry." He kissed her again. "You just make it so difficult sometimes." He kissed her again. "But I should know better than to leave you."

Medallion eagerly nodded her head in agreement. They kissed once more before he pulled the waist of her panties away from her flat stomach to allow his fingers to slip between the softest parts of her well-toned body.

Medallion leaned back on the counter and parted her legs enough for Waymen to touch her. His fingers danced over and around her clitoris which became erect with every little flick from his fingertips.

She closed her eyes and moaned while she focused on the attention he gave her. His fingers now slippery from darting in and out of her wet pussy, he dragged them out of her and placed them in her mouth. Medallion closed her lips around them seductively; flitting and darting her tongue around the two fingers that were just inside of her.

Waymen's knees buckled feeling Medallion's tongue dance and flip on his fingers as he imagined how well she'd perform on his dick. No longer wanting to be teased, he unbuckled his pants and shoved them and his boxers down his legs. He then released Medallion's hold on his fingers to use both hands to relieve her of her cheeky boyshort lace panties. Medallion flipped her sports bra over her head and threw it out of the kitchen, and before she could do anything else, Waymen scooped her up and flipped her upside down. Medallion locked her legs around his neck and attached her mouth to his erect penis while he in turn began sucking her clit.

What felt like eternity in ecstasy, Waymen could no longer stand while Medallion performed her greatest sexual act. She'd slowly taken him all in while fondling his scrotum with one hand and massaging his leg with the other. He could hear her slurping as she slobbed him down making her mouth match the wetness from her vagina he so happily licked and nibbled. Medallion began to wiggle and squirm as he knew she was close to climaxing making it difficult for them to sustain the contorted position. The Luther playlist switched to the classic, "If Only For One Night".

Waymen slowly backed himself up to the refrigerator and slid down the face of it and lay flat on the floor as Medallion straightened up while staying planted on his face. "Waymen... ummmmm I missed this..." She rotated her hips in beat with Luther's band while he continued to please her. "Babe... You hitting the spot... I'm about to cum."

Waymen felt the ripeness of her clitoris signaling how close he was to her climax. He reached around the front of her thigh and rammed his finger into her vaginal opening. Medallion's body began to tremble. "BABE!" She screamed in her highest pitched voice while she exploded all over his face. He felt the flood of her warm orgasm enter his mouth and trickle down his throat.

Not being able to wait any longer, he flipped his wife over, hoisting her rounded derriere into the air and shoving his bulging penis into the place his fingers once were. With both hands gripping her hips, his thrusts reminded Medallion how strong of a man he was. She turned her head to look back at him. She saw the intensity in his eyes. He was ready. She licked her full supple lips and mouthed, "I love you..." sending him into full blast. He pumped her faster and harder. She felt his penis become engorged with each thrust. Waymen clenched his teeth trying to hold in the yell he'd been restraining but it escaped at the moment his orgasm began to spill inside of her.

In exhaustion, Waymen collapsed on Medallion and they laid on the tiled floor both sweaty and satisfied. He kissed the back of her shoulder. "I almost forgot how bendy you are."

"It's the yoga." They both laughed. Waymen squeezed her shoulder once again before rolling her over to bask in their love.

The moment they shared that night was still vivid to her. Medallion shook the memory of that unforgettable moment of love-making out of her head, but the coy smile that crept onto her face told the tale for the both of them.

Waymen also cracked a slight smile as he recalled the steamy encounter. "I do remember."

He stuck his finger down the collar of his shirt to loosen it and let out some of the built-up steam. The sex that night was too hot in the kitchen. After a blissful moment of love-making, he was all ready to throw in the towel about their stand-off and move his things back right then. But after they were done with their romp, he saw the text come through from Rodney saying he was running a little late and would be over in another hour. The message sent him storming out the condo promising to never return.

"Well, I got pregnant that night. I calculated." Avoiding his gaze, Medallion took a sip of her water and went back to eating her salmon. *Oh God... why is telling him this so hard?*

Waymen looked on while she shoveled the food into her mouth while not looking up. He cracked a little smile. Medallion always ate faster when she was nervous. It was so funny to watch her squirm uncomfortably when awaiting her sentence, but the thought of being a father made him realize he wanted that more than being mad at her. He let out a joyous little laugh and she looked up from her plate and straight into his eyes. *Yes! He's mine!* Medallion smiled back and slowly put down her fork. He grabbed her hands from across the table, and the look of adoration for his beautiful wife had returned.

"So you're saying I'm going to be a dad?" He needed her to absolutely confirm what he'd heard before he could finally let the past go.

"Yeah Waymen. I think you're going to be a dad." Medallion smiled from ear to ear as she looked at him fill with pride over his new family member.

Chapter 2

By the end of dinner, it was decided he would move back in the next morning. Waymen escorted Medallion to her car and watched as she drove away before he got in his and drove off as well, but Medallion had another date. In less than ten minutes, Rodney would be pulling up at the restaurant she'd just left. They had a lot to discuss.

Medallion rounded her dark blue Tesla around the block and stopped at its corner just in time to see Waymen drive by and Rodney walking up from across the street. Medallion pulled back into the parking lot of "Jaspers" and met Rodney at the door.

"Ummm…" Rodney sized her up as she breezed through the restaurant's door. Her legs were long, and her stilettos made her as tall as a skyscraper. Rodney loved how she slowly sashayed past him as he held the door open for her. He slyly smiled at her as she planted a juicy lipstick kiss on his lips once they were in the restaurant's foyer.

"As usual, you just took my breath away." He put his hands around her waist grazing her more than usual pronounced stomach. He scrunched his face slightly as he touched her pudge— taken aback by the weight she'd put on.

"Feels like you need to order the salad tonight." Rodney patted Medallion's belly and followed the Maître D to their table in front of the magnificent fireplace.

Self-consciously, Medallion placed her crystal-studded clutch in front of her noticeable baby bump and followed her date. Rodney took his place at the table and waited for her to take a seat.

"Thank you for meeting me here, Rodney."

"No problem at all. When you said you'd pay, I knew I couldn't turn down a good meal." He opened the menu to look for the most expensive entree to order.

Medallion didn't know what attracted her to Rodney other than the fact that he was a very handsome man with a nice thick full beard and amazing in bed. Compared to her husband, Rodney had no redeeming qualities. She sucked her teeth at his comment. *Why did I even waste my time with him? Glad it's about to be over though. I should have never put him before Waymen.*

"Well… I brought you here because I have something to tell you."

Medallion didn't touch her menu since she was full from the dinner she'd just had with Waymen. *I should have told him to meet me at the bar across the street instead of here. Hell, he's not even worth the food I'm about to pay for.*

"Well, can it wait? I'm hungry. I think I'll have the Captain's Feast. It's lobster and steak tonight." Rodney continued to browse the menu looking for something else he could order.

"No, it can't wait. I have something important to tell you, and I have to tell you now." She became agitated by their exchange and wanted it all to be over with. She snatched the menu from Rodney's hand catching his attention.

He stared at her astonished by her actions. "Well what is it woman? You're ruining our night out."

"I'm pregnant." Medallion stated with no emotion or fanfare. They then both sat silent. Both waiting for the other to speak.

Rodney swallowed hard and took a sip of his glass of water. The news of her pregnancy was not a shock, but also not welcoming.

They were having frequent, careless rendezvous, but he didn't want children. The responsibility of it all was more than he wanted from life. Having fun with an attractive woman and hanging out with his friends was what he cared about most.

A child was just not in his cards. But he didn't want to seem callous. His mother always told him a woman with child was by far the most emotional creature on the earth. He wasn't in the mood to deal with Medallion's feelings about her getting knocked up.

"That's good news for you Medallion. I'm assuming your telling me this because you think I'm the father."

"Yes, I think you are the father! We have been intimate on several different occasions without protection! Why wouldn't you assume I thought you were the father?!" Medallion couldn't believe the audacity of Rodney. Besides her husband, he was the only other person she was seeing. "And I'm going back to my husband."

"Your husband?! But you're carrying my baby!"

Rodney wasn't enthused about impending parenthood, but the thought of him losing Medallion to a weak-minded man like Waymen was not something he anticipated. Waymen wasn't strong enough for her by his standards. He'd won Medallion fair and square, and he was not going to let her go that easily.

Medallion shifted her eye's glance away from Rodney as he balked at the thought of someone else raising his child. "Well... that's not entirely true. The baby might be yours. Did you forget that night you showed up at my house and Waymen had already been there? I think I got pregnant around that time."

Rodney's jaw dropped. He assumed Waymen had only come over to pick up a few things from their home. When he saw Waymen leaving in a fit of rage, Rodney thought it was because of their rivalry. He never imagined that she had just had sex with him. If he knew they'd been together that night, he may have reconsidered their plans.

"You mean to tell me, you've been two-timing me with your husband, and now you're pregnant with either one of our child? Medallion… you have taken this situation to a new low."

"Me?!" Medallion couldn't believe she was being chastised by a man she knew had less morals than a slug. "This coming from a man who intentionally showed up at spots my husband hung out at so you could rub it in his face that you were sleeping with his wife!"

She got up from her seat and headed towards the door with Rodney following close behind.

"You are a treacherous woman, and you are going to pay for who you are."

Medallion pushed through the front door of "Jasper's" and hurried to get back to her car not wanting to hear anything else Rodney had to say.

"It's over between us, Rodney. I'm going back to my husband who has already forgiven me for everything… even messing around with you." She looked him up and down in disgust. With her keyless remote, she started the engine to her car and then got in her ride. "My husband has welcomed our child so you don't need to worry about being a father." She closed the car's door and drove away leaving Rodney in the parking lot and finally in her past.

Chapter 3

Medallion pulled up to her Aunt Mary's humble home on the Southside of Richmond. The turn of the fall season was in play and had already begun to change the leaves of the oak tree sitting in the front yard shades of dark red and light yellow. In the fall months, Medallion liked to take a pause before getting out of her car to admire her Aunt's quaint little home. With the tree's leaves falling delicately to the ground and the cottage's perfectly painted yellow door to accent the flowers that bloomed in the spring, it always looked picturesque around that time of year.

From the looks of the tiny and humble brick cottage, no one could fathom the expanse of Aunt Mary's wealth. Her claim to her riches had always been a mystery to Medallion and others close to the illustrious aunt, but she never flaunted her money; only saving and investing it to keep her entire family comfortable. Mary required very little to live. Being frugal showed in her day-to-day life. However, Mary spared no expense on restoring the family home. The grand plantation named Glory Hill was a piece of history Aunt Mary bought back in the 1940's.

Growing up, Medallion always knew the history of where her people were enslaved. On a tobacco growing plantation two hours outside of Richmond, generations of her family worked the land with their blood sweat and tears. Rather than call her ancestors slaves, Aunt Mary taught her the Yoruba term Egungun. A word that was passed to her by her mother meaning the collection of ancestors. For Mary and for Medallion, the title fit better than the word slaves because before America, Africans were healers, priests, tribal leaders, great mothers of the village, and had families that loved them. Once slavery was considered over, Glory Hill was eventually abandoned and stood in ruins until Aunt Mary finally got enough money to buy and restore it.

For many reasons unbeknownst to Medallion, Aunt Mary loved that home. She felt it was only right that it should stay in the family since her ancestors were the ones who maintained it and made it profitable. When Medallion was younger, Aunt Mary would take her to the plantation, and they would spend a week or two cleaning it and adding little touches here and there.

Medallion had asked Aunt Mary why she would never live there like a queen in a castle, and Aunt Mary would only reply, that Glory Hill was an alter and an offering to the ones before her.

"Medallion… people like us aren't seen as kings and queens in this land. Our mansions from where we come are vast and much grander than what you know. This land, our ancestors worked, was not for us but for them to feel like royalty because they weren't. When our people were stolen from our land, Egungun were stripped of their nobility… made to sacrifice who they were to build up this land which was also stolen from the indigenous people. As much as the ancestors hated it, they worked it for many years so that they could survive the wrath of the pilferers and so that you could exist today. I bought this land that Glory Hill stands on back for the ancestors. I restored this home to show their sacrifice was not in vain. I don't live in it because it didn't belong to them then, so it does not belong to me."

Medallion accepted that answer long ago and has never questioned Aunt Mary about it since.

Medallion approached the cottage and used her key to open her aunt's front door. Aunt Mary was an older woman but still had a lot of energy to get around. There was never a dull moment with her, but she had a big fear of dying alone in her home and no one to find her. When Medallion was old enough, Aunt Mary appointed her guardianship, and with that, came a key to her charming abode.

"Coming in, Aunt Mary!"

Medallion never knocked when she came to visit. She only announced her arrival as to not startle her aunt if she were resting. Aunt Mary didn't respond with her cheerful 'Come on in girl! I'm in the kitchen!' or 'Come on in! You're just in time to watch these crazy housewives fighting on this tv', so Medallion let herself in and headed for the fridge to get a bite to eat. The baby inside of her was tugging on her umbilical cord demanding nourishment.

Closing the refrigerator, Medallion spotted Aunt Mary through the patio doors in her garden gathering herbs. *Auntie must have an order…* Medallion took a big bite of a cold piece of fried chicken she'd put on her plate along with a few side entrees and made her way outside.

"Hey Auntie. You don't mind that I made me something to eat do you?" She sat down at the patio table to finish eating while she watched her aunt work.

"Well hey baby girl. Nah… go on and enjoy yourself. You know I can't eat all that food by myself. I don't know why I even cook that much."

Aunt Mary was on her hands and knees yanking out weeds and clipping off the leaves and cloves she needed. She then put them in her basket. Medallion noticed her aunt's feet were bare and muddy. She would have complained to her that the fall air was too brisk for her to be barefoot in the garden, but she knew grounding, her ritual of connecting with nature to reenergize her spirit was an important practice to her aunt, leaving no reason to utter any discontent.

"What brings you by today, Suga? I wasn't expecting you for another couple of days."

Aunt Mary looked up from her work to examine her niece. She could tell Medallion was physically okay, but there was something underneath her cool demeanor that was bothering her favorite loved one.

Medallion finished up the rest of the chicken, potato salad, and the slice of pound cake. Devouring food had become a norm for her since she'd gotten pregnant. She took a gulp of her sweet tea and then patted her belly; satisfied she'd fulfilled the child's request.

"Auntie, I'm just feeling a little down. I think Waymen is still mad at me or something. He said he forgives me for sleeping with Rodney, and that he wants to help me raise this baby, but I think he's changing his mind. He's been acting funny." Medallion put her head in the palm of her hand as she leaned with her elbow on the patio table.

Aunt Mary was very aware of all of her dear niece's marital problems which stemmed from her bad behavior, and she chastised Medallion for all the wrong she'd created in regards to it. Aunt Mary didn't condone Medallion's actions, but she was not going to stop loving her because of it. The best Aunt Mary could do was advise her through her transgressions so she could become a better woman and wife to her husband.

She pulled up a seat at the table beside her niece after she finished tasking in her garden.

"Baby, it's only been three months since you announced the news of the baby and got back with your husband. It's going to take some time for him to warm back up to all of this."

"I know Auntie, but I just feel he's taking too long! It's not like he didn't know what he was getting into when he said 'yes' to raising this baby and coming back home. I'm five months pregnant now. He needs to let go of all that anger and resentment and be the man that I need him to be because this baby will be here in no time."

Medallion folded her arms in a huff as she thought about how distant Waymen had become after he moved back in. Once, she'd caught him staring at her judgmentally as she stepped out of the shower with her belly pronounced and all aglow. She quickly grabbed her towel to shield herself from his opinionated glare, and then picked a fight with him for looking at her in such a way.

Aunt Mary leaned her niece's head onto her shoulder and soothingly patted her up.

"Don't be so hard on him, girl. He's a man who just went through a lot because of you. Yes, he's probably second guessing his steps, but I'm sure he'll come around fully to being your husband again and a father to that beautiful baby you are going to birth."

Medallion put her arm around her aunt and gave her a squeeze. She lifted her head from Aunt Mary's shoulder and got up to stretch her legs.

"I know you think he's going to stay, but Auntie… I'm not too sure. This time feels so different. I feel like he's testing me, and watching me, and waiting for me to mess up so he can leave me again. He can't leave me, Auntie. I gave up Rodney for him."

Aunt Mary rolled her eyes and sucked her teeth at the thought of Medallion being with Rodney and the baby possibly being his.

"How could you even compare Waymen to Rodney? That no-account, no-good, little hooligan is a terrible man! You are lucky to have even gotten Waymen back considering how you treated him."

Aunt Mary removed herself from her chair and went back to her gardening; getting her second wind from such a ridiculous retort from her niece.

"But Aunt Mary! Waymen doesn't love me! I can tell!" Medallion followed her aunt back to the spot in the little garden and began helping pull weeds. "I gotta do something to make him see that he needs us as much as we need him."

Aunt Mary paused her work and looked at her niece in amazement. "Listen to you! There you go again playing with that man's heart!"

"What?" Medallion faked innocence because she knew her aunt saw her intentions before she could even confess them.

"Whatever you got planned, you better unplan it! You promised Waymen you were finished playing games! Be the wife he needs you to be and stop being a spoiled little girl!"

Aunt Mary snatched up her herb basket, marched passed Medallion, and back into the kitchen. Medallion followed never giving up the thought that she had to devise a plan.

Back in the cottage, she sat at the counter and watched her aunt busy herself with grinding up the newly cut plants. She began heating up a pot of water and adding spices and roots… the beginning stages of some concoction to help a poor woman in desperate need. Medallion eyed the pot suspiciously as it began to give her a few ideas.

"Auntie, I thought you didn't do this anymore." she said while waving her hand at the ingredients spread across the table.

It was old knowledge that her aunt would supplement her income by creating potions and doing spells for women who needed them. These women would pay a pretty penny for what her Auntie could do… and undo if they needed it. Aunt Mary had been a practicing Amosu most of her life— only giving it up most recently because her memory had started to give out on her. She refused to use the Book of Wisdom that had been passed down to her to help her "prepare".

"I don't, but I got a friend who has a special request."

"Medallion nodded her head knowing there were no "friends" when it came to magic— only clients, and a "special request" meant magic was the last resort, and the "friend" had already paid a lot for whatever Aunt Mary had decided they needed. She looked up at Medallion while she chopped up her herbs and stirred her simmering pot. She then turned the stove on low and put her knife down noticing that Medallion had a spark in her eye that meant she was thinking up something devious.

"I'm going to warn you again, and I hope you are listening to me." Medallion looked at Aunt Mary whose jaw was now stern, her face just as calm, and her eyes were intense. Mary's signature stare meant she knew what Medallion wasn't saying.

"Don't go playing with fire. You gonna end up getting burned, and Waymen is the one that's gonna end up getting hurt."

Aunt Mary held Medallion's stare for a bit longer before she shook it off. And as quick as Aunt Mary turned down her pot and stopped chopping her herbs, she was back at it once she'd delivered her message.

"And while you're here child… when are you going to finish up these lessons about what I got going on here? My mind ain't as sharp and you gonna miss all this good wisdom I need to share."

"Auntie you know I'm not into all this. This stuff you doing need to die anyway. It can't possibly be legal."

"Legal don't make it right. Remember, slavery was legal but it won't right."

Medallion picked up her pocketbook and leaned in to give a kiss goodbye. "I hear you Auntie. I promise, I'll try to be on my best behavior, but I'm not going to be taking up any lessons about this stuff anytime soon."

"Ummm-hmmm" Aunt Mary said through pursed lips. "I've warned you child. Don't let your sass, get you in a world of trouble. You may have broken your promise to me to learn this 'stuff' but you mind that promise you made to your husband."

"Yes ma'am." Medallion said as she headed back out the door.

Back in the car, she sat behind the wheel thinking about what Aunt Mary's cautionary words meant. Usually her warnings were a foretelling of a revelation. But sometimes, her warnings were just her meddling. Medallion couldn't tell which one it was this time, but she wasn't going to agonize about it much longer. *I need a plan... she* thought.

As she pushed the button to start her ignition, a sleek black Mercedes with tinted windows pulled up in the driveway. Medallion watched as the lady got out of her car and noticed the well-dressed woman had a prominent little baby bump just like hers. *Well, what is she doing here? I know that potion Auntie is cooking isn't for her.* Medallion watched as Aunt Mary opened the door and the woman handed Aunt Mary a small white envelope. *A tribute!* On top of the woman paying for services in advance, she still had to pay a tribute to the ancestors who taught Aunt Mary her craft. Without the tribute, the spell would backfire— causing more harm than good.

A tribute in a white envelope was not a coincidence. White stood for purity. That meant the money was new and crisp. It also meant whatever the spell was for it had to be powerful to undo something harmful. Usually a pregnant woman paying tribute in a white envelope needed to undo something that would harm their situation. *Not all these women want their business known...* Out of respect, Medallion pulled off from Aunt Mary's house and made her way down the street. *I may not have a garden, but I'm sure whatever I need, I can find at the grocery store. All I have to do is put a scare into him, and he'll be focused on me again for sure.*

Chapter 4

Sunta fluttered her eyes open only to see white light around her. *Where am I?* She turned her head and looked behind her. Lightening flashed in the distance reminding her of the lighting she ran towards when she left her body. She looked around. There was nothing. Nothing but white all around her. From what she could tell, there was no ending or beginning to the whiteness making it almost blinding to see if there was anything else around. She crouched down and touched the space near her feet and found that it was solid and white. She stood up and reached her hands far above her head, but her finger tips touched nothing. She began to walk, hoping to reach a door, or a window, or a wall, but the white continued in every direction.

"Hello! Anyone here!" Sunta waited, but there was no response.

"I said, is anyone here! It's me… Sunta! I don't know where I am and I need some help!"

Again, there was no one there to respond. She was alone. She sat down on the white floor and played back her last memory. In the recesses of her thoughts, she heard the faint sound of her baby boy's first cry. *My baby…* She smiled and shed a tear at the thought of seeing his clear blue eyes in contrast to his dark brown skin for the first and last time. *I must be dead,* Sunta thought. *I died giving birth to my baby.* She shed another sorrowful tear as she curled herself up and closed her eyes hoping to catch a glimpse of her son's face once again.

Laying there in the whiteness, she remembered it all. Her last moments with her sisters… being in the middle of "The Circle that Shan't Be Broken" as her sisters tried to save her baby. Then the "Chant of Forever". Sunta smiled to herself. Her sisters risked their lives by revealing their powers to bring her baby into the world. It was the first time they'd done the chant. They'd seen their mother perform it only once before Master took her away from them.

Sunta touched her stomach wanting to feel the little flutters of his kick once again, but only to touch the softness and vacantness that was her own. Even though he was no longer physically with her, she still felt his presence. *He's safe. I can feel it. He will live and I will see him again.* She placed her hands under her head as if to sleep. *I will wait for him here. He's sure to come my way when his life is said and done. He'll be older… a strong man who's lived enough weary days for the both of us. I'll wait for him here, and we'll walk into heaven together.*

Curling up tighter, she began to drift off in thought, her memories of the world she left grew stronger. Then the voices came. Soft faint voices... Mumbles. Mumbling voices all around her... Several voices too soft to understand the words... She ignored them at first thinking they were just her memories scrambled and jammed up in her head, but then she began to understand they were not within her. Instead, they were surrounding her. Now unsettled, Sunta rose from the floor. The White began to swirl in churning ripples and the soft whispers became louder. She stood at attention focused on what might happen next. Then, a ghostly breeze bustled around her; sweeping between her arms and legs engulfing her as it wisped around. The faint scent of the honey suckle's fruity-citrus aroma filled her nose reminding her of her home on Glory which was also her mother's favorite treat. The moment entranced her relaxing her fear of The White. The memory of a melody that her sisters would sing began to surface and the desire to be with her mother who'd passed years before beckoned her. "I know how to get to you, mama.

All I gotta do is listen to this song and I'll get to you." She began to walk. Allowing her feet to forge the path.

But the voices rushed over her as the wind in the white place continued to blow, filling her ears with the chatter of others and overpowering the melody and she lost her way to her mother. The smell of the honey suckles faded away and Sunta stopped walking. She became tense as her fear returned. The voices continued to become more distinct the more she struggled to hold onto the melody and the smell of home. Instead, she found herself concentrating on what was being said by the voices... the mumbles were now all she could hear. The babbling became just louder voices filled with words known and unknown. The voices, there were several. Chattering... mumbling... mixing... louder and then softer. Sunta batted her hands at her ears as if the voices were like flies around her face and buzzing like bees in her ears.

She shook her head vigorously from side to side.

"No. I ain't listening to you."

The voices became louder. Sunta looked all around her. The swirling white continued and mixed with the voices which were now like they were bouncing off of invisible walls. She batted at the voices again and shook her head in refusal.

"Leave me alone!" She shouted her words of frustration upwards. "Leave me alone! Do you hear me! I ain't call out for you! I'm here waiting for my son! Leave me alone and let me be!"

A tingle went up her side. A soft touch on her arm startled her and made her turn and look.

"Who here? Who touched me?"

She held her arm close to her body protecting it from anything or anyone who would try and grab her again. The voices continued to speak to her all at once. The incessant babbling confused her... Distracted her... She began to shiver with fear. Then a grip of an invisible force of her free hand began to pull her from where she stood.

"Come." A whisper of a voice could be heard amongst all the other voices that circled Sunta.

"Come..." Sunta resisted the pull and forced herself not to move.

"Not without my baby. I'm staying right here. When he come I go."

The voices grew angry at Sunta's defiance. The pull on her hand became stronger as she continued to fight against leaving with the voices.

"Just leave me alone 'til my baby come! Leave me for my baby! I can't go with you 'til my baby get here!"

The voices began to subside and the pull on her hand began to ease. Out of exhaustion, Sunta collapsed in the white place beneath her. She curled into herself as the voices faded away.

"Just leave me 'til my baby come." She sobbed for the loss of her child and sisters. "Leave me 'til they all come."

Chapter 5

Back at her high-rise condo, Medallion had returned from her neighborhood's high-priced all-natural produce store where she'd picked out the ingredients that she needed. Since her aunt wouldn't give her the recipe out right, she'd quickly joined a google witchcraft group promoting spells and potions while she walked the store's aisles. Now, in her kitchen, the store-bought herbs collected in jars and presealed bags were all arranged in order by what ingredient was needed first. She pulled out a knife from the utensil caddy on the counter and began chopping the dried tobacco leaf slowly but steadily. The stench from the toxic plant filled her nostrils forcing her to gag with every breath.

"Now, it says here to let the olive oil get hot and then put the chopped tobacco leaf in..."

The pan sizzled as the chopped leaf began to cook while she began cutting the garlic and cracking the pepper. Once the water in the pot came to a boil, she poured in her ingredients to make her tea. She was nervous about what she was attempting to do because she didn't want to bring harm to anyone... especially a defenseless baby.

She stared for a long moment at the beginnings of the concoction she was creating. She'd vaguely remembered seeing Aunt Mary prepare the tea, and trying to piece the memory back together with tips and tricks from a witchcraft google group couldn't possibly be the best way to handle her predicament. But since getting help from Aunt Mary was out of the question, she felt the concoction was the only way.

The contents in the pot began to bubble up. Medallion grabbed a big wooden spoon and began to stir. It was dangerous for a pregnant woman to drink the tea if she wasn't absolutely sure she wanted her baby gone. She thought of her aunt's guest at the door earlier that day. She knew the lady was sure of what she wanted to do because of the tribute she held tightly in her hand. In Medallion's case, she wasn't ready to give her child up. She was only drinking the tea to make the scare of a miscarriage she wanted to fake more believable.

She put the spoon back down and continued to dice up the herbs and soak the ginger root in the heated pot she'd already placed on the stove. She looked at the clock and noted there was only a few hours left until Waymen made it home. *If I drink the tea now, I'll start spotting around the time he's supposed to walk through the door…* Medallion felt slightly uncomfortable playing with a human life the way that she was, but it was the only way to bring her and Waymen closer. *Now, how does this go again…* Medallion closed her eyes as she remembered the words her aunt use to utter so long ago behind closed doors in the little cottage.

"One more thing…" Medallion's eyes popped back open when she remembered she'd forgotten one last step. She grabbed the calamus root, lifted up her shirt, and placed it in between her panty line and her womb. Ready to begin, she closed her eyes and proceeded.

"Aye wa. Aye lọ. Ibukun nikan ni ohun ti wọn tumọ si ọ." She opened her eyes, and then poured the tea into her glass.

"Gods of life. Spirit of death. I give you a soul's vessel." She took her spoon and tapped it to the tea cup three times before drinking her tea in three gulps. "Eck! Auntie never mentioned this tea tasted horrible!" Medallion chased the cup of tea with a glass of citrus water.

She looked down at her belly; placing a hand on her stomach and patted it comfortably.

"Sorry kid, but I'm not trying to hurt you. I just want to get my husband back, and you are the only thing he wants more than me."

Medallion made her way to the back room to get ready for bed. *I hope this plan works.* She thought to herself. She knew how dangerous the tea was, so she'd come up with the idea to cut the recipe in half in hopes of preventing a full abortion. As she laid in the bed, she thought she felt a gurgle in her stomach on her right side.

"Okay… here goes nothing," said as she turned off her light and tried her best to fall asleep.

Chapter 6

"Ahh!"

Medallion woke with an awful pain on the side of her body that shot around to her back. She arched upwards as she griped her belly for dear life.

"Oh God!"

Her face winced as she was in full agony. She jerked herself into a tight ball as another sharp pain raced through her body. "Waymen!" She yelled out. She stretched her hand across the bed to tap Waymen only to find he wasn't there.

"Waymen!" Medallion yelled louder thinking he may have been in the other room working as he usually did if he didn't want to disturb her. Listening through the silence, she didn't get a response from him. She looked at the clock and saw it read 3:00 a.m. The realization of his absence hit her. *He never came home. Where could he be?* She got out of the bed and slowly made her way to the bathroom. She held the small of her back— massaging it, hoping it would ease the intensity of the cramps.

As she reached the door of the bathroom, another pain hit her at the bottom of her belly and shot down her legs. She screamed out in agony and tears fell down her face.

"Why did I do this to myself!" She screamed the words in frustration and painful despair. She didn't know what to do, so she laid on the bathroom floor until the pain subsided.

Once the pain was gone, she gathered herself off the floor and made her way back to her bedroom. She needed to find her phone to call Waymen or an ambulance. Finding her phone, she grabbed it off of her night stand, and hit Waymen's speed dial number. Within two rings, Waymen had answered the phone.

"Hey Medda… I know it's late. I'm on my way home now. I'll see you—"

"No Waymen. I'm in pain. I… I… think I'm losing the baby."

She felt a warm dribble run down her leg; wiping it away with her fingers before it reached the floor. She looked at her hand to see the red on the tips. She began to tremble in fear as the horror of her predicament set in. Her voice waivered as she continued to speak.

"There's blood, and I'm in so much pain. I—". She clenched her teeth and her knuckles turned pale while gripping the phone tight as another pain went through her body.

Waymen heard the agony in Medallion's voice and wished he would have come home instead of staying out late driving around aimlessly just to spite her. Lately, he'd been feeling reluctant about going back home to Medallion being that the baby may not be his. Now, to hear her in desperation, he knew his heart belonged with her.

"Medallion, baby… just breathe." A tear of regret went down Waymen's face as he listened to her suffer in pain on the other end of the call. "You're not going to lose the baby. I'm going to call an ambulance for you and I'm going to meet you at the hospital, okay?"

Hurriedly leaving the park bench he'd found solace in on nights he'd aimlessly ride around the city of Richmond, Waymen got back in the car and buckled himself up. In one swift move, the vehicle was started, put in drive, and was pulling away from the curb.

Waymen took one last look at the bench in his rearview mirror knowing he had no more use for its comfort. The bench in the quiet park under the stars had become his place to resolve his fear about the future with his wife. His nights out to think things through would start out by taking a slow drive up Broad Street. He would then hop onto interstate 64 so he could circle back through downtown and head to Chimborazo Park to his bench under the stars. And once his Drake playlist, which was the soundtrack to his pain, had finally played its last note, he'd pull over and make his way to the bench. His thoughts were always about how life would look like with his wife and raising a child that may not be his. Unfortunately, his new normal would always seem dismal and filled with bitterness. However, in that moment hearing the distress in Medallion's voice, he could no longer picture life without her or their newborn.

Speeding his way through Churchill down 25th street; ignoring the stop signs on every corner, Waymen was determined to make it to Medallion in record time.

"Waymen I'm so scared. I need you…"

"I'm here for you Medallion. Just hang up. I will call the ambulance to come get you and then I'll call you back."

"Okay. You promise you'll meet me at the hospital?" Medallion grabbed her purse and made her way to the front of their condo.

"Yes, I'm going to meet you there. I feel so bad that I left you at home by yourself. I should be there for you."

Medallion sat at the chair by the front door, exhausted from the pain and the events of the night. She waited for the ambulance to arrive.

"I've been a bad wife, Waymen. I don't blame you for not being here."

"Don't beat yourself up, baby. We all make mistakes, and I forgive you for yours. Now hang up so I can call an ambulance. I'll call you right back."

"Okay Waymen. I love you."

"I love you too. I'll see you at the hospital". Waymen ended the call and dialed 9-1-1.

As another smaller pain hit, Medallion wished she hadn't gone this far to get his attention. Still, she was glad it worked. She smiled a little through her self-inflicted ordeal and then grabbed her pocketbook before she headed out the door. Walking slowly down the hall of the high-rise building, she began to feel water running down her leg.

"Oh god… I'm going to have this baby right here in the hall!" Medallion looked down and saw the puddle of water at her feet. "Please don't let this baby die… please don't let this baby come out right here. Waymen has to be here for this."

She heard the bell of the elevator ding and the paramedics rushing her way.

"Mrs. Foster… we got the call that you were having difficulties. We are here to help."

Medallion smiled and said "Thank you. Please take me to the hospital. My husband is waiting for me there."

As she was being rushed through the entrance of the hospital, she spotted Waymen pacing by Triage. He looked up when he heard the automatic sliding doors open and saw his wife on the gurney.

"Medallion!" Waymen exclaimed in anguish upon seeing her pain-filled face. He rushed over and grabbed her hand. "How is she?"

He addressed his question to the paramedics who strolled her in.

"Looks like she's miscarrying. We have to get her to a room for her to be examined." The paramedic said in a rush.

"Waymen…"

Medallion's eyes were rolling as she tried to stay conscious. Even though she cut the recipe in half, she started to consider that she may have either screwed up the tea or the tea was still too strong.

"Waymen… it hurts so much…" she slowly gripped her stomach feeling the child move in a disconcerting way. "I don't want to lose the baby, Waymen…"

"You won't. I promise." He kissed her hand and they all hurried down the hall into a room to check on the baby.

***

Sunta heard the faint echo of a baby crying and she leaped from the bright white ground. "Baby! I'm here, babe! I'm over here, Elijah! Mama is over here!"

Sunta ran to where she thought she heard his voice but saw nothing. Nothing but the white she'd seen when she was laying on the floor...

She heard the baby's cry once more behind her. She swung around sharply and ran in the other direction. She ran, screaming his name knowing it was her child looking for her.

"I'm coming baby! Don't cry no more! I'm on my way! Mama coming!"

She ran frantically through The White- everything around her looking the same until her legs collapsed beneath her. All-the-while, the baby's cry intensified in every direction she turned. She finally sat down and cried out, "Where are you baby! Mama is looking for you!"

Her tears fell fast while she panicked, knowing his helpless plea meant he was in trouble. Suddenly the baby's voice stopped, and she knew he was gone.

"Come back, baby! Mama is here for you! Don't leave me! I'm sorry I left you!"

She wept into her tucked chin not knowing what she needed to do. "I'm sorry, baby…" Sunta spoke softly to herself. She was alone. There was no one anywhere.

"I'm sorry I did this... I'm sorry I let them put that spell on me. He should have just come wit me here. Things would have been better than being here by myself." Sunta laid herself back down in a ball not knowing what was to become of her. "Mama loves you, Elijah. I promise I will wait for you, and we will never be apart again."

Chapter 7

"I'm glad we caught this in time, Mr. and Mrs. Foster. Had we not, I believe we would have lost your son."

The doctor looked up from his clipboard and smiled as he cleverly announced the gender of their child. Waymen looked at the doctor in pure glee at the news. He smiled proudly before he turned his attention back to Medallion.

"Did you hear that babe! It's a boy!"

He gave Medallion a kiss on the forehead as his heart warmed with the thought of his first child being a son.

"Oh, what wonderful news!"

Aunt Mary sat in the corner by the big window which showcased the mighty James River while watching Waymen dote over Medallion while she recovered.

"I do believe this calls for a celebration."

After Medallion called to inform him about the baby's grim circumstance, Waymen called Aunt Mary from his car as soon as he'd hung up with Emergency Dispatch. He knew that if something were to have gone wrong and Medallion would have lost the baby, she would have wanted Aunt Mary by her side.

Aunt Mary was closer to Medallion than any of the other family members since she was the one who raised her. They had a very special bond that Waymen hardly could understand, but he didn't mind it. He loved that Aunt Mary took him under her wing and loved him just as much as she loved her niece. Aunt Mary was their family, so he had to make sure she was involved with any and everything that affected Medallion.

"Yes, indeed it does." The doctor chuckled at Aunt Mary's display of enthusiasm. "The tests we've run on Mrs. Foster could not explain what caused the distress, but we have stopped the bleeding and the baby is no longer under duress. In fact, the baby is quite strong, and I believe he's going to go full term. Now take it easy for the rest of the pregnancy Mrs. Foster. I believe the scare may have been induced by stress."

"Yes Dr. Finn. I'll be sure to take it easy."

Medallion shook the doctor's hand before he left the room. She looked over at Waymen, so happy that he'd made it to her bedside. *Thank God this wasn't worse. Had this little baby died, Waymen wouldn't have a reason to stay.* Even though the whole ordeal was a bit exhausting, Medallion rubbed her belly in satisfaction. *Mission accomplished.*

Aunt Mary watched as Waymen comforted his wife. He fluffed her pillows, ran to the sink to get her a glass of water to drink with her medication, and straightened out the sheets in an effort to keep her at the highest level of comfort possible. For him to be told that he was going to have a boy, put Waymen over the moon… Aunt Mary could tell. And just like she could tell how joyous this occasion was to him, she could also tell, something about the "baby scare" wasn't right. The deathly pains derived from a source that no earthly wound could make, made her more suspicious of the whole ordeal.

When Medallion was a teenager, Aunt Mary began to educate her about the teas and the concoctions that were passed down to her. Medallion, however, never seemed interested in learning the art of healing and blessing. Aunt Mary decided that back then it'd be best that she didn't continue the lessons right way. Even at a young age,

Medallion showed signs of selfishness and manipulation, and Aunt Mary knew if her niece used the art of the Amosu the wrong way, she could do more harm than good.

Not really wanting to believe that her niece would use a mystical tea to abort her child solely to get her husband's attention, Aunt Mary waved away the unnerving thought and focused on the wonderful moment.

"Waymen, you really are happy that it's a boy, aren't you?

"Yes, Ma'am." He squeezed Medallion's hand reassuringly while sitting in the chair beside her. "I couldn't be more overjoyed at the thought of being the father of a son."

With gratefulness, Waymen closed his eyes to ponder his future as a family man.

"I can see your happiness Waymen, and I want it to last." Aunt Mary paused and smiled at the couple before she continued. "I want to give you both a present. I want to do something nice to help your journey along."

The happy couple looked at Aunt Mary in blissful bewilderment. Aunt Mary had always extended her generosity to them, and it always exceeded their expectations. From buying their posh city condo in the newly renovated Shockoe Bottom, to the luxurious cars they drove because she insisted they have the safest most up-to-date vehicles. Aunt Mary never spared any expense when it came to her generous gifts.

"I have watched you two grow together and then apart since you said your vows nine years ago. With this baby on the way, it's going to be harder for either one of you to turn your backs on the tougher issues that await in your future. This is the time for your bond in marriage to grow stronger than it ever has. Now is the time to save what you have and build for the baby that is to come."

Aunt Mary's eyes begged the two of them to listen as her voice quivered with every word.

"Love needs to grow so that the baby can survive…"

Aunt Mary dug into her pocketbook pleasantly placed on her lap and pulled out a set of keys. Medallion's eyes popped as she saw the two familiar keys dangling from the Emerald encrusted key ring. Aunt Mary walked the set of keys over to Waymen and placed them firmly in his palm, then closed his fingers over them.

"My gift to you is family. Take all the time you need to build back up the love you had for each other because family is all you have."

"Aunt Mary… these are the keys to Glory Hill."

Medallion swelled with tears at Aunt Mary's offer. The house was never used as a place to live. No one in the family was permitted to stay more than a week. Being handed the keys to Aunt Mary's most cherished family heirloom was a symbol of love and honor. Medallion didn't know how to take such a present.

Aunt Mary sat back down in her chair across the room—feeling like Glory was where they both needed to be.

"Use the time you are there to find each other. If you don't, all the work you've put into your marriage thus far will be in vain."

She looked at Medallion sternly. As much as she wanted to dismiss the feeling that her niece had used a tea, the truth of the situation tugged at her conscious incessantly.

"We will Aunt Mary."

Waymen left Medallion's side and planted a big kiss on Aunt Mary's cheek as he wrapped his muscular arms around her and embraced her in a grateful hug.

"Oh baby… I know you will." She smiled, but she kept her eyes on her niece, and Medallion knew what only Aunt Mary could know. *I've been found out.*

Chapter 8

Medallion looked at her phone as it began to ring. Rolling her eyes as she thought, *Ugh… Rodney.* She sat up in her bed and leaned forward to peek out her bedroom door listening for Waymen's vicinity in their home as she pressed the answer button on her touch screen phone.

"Yeah…" She said nonchalantly, still tired from the baby ordeal she'd experienced just three days ago.

"Babe! I ran into your girl, Cherie, and she told me you were in the hospital… for a *MISCARRIAGE?!* Please tell me the baby didn't die! Why didn't you call me? I would have come and been by your side!"

Angry at his lame attempt at concern after the fact, Medallion was tempted to hang up the phone, but more eager to give him a piece of her mind. She laid back in the bed; assured that Waymen was out of ear shot.

"No, my baby isn't dead, but how dare you call me now like you care about how me and my child are doing?"

Medallion took a sip of the luke warm water at her bedside. Waymen knew better than to put ice in it. Cold water always hurt her teeth.

"This is our baby, Medallion, not just yours! I have every right to know what is happening to your body while our child is in there."

Medallion almost spit her water back out listening to Rodney chastise her for not notifying him of her distress. She wiped her mouth and put her glass back on the nightstand.

"Don't give me that Rodney. You didn't seem to care about the baby when I told you at dinner. Your only concern then was to keep me from my husband."

"That's unfair Medallion. I love you and you know it! Why would I be calling now if I didn't?"

"You're only calling to be nosey and to stir up some trouble between me and Waymen, but it's not going to work. My husband loves me and my baby! You can save your fake feelings for someone else."

"Babe… who are you in there talking to? Are you okay?" Waymen walked into the bedroom with Medallion's dinner tray. He'd fixed her favorite meal and garnished the tray with rose petals and a candle.

"Nobody, babe. It's just one of the girls. They're giving me hell because they think I'm not resting enough, but I told them you've been taking good care of me." She laughed nervously knowing she was only a few seconds from getting caught with Rodney on the phone. "Alright Dreysia. I'll call you tomorrow. Waymen just walked in with my dinner."

Oh god. I hope Rodney takes the hint and hangs up like he's supposed to when Waymen is around.

"Oh… I'm Dreysia now? Trying to use the code name isn't going to work. I'm not going to be Dreysia anymore. Tell ol' Waymen it's really me on the phone."

Rodney smiled slyly at the position she was in. He loved Medallion, but mostly because she fed into his games. He liked the drama she could produce while trying to hide their affair from her husband.

"Dreysia, girl. Stop playing." She faked a laugh while trying to ease off the phone with Rodney without Waymen catching on. "I'll call you tomorrow. Waymen made me a wonderful dinner."

Waymen happily sat the little dinner tray across Medallion's legs, pulled the napkin from its holder, and tucked it into her nightgown collar.

"Is that Dreysia? Let me speak to her. You guys are always talking on the phone and hanging out shopping, and I've never even met her." He smiled about the opportunity to speak to his wife's best friend. "I'll tell her how good of a man I am to you."

"No Waymen… It's not—" Medallion couldn't get the words out fast enough to stop him from grabbing the phone.

"Hey Dreysia," Waymen said in a sing-song voice. "It's good to finally speak to you. Don't worry about Medda. I'm taking good care of her."

He smiled and began to plant a kiss on Medallion's cheek, when he heard Dreysia speak.

"Nah homie. I already took care of Medda. That's why she's pregnant… with my baby." Rodney maniacally laughed as hard as he could and then hung the phone up.

Waymen's smile dropped, and his lips never touched Medallion's cheek. All he could do was stare into her frightened eyes.

"Waymen… don't be mad. I didn't know he was going to call. Plus I broke it off with him, and he acted like he didn't want the baby. He was only calling to get under your skin. Don't let him, Waymen. We've been doing good. I don't want him. I'm with you now— faithful and committed to make our family work."

Waymen looked at Medallion with an emotionless stare and handed her the phone.

"I'm going out for a couple of hours. If you start having pains, call me, and I'll be back."

Waymen walked out of the room defeated. He wanted to say more. He wanted to yell and scream and make her feel bad for making him look like a fool in front of his rival yet again, but he didn't want to stress her. After all, it wasn't Medallion who was going to feel the turmoil if he yelled and screamed. Delivering a healthy baby was more important than fighting with his unfaithful, lying wife.

"Waymen… please believe me. I didn't ask him to call. I told him to leave me alone!"

Medallion pleaded from her bed for reprieve, but all she heard was the door close as he exited the condo.

Chapter 9

Medallion heard the doorbell ring faintly as her face stayed covered by her pillow. The feeling of defeat laid heavy on her; paralyzing her desire to function. The doorbell rang again. She pushed the pillow from her face and looked at the clock. It was the middle of the next day. Aunt Mary said she'd be over early enough to help out before the ceremony, but with Waymen still gone after the phone call mix up, she knew any plans she'd made with her husband were pointless.

The doorbell rang for a third time. Medallion dragged herself out of the bed and walked lifelessly to the door and answered it.

"You look a mess, Medda. Why aren't you dressed in the outfit I sent over?"

Medallion moved out the way of her front door allowing her Aunt Mary to come inside, then followed her into her home.

Mary looked around the condo confused.

"You haven't prepared the table? Where are the pillows? Nothing is done! The priestess will be here any minute and you are not ready."

Mary put her things down. She looked around the room wondering where she should begin with the set up.

"Can you call her and ask can we do it another day? Waymen left last night and I haven't seen him since."

"Again Medda?! What's going on now?"

"Same stuff… Rodney playing games. I swear it wasn't me this time."

Mary put up her hand to stop Medallion from talking. "I've heard enough". She pulled out her phone and dialed Waymen.

"Hello Auntie."

"Get your butt back here now. We've got a ceremony to prepare for. We've got forty-five minutes before the priestess gets here so whatever you are doing, you need to stop and come home right now."

"Can you just cancel today? Yet again, Medallion has shown—"

"Waymen, get over it. The journey you two are going through comes with a few bumps and bruises until it smooths itself out. This moment is not the moment to indulge in this weak behavior of running away. Now, you said you were going to work through these issues you have with Medda, but you can't do that if you are going to run away every time it gets hard. Today is not the day for you to fold. Get home. Get dressed. We have company coming over and a baby ceremony to perform. You are needed by your wife and your son, and your energy is needed by the ancestors to help confirm this baby's rightful name."

With a conceding huff, Waymen agreed. "I'll be there in ten minutes. I was just at my parents cooling down."

"Good be here in ten. We have a lot to do before the priestess gets here. Make sure your parents come too. You know they have a role in this as well."

"I will." Waymen laughed at how commanding Aunt Mary could be.

Mary hung up the phone before turning her attention back to her niece.

"As for you, go get dressed. Your husband is on the way. I'll get the room prepared. We don't have that much time."

"So he's coming home?" Medallion smiled with grittiness.

"Yes, but I ain't got time for this mess you two keep pulling. I'm going to be so glad when you two are on one accord. Y'all wearing me out."

Medallion walked over to her aunt and marked her cheek with a big kiss.

"Thank you Auntie. Who would I be without you?"

"Broke, homeless, and single." They both laughed. "Now, go on ahead and get dressed. I got a lot to do before the Priestess gets here."

Medallion walked back to her room in time to see her phone light up. "Hey, baby."

"Hey Medda. You probably already know I talked to Auntie. I'm on my way home."

"Waymen, I was so happy to hear it. I can't stand you not being here with us. I'm trying my best, Waymen. I didn't call him and I wanted him to get off the phone."

"Look, I believe you. I'm just tired of him. I'll be so glad when this is all over. When we are finally away from the city... When our baby boy is finally here… I'll be so happy to move on from this chapter of our life."

"Me too, Waymen. We are going to have such a great life together." Medallion walked to her closet and pulled out the traditional matching outfits for her and him.

"Okay, well I'm pulling into the parking lot and I'll be up shortly."

"See you soon. I love you."

Medallion hung up the phone and placed it on the dresser. She went back to the bed where she'd put the outfits down to admire them one last time before she began to get dressed- her purple and gold Gele embellished with traditional symbols of fertility, as well as her Iro and Buba also in the same purple fabric and fertility symbols.

"I'm just in time to help."

Medallion turned to see Waymen at the entrance of her bedroom. She smiled in relief at seeing her tall, handsome, knight in shining armor waiting to assist.

"Babe, you are right on time. I can't wrap this thing around my belly right."

Waymen laughed at his wife's distress. "No worries mama. I'll wrap it."

He walked into the room and gathered her Buba off the bed. He opened the cloth and began the wrap above her belly.

"Is that comfortable?"

"Nothing's comfortable babe, but I'm fine."

Waymen chuckled as he tied the wrap around her. He grabbed her Iro. Medallion put her head through the opening while Waymen fixed it enough to allow it to drape her properly.

"Ummm... girl. You looking real regal."

"I'm feeling pretty special."

They both laughed at themselves. Other than their marriage, this was their first traditional and formal ceremony.

"One more thing, babe. I'll grab it from the closet."

Waymen grabbed the yellow crystal encrusted Pele and draped it over Medallion's shoulders.

"Almost done."

Finally, he placed the pre-sculpted Gele on Medallion's head.

"Now you're ready."

Waymen turned Medallion to the full-sized dressing mirror. Her mouth dropped open in amazement.

"Yup. That's how I feel. You look stunning."

Waymen planted another kiss on Medallion's cheek while she continued to admire her reflection. He swiftly put on his Agbada and met Medallion at the mirror.

"Baby, we look good."

She placed a hand on her stomach. He then placed his hand on hers.

"We are going to make wonderful parents." Medallion said.

"I agree babe. We've come such a long way."

"We have Waymen, but look at us now... we made it. Auntie has made sure of it."

"She has. I am so grateful she keeps us focused on what's important."

"Yes. Family."

They kissed once more and headed out of their master suite and into the living room where Aunt Mary was putting the final touches together.

"Auntie, it looks so cute in here!" Medallion squealed and clapped with excitement.

"It did come together nicely with the little bit of time I had to prepare the room. I'm glad you like it."

Aunt Mary had drawn all of the open curtains together and dimmed the lights all around the home. The shadows that came alive within the darkness bounced off the wall dancing in celebration of the ceremonious occasion. The air in the room was filled with cinnamon and lavender... Medallion's and Waymen's favorite fragrances. The low beat from the congo drum and the rhythmic beats of the shakare from the percussionist Aunt Mary hired for the occasion assisted with setting the mood for the upcoming ceremony.

The doorbell rang. "I'll get it. It's probably the priestess."

Waymen ran to the door and instead of the Priestess found his parents on the other side.

"Mom! Dad! I'm glad you two could make it."

Barbara smiled tightly while his father's never appeared.

"Calm down, Waymen. We just saw each other. However, I'm surprised you actually made it with everything she's put you through."

"Come on dad, be nice." Waymen patted his father on the shoulder and led them into the condo.

"Looks more like a séance than something for a child. And what's that putrid smell? Barbara halted her next spoken thought as she looked him over.

Waymen gave her a big smile and turned around so that she could see all of his Agbada.

"Sweet Jesus, Waymen. What do you have on?"

Realizing fishing for a compliment from his mother was hopeless, he dropped his arms in defeat. His parents never agreed with his marriage to Medallion. In the beginning they were more concerned with Aunt Mary's connection to "other worldly" rituals and habits, but as the relationship became more turbulent, several attempts by his parents to break them up never succeeded. In their eyes, Medallion has always tormented him by toying with his affections. Their only solace was Waymen marrying into one of the wealthiest families known in the state and maybe on the east coast. For that sole reason, they kept their comments about their son's marriage to a minimum.

"It's for the ceremony. What... you don't like it?"

"Of course not." Barbara said frankly.

Barbara handed Waymen her pocketbook and coat.

"I feel stifled, Waymen. Open a window to let some fresh air in."

Waymen shook his head knowing his parents would never fully accept Aunt Mary, Medallion, or their rich culture. He placed his parent's coats and his mother's pocketbook in the hall's coat closet as his parents continued down the main hallway and into the living room.

"Barbara and Henry! Welcome, welcome, welcome! I'm so happy you could make it. This is such a special occasion." Mary opened her arms and surround them in a warm embrace.

"Mary, it is always a pleasure." Barbara patted Mary on the back before she was let go. "I wasn't expecting all of..." She looked around the room. The fireplace glowed from the flames moving slowly and rhythmically and the candles that were placed on the mantle, bookshelves, and on the coffee table all gave the room a mystic ambiance. She then spotted the drummers in the corner beating out what reminded her of a savage's melody. "...this for a naming ceremony."

Mary giggled with delight. She was very aware of Waymen's parent's distaste for her rituals and ceremonies but she never let that bother her. She always got a little pleasure out of making them somewhat uncomfortable due to their dislike of her niece.

"Yes, it's so important to celebrate all aspects of a child's coming. If we don't confirm the baby his name now, how will he know we are talking to him?"

"Dear God..." Barbara mumbled to herself. "Total nonsense."

"Well thank you once again for the invite. I'm sure we will learn something new."

Henry poured himself a drink from the decanter on the table and sat down on the couch before taking a sip of the clear liquid.

"My word... what is this?" He twisted his face into a scowl as he swallowed what felt like the burn of good cognac but the after effect of a scented mineral oil. He then looked at his filled glass with confusion.

"Why it's just a little Florida Water. We'll be using it as part of the ceremony but you can drink what you have poured yourself... if that's your thing. By the way... it's not for drinking." Mary laughed a bit at his blunder.

Henry put the glass down and pushed it away from him in disgust. "No thank you. Son, where is the Gin?"

"I'll grab you a drink, dad." Waymen swiftly made his way to the bar to make his father a glass of his regular libation.

"Mix me a Martini while you are over there, dear."

Waymen gave the thumbs up to his mother's request.

The doorbell rang. Mary headed for the door. "Waymen, is that your brother do you think?"

"No. He couldn't make it today, but he sends his love."

"Well it must be the Priestess! I'm excited." Mary clapped her hands with glee before she opened the door.

"Ifáṣeyì! My darling, it is wonderful to see you once again!" Mary hugged her and then allowed her into the condo.

"Peace and blessings my dear sister. Thank you for allowing me to be a part of this joyous occasion."

Mary took the Priestess' coat and hung it in the closet and they both made their way to the living room.

"Everyone, this is Priestess Ifáṣeyì. She will be performing the naming ceremony."

The Priestess looked around the room. *Sour. Their spirits are sour.* She opened her satchel she carried across her chest and pulled out her smudge stick. She lit it with a candle from the coffee table and made her way to Waymen's parents as a small stream of smoke from the smudge stick followed her.

"Drummers... play a little louder while I take care of this."

She hovered the smudge stick filled with sage and cedar over Barbara and Henry's head. She closed her eyes in meditation while mumbling words of prayer as she waved it over them.

"Excuse me, what do you think you are doing?!" Appalled, Barbara moved herself from under the unfamiliar smoke.

"Unh, unh, child. Come on back here. You need this more than anyone in the room." The Priestess scurried over to Barbara flailing the smoking stick to and fro. "Let me help you clear that ol' nasty energy stuck up in you. We can't have this baby feeling what you done brought up in here."

"No thank you." Barbara took off to the other side of the room with the Priestess right behind her.

Mary doubled in laughter as she watched the two in a chase and the drummers keeping time. Before long the whole room was in laughter.

Barbara laughed her way back to the couch and sat down beside her husband once more; more relaxed after having drunk the Martini. Henry was also relaxed and found the whole scene rather amusing as well. Never had he seen his wife so out of character than in that moment. The scene brought back pleasant memories of the carefree woman he once knew. The woman he fell in love with.

"See... there ya go. That ol' nasty energy gone just like I wanted."

The priestess blew out her smudge stick and placed it in the ash tray on the coffee table. She then raised her hands and lowered them gradually signaling the drummers to bring the beat to a slow pace. The drummers obliged returning the room to a more meditative mood.

Ifáṣeyì turned to Mary with a pleasant smile. "Please bring us Medallion."

Mary nodded and made her way to the master bedroom. She softly knocked on the door. "I'm coming in..." Mary pushed the door open to see Medallion sitting on the bed with her head bowed. Mary smiled at Medallion's vulnerability and innocence. "It's time to begin. You ready?"

Medallion looked up and smiled Aunt Mary's way. She nodded eagerly. "I'm ready. Just thinking a little bit, but I'm ready."

Mary stepped into the room closing the door behind her. "About what, suga?" Mary sat on the bed beside her and held her hand.

"Mama and daddy."

"Oh... yeah. I see." Mary paused understanding Medallion's moment. She patted the top of her hand as she gripped it reassuringly. "Baby, even though I've been guardian most of your life and treat you just like my own, sometimes it can be lonely for you without them being here to honor you on occasions such as these. But don't fret. I'm sure they have been guiding and protecting you through life and haven't missed a thing."

Medallion leaned her head on Mary's shoulder. In turn, Mary leaned her head on Medallion's.

"You're right. It's funny. I never have the feeling of missing them. I always feel them around, but it would be nice to have them here… in the flesh sometimes."

"I'm sure it would be nice. They were good people. You remind me so much of your mom when I look at you. And your daddy. How proud he was of you. I truly believe you got your audacity from him. He was always up to no good and girl could he work a nerve, but he was loved by everyone."

They both laughed at the memories. Mary kissed the top of Medallion's head and then stood up.

"Alright child. Enough is enough. Come on and let's get this show on the road. Barbara and Henry have already started drinking. It ain't going to be long before she get all Northside and we gotta put her out."

Medallion laughed again and began her pregnant wobble to the door. "Yeah she act all sadity but we all know she from them streets across The James."

"Ain't that the truth!"

Chapter 10

Medallion walked into the living with her hand still cradled in her aunt's.

"Hello everyone. Thank you for coming."

Everyone turned to look to look at her when she greeted the room. Medallion's beaming smile accentuated by the ceremonial face paint of intricate white dotting brought a glow to her that neither Waymen nor his parents had ever seen. He proudly walked over and grabbed her other hand.

"Seriously, babe, I never thought you could out do your own beauty, but I was wrong. You have taken my breath away."

He placed a hand on her belly and kissed her cheek.

"Thank you honey. I feel like a whale though."

"Nonsense. You look refined… just like a mother should."

Mary let go of her hand to go stand beside the Priestess. Waymen escorted Medallion to the brown straw peacock chair placed in front of the alter where the Priestess and Mary stood. Instinctively, Barbara and Henry joined the group as the ceremony began.

"You look wonderful dear. Simply beautiful." Barbara patted Medallion's shoulder and gave her a loving smile.

"Thank you for being here with us. You and Mr. Henry." Medallion returned the pleasantry in hushed tones. She sensed the sincerity in Barbara's sentiments and was very pleased they were able to share such a special moment with her.

"Let us quiet our hearts."

Ifáṣeyì lowered her eyes signaling the other participants to do the same. As the room became void of all voices, the family allowed the beat of the drum and the shimmy from the shakare move their bodies and minds.

"As we gather here today in love and honor, we call out the names of our predecessors… our ancestors. We call them as witnesses from a place we know, but yet to see. We call them from our past to glimpse our present as we honor our future generation of the legacy we have created."

Ifáṣeyì's eyes opened. Her head raised. She grabbed the decanter of Florida Water.

"Let us join hands and pray over the water we will use to serve the ancestors we call. Mary, please grab the bowl."

Mary picked up the white porcelain bowl and held it in front of the Priestess.

"Henry, the strongest of your tribe. The man acknowledged as leader. We honor you. Call out to the one who was your protector, your king. Call his name so that he can bear witness.

"I call out to my father, Joseph."

"Ashe." Ifáṣeyì poured from the decanter and into the clean white bowl.

"Barbara, the nurturer of your tribe... The women acknowledged as the wisest and all knowing... We honor you. Call out to the one who was your protector, your king in your home. Call unto him so that he can bear witness."

"I call out to my grandfather, God rest his soul."

A tear fell from Barbara's eye as she remembered the man who raised her and the sacrifices he made so that she never felt the blow of being abandoned. "I call out to my Big Daddy, Earl."

"Ashe" Ifáṣeyì poured from the decanter once more and into the clean white bowl.

"Mary, the keeper of your tribe..."

The Priestess sent Mary a quick look knowing she had to choose her words correctly. She knew what most didn't know about her dear friend and swore the unmentionable part of it would never be hers to tell.

"...the last of your elders, we honor you." Ifáṣeyì poured from the decanter in honor of Mary. "Call out to the one who was your deliverer, your belief, your maker. Call his name."

"I call out to my father. The man who created me. Who was there in spirit more than in the flesh. I call him here today. I call out to Jedidiah, father of the seven sisters... Husband to the great Makeda..."

The air in the room shifted. The candle flames danced to the drums as they grew in sound and power. Ifáṣeyì drew in the air and pronounced, "Ashe!" as loud as she could, knowing that the forefathers had entered as commanded. She poured into the bowl one last time. Mary then took the white ceramic bowl and allowed it to rest on the alter, rejoining the circle after.

"Now for you, Beloved…" The priestess looked at Medallion lovingly and spoke to her with care.

"Place your hand on your belly. Close your eyes and think of your father. The man who loves you unconditionally... You are daddy's little girl. Think of that man. That strong man who could pick you up in one swoop... That brave man who killed the spiders and scared the boogey man away... That sweet man who kissed your bruises and tucked you in at night... Think of him and call his name."

"William." Medallion spoke his name as if it floated from her lips.

"Ashe." Ifáṣeyì walked over to Medallion and grabbed both of her hands. "William is here, Beloved. William is with us."

Ifáṣeyì hugged Medallion before returning to the alter.

"We have called the strongest of our men here to know the name of the boy child born from our daughter, Medallion. They are here to know who will carry on their legacy as the strongest, the wisest, and a future king amongst his own."

Ifáṣeyì lit a match and allowed the flame to grow.

"Medallion and Waymen, the parents of this future man, this flame represents your son. Say his name.

In unison, they both said, "Isaiah Rhakee Foster."

"Ashe!" The Priestess flicked the match into the bowl of water and watched the flame die and the smoke from it rose high.

Medallion lifted her eyes to see all of her family with tears in their eyes. She wiped her tear stained cheeks with the back of her hands.

"The smoke you see- watch it as it drifts through the room. That is the fathers carrying the name with them. They know who he is. While he is with you in your womb, my Beloved, they will come to him and bestow their wisdom through visions while he floats in your amniotic fluid. He will make you proud."

"Thank you. That was beautiful." Medallion placed her hands together and bowed before the Priestess in gratefulness.

"Blessings to you always, my daughter."

Ifáṣeyì gave Medallion a hug before she went around the room giving the others hugs as well.

Mary went over to Medallion and hugged her once more.

"Oh Auntie, this was beautiful. Thank you."

"You are so welcome, honey. How you think that Barbara did over there?"

They both snuck a peek at Waymen's mother. Her eyes full of tears babbling and rambling with the Priestess. They burst into laughter seeing the affect the ceremony had on its toughest critic.

"Oh Priestess, this was absolutely wonderful! I had my doubts, but I am so, so happy I came to see it for myself."

"I knew I could win you over." Ifáṣeyì and Barbara shared another hug. "Mary, I have to get going now. It's freezing outside and you know I don't like it when my bones get too cold."

"Okay Ifá. I'll walk you to the door."

The Priestess gave one last hug to everyone in attendance. With a coy look in her eye, she danced over to the drummers who were still playing in accordance to the happy mood. With a heal toe step and her hands twirling high, she yelled out a quick high-pitched, "YIP! YIP!" before bowing down slowly in honor to their intense and forceful rhythm. She came back up fast, blew them all a kiss, and yelled "ASHE!"

The drummers stopped on queue as the echo of their last beat lingered in the room.

Chapter 11

"I need to see you."

"No. Not with that stunt you pulled with me and Waymen. You almost messed things up for him and me."

"I need to see you… please."

"Rodney, you are trouble. I'm trying to work it out with my husband. You are just going to make things worse."

"Please. I love you… and our baby."

Medallion stared at Rodney's last text. He'd never said 'I love you' before. The words stuck with her; making him just a little more desirable. "Where do you want to meet?"

"Meet me at my house. I'll be waiting for you."

"Okay." Medallion sent the last text and got out of the bed. It had been three months since she almost miscarried. She'd been put on bed rest and instructed by her doctors to eliminate as much stress as possible. Waymen had been in a good mood since the naming ceremony and they'd made it peacefully through their baby shower and baby room shopping. Waymen had been in so good of a mood, he even let go of his dismay over Rodney's call asking about the baby.

Medallion knew her explanation was a lie, but it was believable. Waymen forgave her and began to look forward to being a father once again.

Putting on her clothes and preparing to leave her home, Medallion felt a pain on her side.

"Whoah..."

She gripped the side of her stomach. *Please don't let this be happening right now. Please don't let this baby come right now. Waymen isn't here, and he won't be back for a couple of days…* Just as she started imagining being in the delivery room without Waymen, the pain let go.

"Whew! I am so not prepared for this." Medallion dug through her pocketbook and grabbed her phone, then dialed Rodney.

"Hello…"

"Rod, I don't think it's a good idea to come. I'm having pains in my stomach. I might be going into labor. I'm going to head over to the hospital and get checked out."

"Come over please, Medallion. I want to see you. How far along are you?"

"I'm pretty close to my due date. I wouldn't be surprised if this baby does come today. I'm just going to head to the hospital to get checked out. If I'm not in pre-labor, I'll come over after that."

With Rodney still on the phone, she headed to her car deciding that going to the hospital was best.

"Medallion, that baby is not coming today. You probably have gas. What did you eat today?"

She giggled a little at how convincing Rodney was trying to be. Anything with cheese always made a little uncomfortable and Rodney knew it.

"I did have a couple of slices of a pepperoni pizza…"

"A couple! I'm sure you probably ate the whole pie. Between your cravings and how much you love having a slice, even though you know you shouldn't, you probably just upset your stomach a little. Come over here, and I'll take care of you. I've got some Pepto and some lactaid pills. Come over and we can spend the rest of the evening together. Waymen is out of town right?"

"Yeah. He's out of town for a couple of days as a matter of fact."

When it came to her relationship with Rodney, she'd broken all of the rules. First, she picked a man who worked for the same company Waymen did. Rodney and Waymen were initially friendly business rivals but became more like arch enemies when Waymen discovered his wife and co-worker were in a relationship. The day Rodney showed the men in the engineering department naked pictures of his new conquest changed everything for Waymen. Usually, he would slickly smile at the pictures of random and nameless women placed in soft porn positions for the camera. He'd then give Rodney a pat on the back for being the lucky man to have spent the night with a goddess, but when he looked into the face of his beautiful wife sprawled across Rodney's bed in his phone's camera roll, Waymen broke into a cold sweat and instantly blacked out.

In the beginning of their affair, Rodney had painted a picture for Medallion that he and Waymen were friendly, however, that wasn't the case. Rodney started at the architecture firm after Waymen was already a young seasoned executive. He was very jealous of Waymen's status at the firm, and tried everything to turn the favor to him, but never could. When he met Medallion at an awards banquet in Waymen's honor, he was determined to have her as his. In the beginning of their relationship, he wanted to steal Medallion from Waymen, but then he realized he'd have more fun just being her guy-on-the-side.

Once the fighting and the bickering between her and Waymen started about the affair with Rodney, she welcomed the turmoil. In fact, it was her plan to use the two men's rivalry to make Waymen jealous in hopes his jealously would create more passion in the marriage. At the time, she wasn't feeling like a priority to Waymen. Getting his blood hot for her seemed like the only way to get him to notice her.

Unfortunately, she picked the wrong guy to make her man jealous. Rodney not only grew on her, but he played more head games with her than she did on Waymen. Now, she had feelings for both men and didn't know how to cut the relationship completely off with Rodney.

"Just come Medallion. I know you're in your car already. Just be over here in ten minutes. I can't wait any longer."

Rodney hung up the phone leaving Medallion literally at the cross roads. As she sat in her car at the light, she had a choice to make the left onto Hull Street which would take her to Southside where Rodney lived, or she could make a right and head up the hill to MCV hospital and check in. Lost in thought, she never saw the light turn green, but she did hear the horn from the car behind her blast. Medallion took the turn left and headed towards Southside. *I'll go to Rodney's and if the contractions start up, I'll just head to Chippenham Hospital to get checked out. But like Rodney said, it's probably just a little gas. He's right. I did eat a whole pizza pie.* She smiled as she turned down Rodney's familiar street and pulled into his driveway.

Chapter 12

As Rodney opened the front door, Medallion felt a rush of cold air and the heavy smell of her favorite incense he always burned when she'd come over to visit. *Lavender and vanilla bean. He's pulling out all the stops today.*

"Hey baby. I'm so glad you made it. You don't know how much I've been missing you."

Rodney wrapped his massive arms around Medallion and gave her a warming hug. He then leaned in and affectionately kissed her stomach looking up towards her in a sincere way.

"Come in Medallion and have a seat".

Rodney grabbed her hand and gingerly tugged her towards the living room; assisting her as she sat down on his over-stuffed couch. He sat down beside her and stared at her in awe. She stared back, but more uncomfortable than flattered at the attention she was being showed. *I wonder what he wants… She* didn't want to question his motives, but most of the time, Rodney never did anything without a reason.

Finally, Rodney shook himself out of his haze and smiled at her with a warmth she'd never seen. She smiled back, still not knowing what it was all about.

"Can I get you anything, dear? Water? A pillow for your back? Would you like for me to put your feet up? Oh! How about that Pepto or that lactaid pill? How is your stomach? You still feeling gassy?"

Rodney's barrage of concern felt overwhelming, but charming. Medallion laughed and put her hands out in a halting gesture.

"Slow down Rodney. I'm fine. I just want to know what you want."

A pain hit as she readjusted herself on the couch. She scrunched her face up but didn't let Rodney know. *It's just gas. It's just gas. It's just gas...*

"Baby…" Rodney grabbed Medallion's hand and kissed the top of it. "I was wrong for doing what I did. I knew you were trying to be good for your husband. I should have hung up instead of getting him mad at you. Please forgive me."

She sweetly smiled. Never had she expected him to apologize for his bad behavior.

"You are forgiven. In fact, it's water under the bridge. Waymen and I are really working hard to build our relationship back up. As a matter of fact, me and him plan on leaving Richmond and living at my aunt's plantation for a while. It was her gift to us."

Medallion slid her hand from his and placed it on her lap. Just then, another pain hit her. This one in her back. "Ouch!" She gripped her lower back and begin to rub; hoping to soothe or dull the pain.

"I'll get the Pepto. Looks like you are having a hard time. I'll be right back…"

Rodney left the room and went to his medicine cabinet coming back as swiftly as he could. He handed Medallion a dose of Pepto-Bismal and she drunk it quickly.

"Thank you, Rodney. Now back to what I was saying. Yes. Waymen and I—"

Rodney put a finger to her lips and then one to his signaling for her to hush. She quieted down as Rodney began to speak.

"Medallion, I know all about your little move. It's all Waymen can talk about at the office. When I heard you guys were leaving, I had a feeling I'd lose you for good. I don't want you to go. I need you here with me. Since you've been out of my life, I can't sleep. I haven't eaten, and all I think of is you. I learned that I can't live without you." Rodney grabbed her hand once again and got down on one knee.

She went into shock as Rodney pulled out a four-carat square cut diamond engagement ring.

"Medda… would you do me the honor of—" Just as Medallion was about to grab for the ring and say 'yes' to the impending, another pain hit, and her bladder lost control.

Rodney jumped up when he saw her fluids all over his plush white sofa. "My couch!"

"Rodney! The baby is coming! I have to get to the hospital!" Medallion kicked herself mentally for not going to get checked out when she felt the first contraction.

Rodney grabbed her keys and helped her off the couch.

"You can't have the baby here. You have to go!" Rodney handed Medallion her keys and pushed her towards the door. "Do you think you can make it to the hospital?"

He opened his front door and pushed Medallion through it.

Confused, she put her foot between the door and the doorsill before Rodney could shut it in her face. In between labored breaths, she asked, "Aren't you going with me?"

"Are you serious? Do you see the mess you just made on my couch? I have to get that cleaned up before it stains! That couch cost a lot of money!"

Rodney pushed Medallion further outside the door and shut it before she could stop him.

Chapter 13

"Alright Mrs. Foster, on your next contraction, I'm going to need you to give us a big push."

Dr. Thigaroe looked Medallion in her eyes as he prepared to finally deliver her son, Isaiah.

"It hurts so bad, Doctor! I can't push anymore"

Drenched in sweat, Medallion flopped her head on the hospital pillow as she waited for the signal to push.

Aunt Mary grabbed her hand and patted it reassuringly.

Don't worry, honey. It'll all be over soon. You know, I peeked down there and saw his little head. He's doing just fine."

Aunt Mary giggled in earnest; anticipating the moment where she'd be able to hold her great nephew.

"Aunt Mary, the pain is awful! How much longer?"

"Not much longer. I see a contraction on the monitor now." Aunt Mary's eyes widened as Medallion tightened her grip and bit down on her lip.

"Okay Mrs. Foster. It's time to push! Give us your best one!"

Medallion bellowed a loud moan as she pushed with all the energy she had left. Dr. Thigaroe guided Isaiah out of the birth canal and into his arms.

"It's a healthy baby boy!"

"Oh Medallion, you did it! You're a mom!"

Aunt Mary looked at her niece and quickly knew something wasn't right. Her eyes were droopy and as she laid her head on the pillow, she limply let go of Aunt Mary's hand.

"Medallion..." Aunt Mary patted her cheek to rouse her. "Doctor. I think something is wrong with her."

Dr. Thigaroe turned to look at his patient and saw the blood from the birth canal seeping out.

"Nurse, we need to stabilize Mrs. Foster!"

"Medallion… Honey… don't go. Stay with us. Your baby is here… waiting on you to wake up. Come on Medallion. Your time on this earth is not yet over."

Aunt Mary calmly whispered the words into Medallion's ear. She felt the cold settling into her niece's veins as she looked towards the ceiling for the Shadow of Death that calls a soul to the afterworld. Luckily, she didn't see it just yet, but she knew she hadn't that much time before it would come seeping from the corner of the room making its way to its Charge.

"Ms. Mary, you'll have to leave the room while we stabilize your niece," said one of the nurses attending to Medallion's delivery while she tried to guide Aunt Mary away from her niece and out of the door. Aunt Mary stood firm by Medallion's side regardless.

"I'm not moving out of this room. Go back to helping the doctor stop the blood. My job right now is to keep my niece here."

As the doctor's and the nurses rushed to stabilize Medallion, she took a deep breath and closed her eyes.

"O ti larada ashe."

She prayed to the ancestral mothers to guide her life energy to the death that she touched all over Medallion's body. As Aunt Mary continued to pray, she felt Medallion stir under her hands.

"Good my child. Come back to us. Let the ancestor's guide you back to our world…"

***

Medallion heard Aunt Mary as an echoing whisper within the air around her, and she felt her touch against her skin, but there was a force pulling her away from her aunt's grasp. In between consciousness and death, she stood in wonderment at the space she'd slipped into. *Where am I? She* looked around her and saw nothing but white.

"Medallion… it's okay for you to come back. Come back and be with your son."

She looked up from where she stood in the whiteness hearing Aunt Mary's voice from above.

"Aunt Mary…" Medallion began to walk; her bare feet leading her forward.

"Find the ancestor's Medallion. They will lead you back to us."

Aunt Mary's voice echoed around her instructing her on the task. *Find the ancestors…* Looking around, she saw no one. She continued forward not knowing where to go. As she continued to walk in the white, she noticed it was all around her and had become blinding. She began to fear it. She picked up her pace. *Find the ancestors. I have to find them.* Her faster than normal walk became a slow run as panic began to set in. Suddenly, in her view, she saw something… Someone laying in the white. As she finally approached the person lying curled into herself, a blinding brightness appeared in front of her and through it walked three women in long white robes. The feeling Medallion felt when she saw them comforted her knowing why they'd come. *Egungun… In an awe-fueled trance, she* walked past the woman laying at her feet and the woman laying in the white stirred as she was passed. The woman looked at the ancestor's as well wondering who they were and why they appeared for the strange new woman.

"Medallion, follow us back to life. You don't belong here yet. Follow us back to life."

The ancestor's spoke to Medallion in unison. The woman on the floor in the middle of them tried to grab Medallion's hand, while the ancestor on the right raised theirs; piercing the white and exposing the bright light once more.

***

Sunta stood up when she saw the women come through the light. *Finally, someone has come for me.* She watched as the woman in the middle grabbed the hand of the woman standing beside her. Sunta reached her hand out in hopes that one of the three women would take her hand as well, but they didn't. They spoke in unison to the woman that stood beside her and led her back into the light with them.

"What about me?" Sunta spoke the words mostly to herself, but as she saw the three women take the woman back into the light, she spoke the words louder. "What about me! Take me with you! Take me with you!"

***

Medallion walked with the ancestor's back through the light. She turned her head just in time to see the woman they left. She saw the fear in the woman's eyes, and the tears that fell from them.

"Do not mourn for her soul Medallion, fore she is lost and will never find peace. She is to remain here by choice as she waits for the child she bore so long ago."

Medallion accepted the crying woman's fate and walked through the warm light which was in contrast to the cold white.

Chapter 14

Medallion's eyes fluttered open as she heard the "beep, beep, beep" of the monitor which kept up with her heart rate. She slowly lifted herself into an upright position and saw her Aunt Mary resting in the chair near her hospital bed.

"Auntie…" Medallion stretched her arms and yarned as Aunt Mary woke at the sound of her voice.

"Medallion…" Aunt Mary rose out of her chair and made her way to her niece's bedside. "Thank God you made it back to us."

Aunt Mary kissed her forehead and slicked Medallion's loose hair back behind her ears.

"I had a little help finding my way." she smiled at her aunt; grateful she sent the ancestors to guide her back.

"Trust in them dear, they are there when we need them most."

"I remember you telling me about them. I just never thought I'd ever meet them. There was three. Not the six you've always mentioned."

Aunt Mary walked to the table that held a glass and a pitcher of water. She poured Medallion a drink and handed it to her.

"Not all six will appear all the time. The three that came for you were like the guardian of the gate for our family. You can say they guide you to heaven or guide you to hell."

Medallion nodded her head with understanding.

"And in your case, my beautiful dear, they guided you back to us. We knew it was not your time to leave this earth. You are needed here to raise your son."

"But there was someone else there too."

"Oh… someone else?"

"Yes… she was laying on the ground until the ancestors appeared. She begged for them to take her too, but they ignored her and told me to ignore her too. They said she chooses to stay there and wait for her baby, but she didn't act like she wanted to stay. It was really sad to see her begging to come with us."

"I've never heard of there being someone there just waiting. When I was younger, I heard the elders talk about souls in waiting. She may have been one of them."

"They said she was waiting for her son. I wonder how she got separated from him."

In her heart, Mary felt it had to have been Sunta sitting in The White waiting for Elijah to cross. Medallion almost bore the same fate Sunta had and Mary remembered how Sunta died with her son's name floating off of her lips. It was a tragic night when the sisters had to leave Sunta and every night since, Mary prayed for her sister's soul. Over the years, Mary would reach out to the ancestors through rituals and séance's but none blessed her with vision of Sunta's fate.

"Did the ancestors tell you who she was?"

"They didn't. They told me not to mourn for her."

"Well don't think any more about it my dear. The ancestors bought you safely back to us and that's all that matters."

Medallion frowned and hung her head in thought of the woman begging to come with them. *But they said she's waiting on her son…* And then the thought of her new baby boy popped into her mind. Her near death experience... Her not knowing who his father is... The anguish of it all consumed her.

"Is he okay?"

"Why yes! He's beautiful. He's resting nearby. I can ring a nurse to bring him to you."

Aunt Mary picked up the hospital phone's receiver, but Medallion put her hand on Aunt Mary's forcing the phone back into its cradle.

"Not yet Auntie. I don't want to see him yet."

Medallion rested her hand back in her lap and she stared down at them in silence. Aunt Mary brought her chair closer to her niece's bed; concerned about her.

"What's wrong, dear? Why don't you want to see your son?"

"Is Waymen here?"

"Why no. He's still out of town. But I did call him. He's on his way."

"What did you tell him? How did he sound? Did he sound like he was happy the baby was born?"

"I guess… I mean I told him you had the baby, and there were a few complications, but you were both safe."

"I mean, did he sound like he wanted to come home, did he sound like he wanted to be a father? Be my husband?"

Aunt Mary saw the desperation in Medallion's eyes. She shook her head in shame and let go of her hand.

"Medallion… you almost died giving birth to your son, and all you can think about is Waymen? Why don't you take a moment and bond with your child."

Medallion sucked her teeth and rolled her eyes as she folded her arms in a pout.

"I'm going to. I just want to know about my husband. I want him here. He belongs here with me. Not in some other city."

"Well, do you blame him?!"

Aunt Mary felt her temperature rise as her agitation with Medallion grew over how she ignored her son and was more focused on Waymen.

"You have played so many games with his heart and taken him through so many twists and turns, why do you think he'd want to be by your side? I'm sure when he gets here, he'll be supportive and be the husband and father he has to be, but honestly, you don't deserve it. You don't deserve him or that precious child you just bore. And sometimes, I feel like you don't even deserve the love I give you. You're just selfish, Medallion. Plain and simple, selfish."

She grabbed her things and headed towards the door.

"I hope you figure out what is really important before Waymen gets here, and here is a clue. That baby takes precedence over any drama you're cooking up."

Aunt Mary turned on her heels and walked out of the room closing the door behind her.

Medallion couldn't believe her aunt left the way she did. They've had differences before, but none ever led to either one of them leaving in anger. *How can she doubt my love for that kid? I love him… well… I love what he represents. He can mend this marriage that I screwed up. Can't she see I'm trying to get my family back together? I mean… I care for the baby, but the baby isn't for me. It's for him… for us. That's all.* Medallion picked up her cell phone when she heard it vibrate on her bedside table.

"What do you want?"

"You had that baby yet?"

"What do you care?" She contemplated hanging up the phone on Rodney. The way he left her standing on the front porch showed once again how callous he could really be.

"You know I care. Don't be like that."

"Yeah, I had him. I almost died in the process but he's here."

"Died?"

"Yes, but I'm fine now."

"Can I come see you guys? I want to apologize for the way I treated you earlier. You know I didn't mean it. It's just… That was a new couch. I freaked out."

Medallion smiled a little as she thought that maybe she didn't need to make things right with Waymen. Maybe all she needed was Rodney. *After all… it may be his child…*

"Yes. You can come see us. I'm in room 326."

"Great. I'll be there in a bit."

Medallion put her cell back on the bedside stand and prepared herself for Rodney to come through the door.

"Ma'am. How are you feeling?" Medallion looked up and saw the face of a happy plump nurse standing in the entrance.

"I'm fine."

She gave the nurse a relaxed smile; hoping she was just doing rounds and not trying to bother her.

"That's good to hear. I'm Nurse Jackie by the way and I have your baby with me. Would you like some snuggle time with him before we get him changed and prepared for his feeding?"

Before she could respond, the nurse was already backing into the room with the baby in the rolling bassinette.

"Umm… nurse… NURSE. Please don't bring him here right now. I'm still a little tired from earlier."

"Oh it's okay!" The nurse said cheerfully. "The doctor said even though you gave us a scare, you're quite alright for a visit."

"But I don't want him right now! Please take him away!"

"Oh…"

The nurse looked confused; not understanding how cold the young woman was being towards her own child. Instead of meddling, the nurse smiled politely and put the baby back in the bassinette.

"Of course dear. Get your rest. Maybe you'll be up to seeing him a little later."

Chapter 15

"Driver, this is my house here on the left."

Mary's Uber slowed down as it prepared to stop.

"Yes, you can let me out right in front of the driveway."

The Uber came to a full stop allowing Mary to depart the vehicle. She tipped her driver and made her way into her cozy Southside home. Mary went to the kitchen and grabbed the glass jar from the shelf and placed it on the counter. She opened the jar and took a whiff of the bloom's aroma before grabbing a few of the clumped together dried leaves and placed them on the counter.

"That girl child of mine…"

Tears of frustration swelled in her eyes. Her hands trembled with anxiety while she contemplated Medallion's situation. Mary grabbed her small wooden decorative "robin's egg" blue box sitting on the counter. In it was her rolling paper, a few cigarillos with the plastic tips, along with her favorite multi-colored jewel encrusted lighter. Deciding not to use the cigarillo's, she pulled out her rolling strips and then grabbed the dried pieces of plants she'd left sitting on the counter.

"Why must she continue to be this way? Can't she see what she is doing to her life? She's ruining everything."

With everything she needed for a vision quest, Mary turned around and opened the kitchen's knick-knack drawer pulling out her leaf grinder and headed to the den. She flipped the light switch for her special red light to brighten the room and finally sitting down in her favorite comfy recliner with the side table beside it. Comfortable in her chair, she began to roll a perfect cylindrical blunt. Once done, she looked it over in satisfaction admiring her masterpiece before she lit it to smoke.

As her mood began to shift, Mary began to meditate on Medallion's behavior while she exhaled the thin smoke from her first pull of the rolled and grinded plant. *For all that has been passed down to me, I'm at the mercy of a child who ain't willing to take her place in the line. She out here messing up everybody life over a man.*

She took another pull and exhaled. Mary watched the smoke droll upwards; watching it for the formation of clues into the future for Medallion and her family. The smoke moved slowly like clouds traveling in the sky, but nothing could be made of the message she received from them. Mary withdrew the blunt from her lips and looked at it with a questioning glare.

"This blend isn't working strong enough. I need something heavier than this."

She put her blunt in the ashtray letting its energy die with the dimming of the embers. She then pulled her cellphone out of her pocket to make a call. "Let me see if he picks up…"

"Hey Mrs. Mary Mack! What it do!"

Mary smiled at the greeting. "Hello Kyhiem. How's my favorite guy?"

"I'm good now that you calling! Shoooooot Mrs. Mack What you finna do?"

Mary laughed at her dear young friend. Kyhiem worked at the grocery store she frequented as a bagging clerk. Their relationship began when he overheard Mary making a fuss to the store manager about baggers no longer taking the groceries out to cars as a curtesy to its patrons. Admiring her liveliness, Kyhiem made it his priority to take her groceries to her car whenever she visited the store. And when he wasn't there, he made sure his teammates did the same.

During those short walks to her car through the parking lot, Kyhiem and Mary exchanged stories about their lives and laughed at the way of the world. Mary found him refreshing but also sensed he was a young man full of potential for something greater. Learning that Kyhiem was top of his class at Virginia State with a major in Agriculture and a minor in Chemistry delighted Mary to see black excellence in a S.T.E.M. profession.

What Mary admired about him most was his desire to be great. When he talked about his school work, she felt his excitement and passion for his chosen field. He was dedicated to his studies but was also so grounded when it came to his friends and family. With his non-conforming locs, oversized jeans, and colorful sneaker choices, the average person wouldn't see his intelligence or how well his parents raised him. But she knew with his skin the color of day, and eyes as meek as a lamb, he would prove his naysayers wrong every chance he could.

Kyhiem was on the verge of creating a hybrid plant with more potency and super power than the regular grown cannabis when he learned that Mary was an expert in herbs and plants. Mary encouraged him to pursue his dream in Botanical Engineering and she would happily test his strains for potency. For four years, Mary was his only test subject as she had been the only person he'd trusted with his most important work. She also decided to be his financial backer once she learned of his ambitions.

"Well… I'm sitting her smoking something from my garden, but I feel it's not strong enough for my needs. Would you mind bringing me a batch of trial 7B? I smoked the last of it a month ago."

"Wait… We lighting up tonight? You must got something heavy on your mind if we about to get lit. You need me to bring anything else? I'm at the store so I can grab us some snacks. Your favorite marshmallow snowball is in stock and the new Oreo is back out!

"Thank you my dear, but I'll have something prepared for us to eat when you get here. I've been consuming too much junk food lately and I think it's messing with my premonitions. Can't seem to focus lately. That's why I need you to come over with that strand we created. Something about that blend really helped me see my visions better."

"Fo sho! I feel you Mrs. Mack. I remember when we smoked it, you were seeing all types of things for me and that shit was real too. Yo… That connect you said to cut the deal with? You were right! He was not anything I thought he was. I'm going to finish up here and when I get off, I'm going hit my crib up to grab that for you and I'll be right over.

"Great. I'll see you soon."

"Hold up Mrs. Mack… Is Medda gonna be there? You know that's my future wifey."

"Oh Kyhiem!" Mary let out a chuckle. "Now you know she's married. Plus you are way too young for her."

"Man! I know she married and everything but you can put in a good word for me! You already know I'm going to be the next billionaire! You told me yourself I'm gonna be rich and take care of my whole family so I know I can take care of her and everything she need. Tell her I love her so I can shoot my shot."

"Kyhiem! You are a mess! You've never even met her. How can you tell you love her if you've only seen her picture?"

Mary bellowed over in laughter. Kyhiem was such a character and she loved how his sincerity could come off so hilarious. The best part about him was that he never took himself too seriously, so he never minded her laughing at his intentions to be with Medallion.

"Don't worry my dear. You focus on your studies and don't think about Medda. When you graduate, I know just the young lady for you. I hand-picked her myself."

"For real Mrs. Mack! She fine like my baby mama, Medda?"

"I can say for a fact she is. She's one of my other nieces and I'm sure you two will be perfect for each other."

"Bet! I'll see you in two hours. Write her number down for when I get over there!"

"No Kyhiem! Not until you graduate!" They both laughed, said their goodbyes and hung up the phone.

Two hours later, Mary's doorbell rang, and as promised, Kyhiem was on the other side.

"Why Mrs. Mary Mack! You looking good in all that black! You know I gotta thang for you."

Kyhiem gave Mary a welcoming hug and a kiss on the cheek. He'd been calling her 'Mrs. Mack' since they first met. He admired her class and distinction and how people respected her presence; like the respect a Mack would receive from all the pimps and players on the block. Whenever she came into the grocery store, she always got first-class treatment from the manager. And when the manager noticed their friendship, his status at the store rose as well.

"Kyhiem, it's so good to see you. I'm so glad you could make it over. It's been a while."

"I know. School and work have been hard, but I'm almost done. And when it's over I get to work for the largest bio company in VA, thanks to you."

Mary opened the door wider and let him walk in to find his plate of food waiting at the kitchen's bar.

"It was my pleasure dear. There are so few black men working in agriculture this day in age. You are a diamond in the rough. This company will definitely help you on your journey."

Kyhiem took off his coat and hung it on the back of his chair. When he took his hat off, his locs expanded from their smooshed position and sprawled around his head in an incohesive pattern. They finally laid scattered around his dome crowning and framing his face. As he sat down, he pulled out the cannabis from his back pocket and placed it on the counter beside his plate.

"You want me to roll or are you going to do it?" Kyhiem offered Mary the bagged cannabis but she pushed it back to him.

"You can do the honors."

Mary went to the cabinet to grab the lavender oil and two cups of sweet iced tea to complement their dinner. She handed him the wrapping strips, but he declined them with a head nod.

"I got a black I'm going to slice open for this batch. It's better with the cigarillo paper."

"Okay. Well add a few drops of this in it."

She handed him the lavender oil and watched while he slit open the cigarillo with his thumb nail and dumped the tobacco in the waste can beside the edge of the counter. He then put a few drops of lavender oil on the cigar paper and allowed it to seep in as he chopped the leaf up into smaller bits for rolling. After he was done preparing it, he lit the blunt and handed it to Mary to pull from it first.

"Here you go. Let that get all in your system..."

Mary watched the blunt burn for a moment. Its embers danced around while smoldering in the cigarillo paper. She smelled the lavender oil blending with the cedar smoked leaf infused with eucalyptus heightening her anticipation to smoke. She pulled long and hard from it. The smoke filled her mouth and as she breathed in, it began to fill her lungs. She felt the vapors circle around in her body and then she slowly blew out; nodding her head in approval.

"Ummm... That's better than I thought." She took another pull and then passed it to Kyhiem. "You are going to like this."

Kyhiem pulled from the blunt and instantly felt the mellow vibe the lavender contributed, intensifying the eucalyptus and the spice blend from the original batch. He inhaled the smoke deeper; feeling it slowly roll around in his mouth. The experience was smooth like satin with a warmth that comforted him. He began to feel his body relax, and as he blew the smoke outward, he felt his cares float away on its trail.

"Whoah... I ain't never felt this good off one pull." He pulled one more time before passing it back to Mary.

"It does have a stronger affect than what I expected, but it is just what I needed. Come, let's settle in the den while we enjoy this."

Kyhiem grabbed their plates and followed Mary into the next room.

"Mrs. Mack, I think that's what this batch needed. That lavender put something to it."

"It did. Next time you are in your lab, add that and hydrate the plant with rose water and see what comes of it."

"Ah man! I never thought about rose water! I could use it since it's known to enhance moods and boost antioxidants."

Kyhiem grabbed his phone and made a note in his memo app to massage the plant leaf with lavender oil and nourish it with rose water. He smiled at the revelation and put his phone away in time for his turn to pull. As he did, he looked over to see Mary lost in thought. Her head tilted back in the recliner as she stared at the ceiling. He nudged her for her turn. Without looking his way, she took the blunt taking her pull.

"Mrs. Mack… what's on your mind? You said earlier you were stressing over something. So, what's up?"

Mary looked his way when she blew out her smoke while discerning her woes.

"It's frustrating you know." She took another pull. "To watch someone you love ruin their life and you can't do anything about it."

"I feel you Mrs. Mack, but you gotta let them stumble and fall so they never make the same mistake twice."

Mary chuckled at the advice and passed the blunt. "You are wise beyond your years, Kyhiem."

"Yeah my mama be telling me my soul old and stuff."

He pulled once more and passed it back to Mary. She looked at the last of it knowing she would get the final pull. She held it out for him to take.

"Do you want the last of this?"

"Nah, you can have it. I gotta hit the road. My girl mad I came to smoke instead of kicking it with her." A sly grin came over his face before he spoke again. "I think she a lil' jealous of you and me."

Mary turned in shock at the comment. "Are you serious about that?! Jealous of me?!" She pulled the last of the blunt and put the endings of it out in the ash tray. "What is she jealous of? I'm probably closer to your great grandma's age. Ain't nothing here for her to be jealous of."

Kyhiem bellowed over in laughter watching Mary's facial expressions.

"Yeah she jealous. She don't even care how old you are. She keep calling you my 'Sugar Mama' and whatnot."

Mary couldn't hold in her giggles at the thought of using Kyhiem for sexual desires and belted out a laugh she hadn't heard from herself in a long time. Tears of amusement began to flow. As she laughed, Kyhiem began to laugh to the point they were both falling over each other in a fit of humor. When Mary could finally catch her breath, she said in between gasps, "Let your young lady know I am not a threat, but if I wanted you I could have you… even without the suga." They both laughed once again.

Kyhiem walked back to the kitchen where his coat and hat lay. Mary followed with the plates. She scrapped the remnants of their meal into the trash and put the dishes in the sink. When she turned around, Kyhiem was ready to go and his arms stretched out wide for a goodbye hug. Mary walked into his arms and wrapped hers around him and patted him on the back.

"Thank you for spending some time with me."

"It was my pleasure Mrs. Mack. Thanks for the enhancements on the weed. I think this the one."

"I think so too. It sure took the edge off. My vision is clearer so I have some work I have to do."

"Well I'm going to leave you to it. I'll catch you later Mrs. Mack! Oh, I'll drop off some of the new batch when it's ready."

Kyhiem headed out the door. Mary watched him drive off before she shut the door and locked it.

Heading back into the den, she picked up the blunt she started before she invited Kyhiem over. She lit and pulled from it ready to focus her thoughts and center herself. She closed her eyes, allowing her mind to relax and release the emotion and frustration of her day. As she breathed in and out, she kept her eyes closed while acknowledging and accepting all that Medallion said in the delivery room about her dealings with Waymen… her feelings about her own child… and her questionable relationship with Rodney. Mary exhaled and released the tension that dynamic had brought her. She inhaled again ready to understand what she nor Medallion could not.

From the darkness found behind her closed eyes, she began to see hints and flashes of light. Eyelids closed, she watched formless shapes become more defined. Lights of amber haze began to create a backlight, and as they grew in intensity, their hues started to magnify. She saw blurs of blues and reds and yellows as the scene materialized. Flashes of objects appeared as the lights circled creating the beautiful story that was her own.

She inhaled the fumes from the blunt triggering a memory of springtime at Glory Hill, surrounded by her sisters under the great willow tree near the lake. She saw them sitting there waiting for their mama to come teach them the magic. Mary walked over and stood and observed the scene in silence. She watched she and her sister's sit in a circle preparing for their lesson. Bettye handed out their bowls and pumice sticks to begin a session of mixing herbs, plants, and oils. Then she saw the baby of the bunch, no more than seven years of age, run down the hill to sit with them. Their mother Makeda followed behind.

Mary remembered that day. It was the day her mother told them all that she wasn't going to be able to watch over them any longer. She said that she was being sent to another place far away and they would have to look after each other. She placed Bettye in charge of seeing after their care. Mary watched the scene play out like a silent movie. No one noticed her. She saw her and her sisters cry and beg their mama to take them with her but all of them knew it couldn't be done. And then Mary, as she looked at her younger self with her sisters struggling to accept the imminent departure of their mother, understood why she had to accept Medallions situation the way it was.

She opened her eyes and was back in her home. Her mind and soul at rest; understanding the purpose and knowing the turmoil surrounding Medallion was not hers. Mary finally accepted that what Medallion had to go through to save her family, she would have to do on her own. Mary never knew the details around her mother leaving. What she remembered, was her mother was one of the Master's favorites. Talk on the land rumored that the Misses was jealous and had arranged for her mother to be moved. None of what happened to Makeda and her sisters mattered. What mattered was now Medallion would have to find her way to save her family just as she did when it was time to escape Glory Hill, and just as Makeda did when they tore her from her children.

Chapter 16

"Alright, take your time, take your time." Aunt Mary braced Medallion's back as they walked slowly into her condo.

"Nurse, you can put the baby in that bassinette right over there."

Aunt Mary smiled kindly at the nurse who carried Medallion's son to the bassinette next to the couch and laid him down in it.

"He's such a precious little one." The nurse tucked him in and then went to the kitchen to prepare his bottle.

"When is she leaving?" Medallion eyed the nurse in irritation as she passed them by.

"She wouldn't have had to come in the first place had you shown a little enthusiasm about the birth of your son."

Medallion sucked her teeth in disgust at how she was treated at the hospital. She was shocked that a child protective services counselor knocked on her hospital door wanting to "talk" with her about the demands of being a new mother. Apparently, her nonchalant attitude about nursing and cuddling with her son didn't go over well with the nurses attending to her care, and they found it to be a great idea to let CPS intervene on the hospital's behalf.

In the end, the visit amounted to a couple of days more in the hospital, and a diagnosis of post-partum depression. Aunt Mary assured the hospital facilitators and the CPS agent that she was going to look after her niece and her great-great nephew, and that no harm would come to the child or the mother. But even with that type of reassurance, the authorities were a bit leery about agreeing to release Medallion and the baby to Aunt Mary. Finally, the matter was settled when Aunt Mary hired an at home nurse to come and help Medallion with the heavy duties.

"Alright Medallion, slowly ease yourself down to the couch and we'll stretch your legs out so that you can relax."

Medallion gave a tight-lipped smile to her aunt as the pain of her stitches from her undercarriage increased with every move she made.

"Have you heard from Waymen?" she asked Aunt Mary once she was settled on the couch.

Aunt Mary eyed Medallion with her "uh-huh" smirk on her face as she finished fluffing the pillows behind her back.

"Yeah. I heard from him."

"Well what did he say? Why hasn't he come home yet? It's been days since he was supposed to come back. At first, he was supposed to meet me at the hospital, but he got caught up at work and said he'd meet me here."

Medallion grabbed the remote for the tv off of the coffee table and began flipping the channels as soon as the television screen lit up.

"Well, he's in flight now. Something about the foreign buyers couldn't agree on design specs for the new building and it held up negotiations. He called me from the airport this morning and said he would be here later tonight."

Aunt Mary grabbed the remote from Medallion knowing that her niece wasn't really watching television and powered it back off. Medallion gave Aunt Mary the 'why'd you do that?' look but didn't dispute her aunt's actions. There had been a conversation brewing in Aunt Mary since her stay at the hospital, and Medallion knew her aunt's agitation had to do with her walking in on her and Rodney sharing a kiss goodbye.

"Jackie… I think we are fine right now. If you'd like to take a break and come back in a few hours, I'd like to have some privacy with my niece."

"Oh no problem. I'll just make a run to the store for a few things I see the baby needs and I'll be right back."

Nurse Jackie grabbed her coat and her pocketbook and headed for the door.

"Thank you Jackie. Don't worry about locking the door. It'll lock once you shut it." Aunt Mary assured the nurse as she made her way down the entry hall and out of the front door.

Once Medallion heard the door click from the lock, she began explaining before Aunt Mary could begin to speak.

"Now, Auntie, I know what you want to talk about, and I'm not really trying to hear it. Yes, Rodney was at the hospital 'cause he was with me when I went into labor."

Aunt Mary's eyes grew big at the revelation, but she did not interrupt Medallion as she continued with her explanation.

"And yes, you saw me and Rodney kissing, but what you don't know is that Rodney came to tell me that if the baby is his, or not, he is ready to take full responsibility, and be my husband. He even gave me a ring. Yes, Auntie. Rodney proposed, and I accepted."

"You what?!" Aunt Mary was in full shock listening to Medallion speak. "How foolish can you be, girl? The ancestor's told me to stay out of this but I can't hold my tongue about your trifling stupidity. Child, can't you see Rodney is playing games?! He's just stringing you along because he likes the drama!"

"You are wrong, Auntie! While he was there, he gave a sample of his DNA, and Look. He brought the ring with him too. I would have had it on my finger when I came to labor and delivery, but we had a mishap at his house and I accidently left it there."

Medallion held up the piece of jewelry that had been hanging from her gold necklace to display the diamond that dangled and twirled around.

Aunt Mary slapped the hand that held the ring letting it flop back down on Medallion's chest.

"That don't mean nothing to me. And you know it don't mean nothing to you! How are you going to accept a proposal and you are already MARRIED?! I thought you wanted to be a better woman for Waymen. What happened to that promise?"

"It went out the window when Waymen left town... AGAIN for some business trip… right in the middle of my pregnancy. He knew I was due any day now and he left! Not to mention, he acts like he doesn't want me anyway, so why should I change if he's not even trying?"

"You know why he isn't trying? Because you haven't changed— at ALL! Medallion, you keep pushing that man to his limits, and I'm warning you, you are going to push him too far!"

"Auntie! You always take his side! Can't you see my side of things for once! Waymen married me for better or worse. Yeah, I've done some pretty messed up things, but I planned to right my wrongs. But Waymen acts like what I've done to make things right aren't good enough. I had this baby for him! Do you think I want to be tied down to some kid?! Babies aren't my thing, but I didn't have an abortion because I know Waymen wanted a little brat to take care of. Now... I may have gone about it the wrong way, and the baby may not be his, but I had this kid because there is a fifty percent chance that it might be, and if this baby can save what me and Waymen had, I was going to take that gamble. But now?! Now Waymen acts like he doesn't want me or this baby! If he's not going to take care of him, then I have to go with the next best thing, and Rodney is it."

"Medallion, the things you say sometimes sickens me. I didn't raise you to be this vile person you've turned out to be."

"Don't say that, Auntie. I mean… I like the kid, and eventually I'll love it, but I didn't have this kid for me. I gave birth for Waymen."

"The way you talk, I should have never had the ancestors bring you back." Aunt Mary stood up and went to grab her things.

"Where are you going?" Medallion watched Aunt Mary walk to the door.

"Away from here. I need to go pray. You've got me thinking some evil things, girl, and no good will come if I stay. I'm going to go pray that you find some sense in that brain of yours. I pray that baby is Waymen's so he can get full custody of him when he finally wises up and divorces you, and I pray the ancestor's had a reason for bringing you back because even though I asked them to help you find your way, they didn't have to. There must be something meaningful on this earth you have to do before your time here is up."

"Well who's going to watch this kid until the nurse comes back?"

"Lord have mercy and HELP this child!"

Aunt Mary shook her head in shame for Medallion and walked out the door unable to say anything to make her niece see what she was doing to herself, her son, and to the two men mixed up in her drama.

Aunt Mary doesn't understand. This is about what I want, and what's going to make me happy. I'll do anything for my happiness, and keeping a man is what's going to make me happy. Medallion grabbed for the television remote once again, but noticed a pile of mail on the coffee table as well. Instead of picking up the remote, she picked up the mail noticing the light blue tinted envelope stamped with the logo for the City of Richmond and the initials for the Department of Child Services underneath. "This has got to be the results..." Medallion muttered to herself. She lifted the envelope out of the pile of mail which were mostly hallmark cards congratulating her bundle of joy.

Hesitating about opening the life-changing envelope right away, she allowed it to float on her fingertips shifting from one hand to the other; pondering what the results would actually mean for her future.

"I'm not scared of what it says. I come out the winner no matter who the dad is going to be."

After taking a deep breath, Medallion opened the envelope without any more lingering thoughts and read down the page; allowing her glance to linger on the results.

"It's what I thought." She folded the paper back up and stuck it back in the envelope. "Your daddy is not my husband." Medallion spoke the words as she looked towards the baby in the bassinette. "But don't worry. Your daddy wants the both of us, so I'm not bothered."

Medallion grabbed for her pocketbook sitting on the floor by the corner of the couch and pulled her phone out of it. She hit speed dial #2 for Rodney and waited for him to pick up.

"Hey baby. You home?" Rodney's voice bellowed joyously through the receiver motivating Medallion to tell him the good news.

"Yeah, I got in about an hour or two ago. Guess what. I got the results in the mail."

"So what's the verdict?" Rodney asked the question with anticipation.

"Are you sure you want to know? I mean, this test is going to change everyone's life." Medallion desperately wanted to tell him, but also wanted to toy with him just a bit.

"You know I'm ready. Go on and tell me. I can't wait any longer."

"Okay, okay. Rodney… my son… is… your son too!" Medallion giggled and laughed as she waited for Rodney to respond, but he fell silent, and the silence silenced Medallion's giggles.

"Rodney. Did you hear me? This baby is biologically yours."

"Yeah. I heard you." Rodney said in an irritated tone.

"Well, what's the problem? Aren't you happy? Now, when I divorce Waymen, I have no reason to contact him. He's out of the picture for good."

"Wait— what? You are divorcing Waymen?"

"Yeah. Wasn't that the plan? Didn't you come to the hospital to be there for us? And what about the proposal at your house? I mean, you did give me a ring and say I can't wait for us to be together."

"Yeah… sexually… after you've healed from the baby stuff. I never said anything about marriage."

"Huh?! You didn't propose?! Well what was the ring for?"

"That thing?" Rodney laughed at her assumption. "That was a leftover gift I was going to give to my mama. I saw it on the QVC channel and bought it for her. Lucky for you, she didn't like it. I don't even think it's real. It's like a diamonique or something like that, but it ain't no engagement ring!" Rodney continued to laugh; finding it funny Medallion was ready to change her life over a fake diamond and a presumed marriage proposal.

"Rodney! This is the last straw! I am so tired of your games! I should have never messed around on Waymen with you! You only want me because Waymen has me. You've got some sick, warped obsession with getting under Waymen's skin and you're using me to do it!"

"You just figuring that out? I thought you were in on the plan. Weren't you doing that in the first place?"

Medallion couldn't respond because in fact, she had done the same thing, but it all backfired. With all the time she and Rodney spent playing games on Waymen, she had grown to have some real feelings for him and thought he'd developed the same.

"Look Rod. We are done. I can see now that I have made a terrible mistake messing around with you. Luckily Waymen and I plan on working things out, and he has said he'll be this baby's father whether it's biologically his or not."

"Good. Because I wasn't planning on taking care of him anyway. I'm glad that boy's going to have a good man to call daddy. I'll holla at you later. I got my girl coming over in an hour and you killing the vibe with all this marriage and baby daddy crap. I hope you and Waymen have a great Leave-it-to-Beaver life together." Rodney hung up the phone before Medallion could say another word.

"Ugh!" In frustration, Medallion threw the phone across the room; barely missing the bassinette the baby slept comfortably in.

"Whoa! What's gotten under your skin?"

She turned her head towards the door to see Waymen standing in the entryway to their living room. Medallion took one look at him and burst into tears. “Baby you’re home!” She didn’t know if she was crying happy tears or sad ones, but Waymen only saw them as a welcoming show of affection.

“Yes mama, daddy’s home.”

Waymen dropped his bags and made his way to the couch. Crouching down to kiss Medallion on her lips, he stopped and stared at how wonderfully her skin glowed, and how her eyes sparkled even if they were full of tears. “I’ve missed you so much.” He kissed away the tears that were already splattered one her cheeks, and then passionately planted his lips on hers.

Medallion embraced Waymen within her arms wondering why she ever doubted his commitment to being the loving husband he’d promised to be when they got back together.

“I’ll never leave like that again, Medallion. I should have been there for you, and I’m sorry I wasn’t, but I’m here now. You and our son have me for the rest of our lives.”

“I’m sorry, Waymen. I’m so sorry I put you through all of this. From now on it’s just you and me— and our son.”

Medallion laughed at the inclusion of Waymen’s new bundle of joy. Waymen lifted himself from his crouched position by the couch and made his way to the crib to get a look at his baby boy.

“He’s beautiful, Medallion. I can’t believe we made a little one.”

He scooped up the baby and held him in his arms. He gingerly touched his little fingers imagining them catching the football he’d toss to them. He then took off the baby’s little fluffy cotton socks and looked at his splayed out toes excited about the first pair of Jordan’s he’d be able to put on them. “My boy.” He said proudly to himself. He kissed the little one on the forehead before placing him back in the bassinette. Waymen turned back to Medallion with a beaming smile, and announced, “I’m going to make dinner.”

Medallion wiped the rest of her tears away and shook her head no.

"You don't have to. You just got back in. I can just order us some Chinese from Jhangs."

"Nope. I'm ready to jump in and be a dad. I'm going to cook your favorite meal, and then carry you into the bedroom and get you ready for bed." He gave her a wink of his eye and headed towards the kitchen.

Medallion smiled as she thought, *and to think, I was about to turn my back on all of this.* Just as she was about to stretch back and relax into the couch, she spotted the letter from the child support office which held the DNA results. She quickly grabbed it and shuffled it underneath the couch.

"What do you have over there, Medallion? Is that the mail?" Waymen peered over the counter while he dug around looking for the right pots and pans he needed to begin his food preparation.

"Uh, yeah. Looks like a lot of cards and junk mail." She held up the bundle of mail she had in her hand.

"Well, go ahead and start cracking those congratulatory cards open. I hope that they have some money in them because I think we are going to go broke from me spoiling him rotten!"

Waymen laughed and hit the sound system's remote; filling the apartment with the sound of hip-hop infused jazz music. He bopped his head to the beat of the jazz version of Big Poppa's song "Get Money" as he whisked around to turn on the stove.

As Medallion began opening the cards and reading them aloud, the doorbell rang startling them both. Waymen looked at Medallion with a 'who could that be' look. Medallion thought for a moment, and then remembered.

"It's the nurse assigned to take care of me." Waymen ran to get the door.

Nurse Jackie entered the room, put her bags down, and headed straight for the kitchen. "Something smells delightful!" Nurse Jackie stirred the sauce Waymen had started and turned down the heat on the sautéing onions and peppers.

"Yeah. I'm cooking for my babies and then I'm going to escort my wife into the room and get her ready for a bedside romantic dinner for two."

Waymen attempted to join Nurse Jackie in the kitchen, but she shooed him away.

"Mr. Waymen, you've been flying all day. I can see you just got here. Why don't you let me finish up in the kitchen? I'll feed the baby while the food cooks, and you can tend to your wife. It's not hard to tell you both miss each other.

"Why thank you Nurse Jackie. I think I'll take you up on your offer."

Waymen scooped Medallion off of the couch and they both kissed each other and giggled as they made their way to the bedroom. Nurse Jackie turned down the heat under the pots and pans on the stove and went to the living room to straighten up before she settled the baby into his bedroom crib. As she picked up around the couch, she spotted the light blue envelope peeping from underneath. She placed the envelope on top of the congratulation cards before she went to the bassinette. She then picked up the baby and headed to his room for his feeding and bed time.

Chapter 17

"Mr. Foster…"

Nurse Jackie knocked lightly on the closed double doors of the master bedroom. *No answer.* She knocked a little harder on her second round when she realized she could hear the rush of the bathtub water running. "Mr. Foster…" She spoke up a little more hoping she didn't have to intrude any further on the couple's intimate time together.

"Hold on Jackie!"

Waymen heard the knocks and the delightful voice of the home nurse at their bedroom door.

"Baby, that's probably the nurse letting me know that she is on her way out for the evening. I'm going to walk her out and I'll be right back."

Waymen had placed Medallion in the bath full of bubbles allowing the running water from the faucet to cascade over her feet. He enjoyed tending to her every need during these moments of joy with his new family. He stood up from the tub and kissed Medallion on the forehead before he left her. He opened the door of the room and greeted the nurse with a relaxed smile.

"Thank you so much for dinner Ms. Jackie. Everything tasted great."

"Oh, it was my pleasure. Seeing how excited you were to be with your wife and your son is all the thanks I need."

She turned around and made her way back down the hall with Waymen following.

"I've put Isaiah down for the evening. He took his bottle nicely." Nurse Jackie grabbed her pocketbook from the counter and headed to the hall closet for her coat. "Isaiah also took his bath just as perfectly."

She let a slight chuckle escape her lips before she continued. "Oh how I love babies, and you've got a beautiful one to look after."

"Thank you Mrs. Jackie. I'm a lucky guy."

"The real lucky one is your wife."

She turned to look at Waymen with concern before she opened the door to the hall closet. She placed her hand on his arm in a moment of empathy before she continued.

"Mr. Foster, I'm a nurse, not a psychiatrist, but my eyes have seen a lot of things while working in the baby ward. Watching women bond with their child is what I love. It brings me real joy to see that first hug, that first kiss— the real image of love-at-first-sight."

She bowed her head in sorrow as she spoke her next words.

"I didn't see that when your wife held your son. There were no hugs or kisses. She just laid there— even after they saved her life, she didn't want to be bothered by him."

Waymen bristled at her words wanting to retort the negative assumption of his wife. However, a cool head conquered his emotions allowing him to listen for understanding as he continued to let the nurse speak. She looked up with hope in her eyes as she continued on.

"Now, don't get me wrong, it's not the first time I've seen a woman respond like this. In fact, it's a natural thing for a woman not to bond right away with their new born baby. They call it the Baby Blues."

She smiled gently and squeezed his arm just a bit for emphasis.

"Mrs. Foster may seem distant, and at times downright unloving to you and your son, but stick it out with her. Be patient. Show her you love her just as much as you love that boy and I'm positive she'll pull right out of it."

Waymen relaxed his shoulders in relief as he received her encouraging words.

"I will Mrs. Jackie. I appreciate your concern."

But then the nurse's face turned grim and she gripped his arm a little stronger.

"But protect your son... If for one moment you think Mrs. Foster may harm that child— 'cause you think she's acting a bit strange, or she's said something that just don't sit right by you, you get your guard up. It's nothing wrong with reacting 'cause you think she might do something to harm herself or that precious baby. It's better to overreact than underreact."

Nurse Jackie shook her head once more as she thought about the horrors some new moms succumb to. Too many times she'd seen and heard of cases where a mom drowned herself because she couldn't handle the stress of being a mother. Even more dreadful was hearing of a mother who tried to put a child in the microwave because the voices in her head told her it was for the work of the Lord.

"Mrs. Jackie, you have my promise that I will not let any harm come to my son or my wife."

Waymen gave the nurse a grateful hug. He then opened the closet, handed her, her coat, and then grabbed his.

"What you putting your jacket on for?"

Nurse Jackie looked at Waymen strangely as he put his jacket on in one swoop and was now straightening out his collar.

"Why, I'm going to escort one of the prettiest nurses to her chariot."

They both laughed at his charismatic words while he helped her with her coat.

"Nonsense! I'll be fine. There's a doorman in the lobby and I'm sure he'll watch me to my car. You get yourself back in there and tend to your wife."

Waymen laughed at Nurse Jackie's spunk and agreed to her orders.

"Yes ma'am. I'll do just that."

He opened the front door for her and watched her pass through.

"I'll be back in the morning to help out," she said while turning around to say her goodbyes.

"No need, Mrs. Jackie. I think I can handle it from here. I'm on hiatus from work starting today, and the movers will be here in the morning to help us with our things.

"Oh, that's right! Your aunt did tell me you all won't be staying here long— that'd you'd be moving somewhere out in the country. Fresh air and relaxation will do you all some good."

"I believe it will too. And with winter here, it'll be a great place to snuggle up and get cozy."

"You're absolutely right about that." She laughed and gave him a hug. "Well Mr. Foster it was a pleasure meeting you. I wish you and your family the best."

"Thank you. I'll make sure to pay the agency for today and tomorrow."

"Well isn't that nice of you!"

Nurse Jackie gave him a kiss on the cheek, and then turned and headed down the hall towards the elevators.

What a nice lady… Waymen thought as he stepped back into the condo and closed the door behind him. Heading back to the master bedroom, he grabbed a few things in his path and put them away. He turned off the hall light and headed to the kitchen. Nurse Jackie had done a great job of straightening things up, but Waymen was meticulous and liked things to be in the places he'd predetermined. He put the clean and dried dishes in the cabinet and then placed the dish rag back in its usual spot near the dish soap. He then headed through the living room and tidied up a little bit more.

He walked over to the bassinette and found a new place for it near the couch knowing Medallion would be spending a lot of time on the sofa while she healed. *She'll want to at least peek at him while she's laying here.*

He gathered up all of the mail and stacked the cards and letters neatly on top of each other so that the corners of each piece lined up perfectly. He noticed the light blue envelope that was more rectangular than square like the other cards and pulled it out so he could lay it beside the neatly stacked greetings. His interest piqued when he saw the addressor. *Department of Social Services. Must be the paternity test results. Didn't know they would come back so soon.*

Waymen's heart began to beat rapidly while his hands trembled with anticipation. With shaking hands, he began to open the envelope containing the results. However, he hesitated and looked in the direction of his bedroom door and wondered to himself. *Why didn't she tell me she got the results back?* He frowned at the possibility that she would be keeping something from him, but then he graciously smiled as his shoulders broadened and his chest began to rise in pride. *I didn't give her time to even tell me. I've been hogging the spotlight since I got back. She probably was going to tell me and it just slipped her mind. Maybe she'll tell me once we get settled in the bed.* Waymen put the envelope back down on the table and made his way back to the bedroom.

"What took you so long?" Medallion said to Waymen in a dreamy sing-song voice.

As she watched him walk through their bedroom and arrive on his side of the bed, she thought, *he is so fine. I can't believe I even second guessed his love for me. I should have trusted my gut and never even called Rodney.* She rolled her eyes and sucked her teeth softly in disgust at the thought of her blunderous relationship with her lover.

Waymen caught her eye roll as he got in the bed beside her. "Are you okay?"

"Oh— yes I'm fine." she smiled at him and planted a sweet kiss on his cheek.

"I thought you might be in pain. You didn't have to get out of the tub. I was coming right back."

"I know. But I was tired of waiting. Really Waymen. You don't have to wait on me hand-and-foot… even though I like it, it's not necessary."

She looked at her clock on the bedside table. *9:00. Just in time.* Medallion grabbed her tv remote and tuned in to watch her favorite show, *Scandal.*

Waymen propped himself up beside her and began watching the show with her, but his mind was restless thinking about the test results. *I wonder when she's going to give me the good news.*

"So why were you taking so long with that nosey old hag?" Medallion said while the show was on commercial break.

"Aww… don't call Nurse Jackie that. She's just looking out for our best interest."

"But what did she want? I know she probably said something bad about me. I can tell she doesn't like me."

Waymen chuckled at his wife but patted her knee assuringly.

"She didn't want nothing much. Just wishing us well. She also told me I was a lucky man to have you."

He gave Medallion a kiss on the cheek while he stared at the television not really watching.

"Well… I didn't like her. I'm glad you're here so she doesn't have to come back."

She sat quiet as she watched the next commercial; all while stewing over her disdain for the meddling nurse.

"You know that bitch had the nerve to call CPS on me because she said I was acting 'weird' and 'strange'? Just because I didn't want to hold the baby? I mean… I was just in the worst pain of my life and I almost died giving birth to that boy! Obviously, she's never gone through what I went through."

Waymen put his arm around Medallion's shoulders and gave her a small squeeze.

"Don't be so hard on her. She was just doing her job. She's a fine nurse and was just concerned."

He went back to watching the television almost scared to ask his next question, but couldn't wait any longer for Medallion to bring the subject up.

"Speaking of CPS… I saw the letter from the paternity division."

Oh shit! Where did he find that!

"Waymen! Did you just see that! Huck just pulled that girls tooth out!"

Medallion tried deflecting Waymen's attention from the letter. She hadn't planned on telling him that the baby wasn't his... especially not then.

"Yeah, I saw it. Pretty gruesome. But back to the letter…"

"In a minute Waymen, the show is getting too good."

Oh my God. I'm about to lose both men in one night. Having this kid wasn't worth the hassle.

"Bae, turn the tv off and let's talk. We can watch it later with On-Demand". Waymen took the remote from Medallion and powered off the television. "I know you saw the results—"

"Waymen, now, let me explain. See… I was going to tell you and everything, but you know how things go. You came in, we came in here, and you know, I just forgot to mention it—"

Waymen held up his hand for her to pause, and she quieted down as she braced herself for his explosion of emotions.

"I haven't read the results yet. I was waiting for you to surprise me with them. I know it's been a whirlwind afternoon, but I can't wait any longer. You've got to give me the good news."

He looked excitedly at Medallion knowing exactly what she was going to say.

"You caught me, Waymen." Medallion smiled guilty. "He's… ummm…."

Just tell him what he wants to hear and figure out how to cover up the truth later. "Well, he's yours!"

She stretched her arms out and Waymen lovingly embraced her.

"I really have a son! He's my boy! I knew it!" He let go of Medallion and looked at her with pride. "I am so glad this tug of war between Rodney and me is over. I'm going to get us some sparkling cider to celebrate.

"No! Stay with me and let's snuggle."

"We will. I'll just go get the cider, and the letter. We can frame it with one of the unused fancy frames lying around that huge closet of yours and then we can snuggle and catch the end of Scandal."

He got out of the bed and headed for the bedroom door.

"Ouch!" Medallion dramatically held her side in pain with one hand and held out her other indicating she wanted him to hold it. "Don't leave me Waymen. I've got a pain."

Waymen rushed to her aide and held her hand, scanning her quickly to see if he could find the affliction.

"It's probably from all that moving you did when you got out of the tub."

He let go of her hand and rushed to the bedroom door.

"I saw your pain medication on the kitchen counter top. I'll go get that along with the letter and the drinks, and be right back."

Before Medallion could respond with a rebuttal he was out of the door. *Oh God. This is it. He's going to find out.* Waymen returned to the room with just the pain killers and a glass of water.

"What happened to the other stuff?"

"I left it. We can celebrate tomorrow. Take these and we'll finish watching Scandal."

Waymen turned the television back on and Medallion took her medication and laid back in the bed, snuggling up under his arm. By the time the ending credits rolled, she was snoring heavily. He laughed to himself as he gently pushed her onto her side of the bed; resting her head on her pillow.

Glad I gave her that sleeping pill too. She seems a bit riled up. Waymen turned the television off and went to Medallion's closet finding the box with the unused frames. He picked out a cherry wood finished frame with silver trim he could put the DNA test in. *I'll take it to work and put it on my desk that way Rodney can look at it every time he walks pass.*

Waymen left the closet and tiptoed out of the room to go get the letter. He grabbed the envelope and sat down on the couch. He looked at the addressee and the addresser one more time before he flipped the envelope over and opened it to reveal its contents. He pulled the letter out and unfolded it, then reading each line slowly to absorb the fulfilling feeling from finally winning in a game of love he was forced to play. But as he read, the information he assumed would be there wasn't. *This can't be right...* He continued to read slowly but steadily; his smile became a frown, and then a grimace. *99.9 percent positive that Rodney Maurielle Daniels is the father of Isaiah Rhakee Foster?!*

"This can't be right." Waymen mumbled to himself in bewilderment. "She just told me Isaiah was mine."

He reread the letter and his consciousness finally caught up with his actuality. *She lied to me.* Waymen put his head in his hand. The weight of the situation bore down on his shoulders and he knew he didn't have the energy to forgive her once again. He lifted his head just enough to look sorrowfully at the master bedroom door. *I don't want to go back in there.* He stood up and looked down at his bare chest, legs, and feet; his boxers were the only piece of clothing he wore. *The front hallway closet.* He went to it and opened its door. There on the floor sat a bag which contained a couple of pair of slacks and a polo shirt he'd bought on sale at Brooks Brother's before he left town. They were to be a gift for his brother, but tonight they would be resourceful with leaving and never looking back.

He put the pants and shirt on, grabbed his coat, keys and hat, and then headed for the front door. As he turned the lock, he hesitated as he looked towards the back hallway.

"Protect that baby with everything you got. He's your son." The words Nurse Jackie spoke earlier haunted his soul. Waymen sighed a helpless sigh and turned the lock until it clicked. *I can't leave him like this.* He backed away from the door and headed down the hallway. He opened Isaiah's bedroom door where he found him sound asleep. Waymen walked into the baby's room and watched him from overhead. Without warning, Waymen began to weep, and his tears dropped with a thunk in the baby's crib.

"I wanted so much for you to be my child." He picked him up and snuggled the child close. "Little man, I loved you. I pray that your mother does better by you than she did by me. I hope she'll put you first in her life instead of first thinking of herself. I hope you can change her because I wasn't able to do it."

He kissed the baby on his cheek and laid him back in his crib. Once he wiped away his tears, He left the room closing the nursery door behind him.

"Good luck little man."

He took on more look at the master bedroom door, and then quietly made his exit.

Chapter 18

"Bae," Medallion said in half a whisper as she rolled over in the bed to flop her arm over Waymen.

She could hear the baby crying and needed him to stop his son from fussing.

"Bae," she said a little louder assuming he was in the bathroom since her arm landed on the mattress and not on his smooth muscular chest.

"Ugh! Will that baby ever shut up!" Medallion said in a mumble to herself waiting for Waymen to respond.

After a few more scream-filled moments, she finally opened her eyes in the dark room. No light came from the bathroom. Waymen wasn't in their bedroom.

"WAYMEN! THE BABY IS CRYING!" Medallion shouted loudly thinking maybe he was in the kitchen. But after a moment of just hearing the baby screaming more, she knew he wasn't in their home at all.

"Where is he?!" Medallion flopped her head back on the pillow as she tried to ignore her wailing son. *"Maybe if I wait him out he'll cry*

himself back to sleep. Hopefully Waymen just ran out to the corner store for a midnight snack and he's on his way back."

Medallion turned over in the bed trying to ignore the desperate screams coming from the other room, but it was no use. She checked the clock on the dresser.

"2:15 in the morning! I can't believe he would go to the store this late at night!"

She slowly rolled out of the bed not wanting to agitate her stitches and then began the slow walk from her room to the nursery.

"Alright, alright, ALRIGHT! I hear you! Hell, the whole building probably hears you! Geesh!" She said in an irritated tone as she opened the door of the nursery and saw the baby laying in the crib illuminated by the nightlight plugged in by the bed.

Medallion scooped up her son and held him to her chest. Instinctively she began to rock in an attempt to quiet her little bundle.

"Your daddy is supposed to be handling you. Not me."

She rolled her eyes at the helpless child, and then sat down in the rocking chair with him cradled in her arms. She leaned back enough in the rocking chair to set it in motion. Isaiah slowly began to quiet down. Medallion looked closely at him for the first time. She took in his features and his smooth skin. She smiled a half smile allowing his little fingers to wrap around her index.

Look at him. He's so little. His dark brown skin glowed even though it itself was the color of darkness. She placed her finger lightly on the top of his head and smoothed down the soft sparse silk-like hair that had begun to create a slight upward curve. She held him a little tighter as he finally opened his eyes and looked at her which were a dark grey; a trait the doctors assured her would eventually change to a darker brown. However, Aunt Mary didn't believe so. She mentioned his skin tone and eye color were reminiscent of a family member of long ago.

He is rather cute. Unfortunately, he looks a lot like his daddy. Medallion looked harder at Isaiah's sparkling grey eyes admiring how stunning they were.

"One thing your daddy doesn't have are those eyes of yours."

She stroked the top of his head as he continued to stare dreamily at her. *I hope Waymen doesn't notice how much our son doesn't look anything like him. Maybe he'll look more like me than Rodney, and Waymen will just settle with that.*

Medallion undid her pajama top and loosened her nursing bra. "Guess you might be a little hungry."

As he latched on for the first time, Medallion felt the sensation of their connection. The feeling was of undeniable love and protection towards her son. *"This is my son," she* said proudly to herself. She smiled at her accomplishment of bringing such a tiny life into the world. She rocked him soothingly while he drank, and the act of it allowed her to drift into a dreamy state.

Her eyes closed gradually and heavily and as they did, she saw herself falling backwards into the nothing of darkness. The decent was slow and she felt as if she was floating more than falling. The darkness began to cradle her and she felt comforted. She opened her eyes in the darkness to see her mother looking back at her smiling. Medallion smiled back at her feeling nurtured and safe.

The darkness began to make sounds all around her. The sounds of bells in chorus made her restless within her mother's arms. Her mother's face soon began to dissipate as the ringing bells continued. The darkness began to fade, and the bells continued to ring, pulling her from the darkness. Finally, she opened her eyes realizing the bells were the sound of her phone ringing from her bedroom. The ringing phone finally woke her from the comfortable rest and the visit from her mother she received while in the rocking chair. With her son sound asleep, she placed him back in his crib and walked her way back to her room. As expected, her phone was vibrating violently and beeping all at once. She picked it up to silence it and saw she'd missed a text and a call. *I must have been really tired because Waymen sent me a message about an hour ago.* She opened the text and read it:

"Medda, I tried to call and tell you. I had to leave on business. I'll meet you at Glory Hill in about a week. I called the agency to have them send Nurse Jackie back. I'll see you soon."

Medallion rubbed her eyes and re-read the message upset that Waymen would leave her yet again in her hour of need.

"I'm so tired of him and that job. I hope he doesn't expect me to raise this child with him always flying out of town."

She haphazardly tossed the phone back on the bed and made her way to the bathroom.

Chapter 19

Medallion opened her eyes to see the time on the clock change to seven. It was already morning, but she felt like she'd just laid down from the night before. Sitting up in her bed, she smelled the aroma of a freshly made breakfast along with the sound of pots and pans clanging gently against each other as they were moved around. Voices of others could also be heard as feet shuffled around her home. Automatically, her face lit up with the thought of Waymen changing his mind about going out of town for business. *Please let that be him in the kitchen.* But then she remembered the rest of the text where he noted that Nurse Jackie would be at the condo in the morning. Medallion's smile left her face at the thought of the nosey nurse making her feel uncomfortable about how she "ignores" her child.

"Ugh!"

She flopped her head back on her pillow in disgust. Nurse Jackie was not the person she wanted to wake up to. She picked up her phone and viewed her call log. Waymen hadn't called her yet. She quickly dialed his number and waited for him to pick up. The phone rang twice and then the call was sent to voicemail.

"You've reached Waymen. Leave a message. I'll call you back."

"Hey Way-Bae. You know if the phone rings and then goes to voicemail, it's a clear indication that you don't want to talk to me. Everyone knows not to hit the ignore button if you don't want the caller to know you are ignoring them. Either way, I'm sorry I missed you leaving last night. Wherever you had to go must have been more important than staying here with me and our son. I see you got that nurse here too. I don't want her here. I want you. Please hurry and tie things up and meet us at Glory. I can't wait to have you all to myself."

Medallion disconnected the phone call and finally got out of the bed. Taking her time down the hallway, she surveyed the movers as they worked hastily to pack up most of their essentials. She and Waymen weren't packing much— mostly clothes, important papers, and a few home accessories to make Glory their own. Since the plantation was not going to be their permanent residence, they ordered the movers to cover their furniture in muslin cloths in the condo so the dust wouldn't settle on their things while they were away.

The movers appeared to be handling things well, so Medallion didn't bother to hover and pry as they worked. She headed towards the kitchen's countertop bar and sat on one of the stools to watch Nurse Jackie methodically make pancakes and eggs while cradling Isaiah in the nook of her other arm. As the nurse placed the completed pancakes on a plate and turned to place them on the countertop, she was happily surprised to see Medallion sitting there watching her.

"Well good morning to you," Nurse Jackie said with a smile.

She placed the plate of pancakes in front of Medallion and put the baby in his cradle seat sitting on the counter nearby.

"Would you like a plate of pancakes and some of these delicious eggs? You know, I have a small chicken coop so I get my eggs fresh."

Medallion nodded yes, and Nurse Jackie got busy making her a plate.

"I thought you lived in the city… Church Hill, right? How do you have a chicken coop?"

"Oh it's nothing to have one of those in the city".

The nurse always laughed every time someone asked her about her cherished chicken coop.

"I have a good size yard so I just carved a little place in the corner of it to raise a few chickens. I used to tend to my daddy's chickens when I was younger, so I thought I'd bring a little piece of home with me when I moved here when I was about your age."

She placed the plate full of breakfast in front of Medallion and handed her a fork.

"Do you want some juice too?"

"Is there some milk?"

Nurse Jackie thought for a minute and then headed to the fridge to grab the milk carton. She got Medallion a cup and brought them back and poured Medallion's drink.

"My grandkids love the chickens. In fact, a few chicks just hatched, and my grand babies couldn't be more excited."

Medallion nodded and gave her a tight smile. She hated idle chatting and it appeared Nurse Jackie was full of it.

Breakfast anywhere other than in front of the television felt odd to her so she took her plate from the counter and made her way to the living room to sit on the couch and aimlessly flick through the channels. Plus, she was happy to move out of ear-shot of "Chatty Jackie". As she sat down to get more comfortable, the nurse was right there behind her with Isaiah in tow. The nurse put the baby's chair beside Medallion on the couch and walked back to the kitchen.

"Why did you put him there? I was just about to stretch out?"

Nurse Jackie stopped in her tracks and turned around surprised. She headed back to Medallion and the child.

"Oh, I'm sorry. I thought you might want some company while you ate. He's such a cute little thing."

"Yeah, well. I'm not in the mood for all of that. Please take him back with you into the kitchen. Isn't my husband paying you to watch him?"

Medallion looked at Isaiah. His eyes were wide open gazing around the room.

"He kept me up all night. I'm too tired to deal with him after all that."

"Aww. You don't mean that. It's natural for a baby to cry. He was just missing you was all. You got to remember, you were his world for almost a year. He don't know much else but you. Go on and snuggle with him after you eat. It'll make the both of you feel real good."

Nurse Jackie smiled pleasantly hoping her words would warm Medallion up to being a mother a little more. Her experience with new mothers helped her see Medallion was having a hard time adjusting to Isaiah and she could also tell there was something else keeping her from loving on her son.

"I said take him back in the kitchen with you. I don't want to hug him or snuggle on him. I want to eat my breakfast in peace, and then I want to get ready to go to Glory."

Nurse Jackie frowned at Medallion's response but didn't say a word. She picked up the baby and returned to the kitchen, placing him back on the counter in his seat. After their exchange, there was an awkward silence between the two that Nurse Jackie couldn't resist filling.

"You know, I've never been to Shenandoah County." She felt more comfortable talking than not, so she made an attempt to change the subject. "I've lived in Virginia all my life and the only places I've ever been are Drewyville and here."

Proudly, Nurse Jackie smiled to herself at her simple life. Others would have characterized her mundane existence as dull and uninteresting, but she viewed it as pleasant and cozy.

"This will be my first big trip since I left home when I was younger. I always say I'm going to take a long trip somewhere like the islands or the Grand Canyon, but life here in Richmond keeps me so busy. I just can't seem to find the time to leave. It's okay though. Daydreaming about those places is good enough for me. You know, I–"

"Mrs. Jackie. Ummm… no offense, but I'm not a morning person. I'd rather not hear you go on and on about this and that so early."

"Oh… I'm sorry, Honey. I just get nervous when I get excited. I do tend to ramble more when I'm bubbling over with nerves."

"Well, try to keep your rambling to a minimum. It's bad enough there's a crying baby around, and now you have diarrhea of the mouth."

Medallion put the last fork full of eggs in her mouth and turned the television on. "I'm all done with my plate. You can come get it now."

Shocked and appalled by how Medallion spoke to her and then to have ordered her to retrieve her plate, the nurse's happy demeanor changed. She'd never been treated so rudely by any client of hers, and the nerve of the young arrogant woman was something she couldn't tolerate. Nurse Jackie put down the kitchen appliances she was preparing to pack and walked over to Medallion with a stern look on her face. She snatched the remote out of Medallion's hand and turned the television off.

"Hey! How dare you take that from me!"

"And how dare you talk to me the way you do? I have never in all my life encountered someone as disrespectful as you. May I remind you that I am a nurse hired to help you heal and handle the baby. I am not your servant or the cook. I may be cooking and cleaning, but that's only because your husband is a fine gentleman and I'm doing the extra out of the kindness of my heart. Don't ruin a good thing by showing your behind to the kindness of a stranger 'cause you never know if that stranger is going to kick you in it!"

Nurse Jackie grabbed the plate from Medallion, turned on her heels, and went back into the kitchen.

Medallion bowed her head in remorse realizing how bad she'd treated the nice lady.

"I'm sorry, Mrs. Jackie. I guess I have been a little bit of a monster."

"I little bit? That's an understatement." Nurse Jackie said with a forgiving smirk. "Don't worry about it. You're a new mom. It's got to be a stressful time for you right now. Go on and get yourself ready for the day, and I'll finish up with the movers and the baby. We have a long drive ahead of us."

Chapter 20

The nearly two-hour drive in the chauffeured black Suburban afforded Medallion and the nurse an opportunity to get to know each other a little better. As Isaiah rested in the car seat between them, Nurse Jackie took advantage of the light-hearted moments to give Medallion tips on taking care of her new son.

"Okay, okay, okay!" Medallion said in between laughing. "I get it. It's best to check him every two or three hours to see if he's hungry."

She scrunched her face at Isaiah as she thought about having to pull a breast out every time his desire to be fed beckoned."

"Well don't look at him like that! He probably don't like crying every two to three hours either. Besides, them breast gonna let you know before he does anyway. They gonna get to hurting and leaking so much that you gonna actually want him to nurse just to take the pain away."

"Oh my God don't tell me that! It sounds horrible!"

"Girl please! Ain't nothing but nature doing its job." Both women laughed at the thought of it all; Nurse Jackie at remembering her days of being a mother of a newborn and Medallion at all she didn't know about being a new mom.

"And check... when it's time to wean him off..." The nurse shook her head at the thought. "It's the worst time in your life. Them breast gonna hurt more, but just wrap them with raw cabbage leaves. That will draw the milk out and relieve you of that pain."

"Cabbage?" Medallion spoke with confusion and shock.

"Yup. Does the trick every time."

"The things y'all old folks come up with..." Medallion said under her breath.

As they both grew silent in thought, Medallion let out a whimsical sigh. Peering out her window, she began to see the start of Glory over a low hill.

"Mrs. Jackie... look. We are almost there."

Looking in the opposite direction, the nurse turned her head and looked out of Medallion's window. What she saw was the rounded rolling hills exposing Glory the more they made their way down the road. "Is that the house?"

"Yup. This street coming up is basically the driveway."

Passing a sign saying, "Welcome to Glory Hill", the driver made a left onto Auburn Road. The Suburban slowed as it paced its way down the graveled driveway lined with a row of bare leaved oak trees on each side.

"This is my favorite part about arriving at Glory, Mrs. Jackie. I love how the limbs on the oak tree bow over us like they are tipping their leaves to say 'Welcome'."

Medallion beamed with delight as they continued down the long drive way.

"I see what you mean. It does sort of look like that."

Being from the south, Nurse Jackie had only seen plantations from the street as she travelled by bus, or in the back of a pickup truck. She was never interested in visiting one due to her ancestor's working them during slavery and then as indentured servants. To know a black person to actually own one was a foreign reality to her.

"Look Mrs. Jackie, there is the house coming up."

Medallion hadn't been to Glory in so long it dawned on her how much she missed it. Getting closer, the bowing oak trees began to give way to a palatial circular driveway.

"Whoah… Who lives here?"

Dean, the driver of the Suburban would usually keep his composure when it came to exquisite homes. This time he couldn't hold in his commentary. He'd never come across a home so grand and so historic. It even had a welcoming feeling that other homes of its statue didn't possess.

"This is our family home. My Aunt Mary owns it," Medallion spoke with pride as the driver slowed down to park the SUV in front of the elevated main entrance.

She began to gather her things just as the phone rang. She looked down at it in hopes that it was Waymen, but it was her aunt instead.

"Driver, don't pull our things out just yet. I'm going to take this call first. I'll let the movers pull around the back of the house to unload and to begin setting up things in the house while I take this call."

The driver nodded in acceptance and turned the ignition off.

"Hey Auntie. We just rolled into the driveway…"

While Medallion took the call, Nurse Jackie took in the site that was Glory Hill Plantation. Trying to remember all the features Medallion listed off just as a realtor would to pique a buyer's interest, Nurse Jackie allowed her eyes to slowly stroll Glory's façade.

The front of the home boasted huge white columns that supported the double decker porch. From where she sat in the car, she could see the main entry was a pair of three panel oak doors with fixed glass top panels.

"Yes, the outside looks fine…" Medallion nodded her head in agreement to no one in particular as she continued her conversation with her aunt.

Nurse Jackie continued to survey the grounds of the house from her window seat. The land extended as far as she could see, yet in the distance she saw the hint of "the big willow tree by the lake" as Medallion would say it. *And there's a lake there we all go fishing in. Auntie keeps it stocked with trout.*

"Yes, I'll call you back when we get in and settled. No… Remember. I told you earlier, Waymen is out of town on business. Yes, the nurse came with me. She'll probably stay until Waymen gets here and then we'll have the car that brings him take her back to the city. Yes. I'll let her know how much you appreciate her being here. Okay. Love you too." Medallion hit the "end" button on her phone and then shook her head with a smile. "My auntie worries so much."

"Oh, it's only because she loves you so much." Nurse Jackie turned her attention back to Medallion as her eye browsing tour came to an end.

"Yeah. She does. She would have been here herself taking care of me until Waymen came back, but this is her busy season. She's got parties to host, and social events to prepare for. Aunt Mary has a lot of friends and keeps a full calendar."

"Oh, I know. Your aunt and I were close when we were younger. She was the one who helped me get on my feet in Richmond."

Medallion looked a bit surprised at that tidbit of information. "I didn't know you knew Aunt Mary. You two acted like strangers at the hospital."

Nurse Jackie laughed. "Oh no! We have a great respect for each other. She taught me a few things about healing and how to call upon the ancestors. With her blessing and her teachings, I turned a pretty profit, put myself through school, and live a humble life."

"So, you know a little about auntie's business."

"Just a little. I helped her on an assignment or two when she needed the strength of another to fuel her powers. Your Aunt has a calling for who she is. I only have the knowledge, and because of that, my ability to do what she does will only do more harm than good."

"How so?"

Listening to Nurse Jackie speak about learning spells and practicing her Aunt's craft was intriguing. She'd never met another person talk about what Aunt Mary did firsthand.

"Well, at the very least, I could screw up a spell, but at the very most, I can be manipulated by the dark spirits. They know the ones who are called and the ones who are not. Dark spirits take over the ones who aren't innate to the craft. Someone like myself has to be careful not to play around with it. So, I stay away from digging too deep. Your aunt understood and just showed me enough to get where I needed to go in life."

"Wow. I never knew that. She never even said she had a student. I mean… she taught me a thing or two, but I just thought I was the only one."

"You weren't, and in fact, I'm not either. There's a few of us who have studied under her. We don't keep in touch, and that's fine. We were never meant to. But I do remember a time when she called on us all to gather. There was about seven or eight of us. There was a darkness— a danger lurking. She knew she couldn't handle it alone. She needed the strength of us all to get it away from there. It was late when we all arrived, and we came together in her garden. That night, we chanted and we called upon the ancestors, and our beloved Ogun to help. There was a lot of turmoil from that darkness when we were at our strongest, but we knocked it back to where it had come. By morning time, the place was at rest. After that, we all went back our separate ways. I believe that was the last time I saw your aunt up until you came to the hospital ready to deliver."

Medallion sat quiet thinking about what Nurse Jackie remembered. Then a thought crept in. "So, it's probably no accident you were my nurse at the hospital, and my nurse at home."

The nurse smiled slyly. "I guess not." They both laughed at Aunt Mary's antics as they got out the car and made their way to the front door of the beautiful plantation home.

Chapter 21

"Allow me to assist you two lovely ladies out of my chariot," the chauffeur said as he left the driver's seat.

He moved swiftly to open Medallion's door. He offered his hand for balance as she scooted out the back seat. He then went to the passenger side of the Suburban and opened the backdoor of which Nurse Jackie climbed out.

"Oh no ma'am. Allow me to gather the baby for you. There may be some black ice I would hate for you to slip on."

"Oh you're so kind. Thank you."

Nurse Jackie waited for the driver to take the car seat with the baby in it out of its chassis. He then stuck both of his elbows out for each of the ladies to grab.

"Such wonderful service!"

Jackie relished in such attention. *Having money really makes the simple things so much grander...* As they made their way up the steps to the front porch, Nurse Jackie noticed the huge windows on each side of the thick oak doors. A beautiful wooden porch swing that could easily sit three people was stationed on the left side of the door, and on the right, a small table with two chairs looked ready for summertime guests.

"Don't you just love it, Mrs. Jackie? The porch in the warmer seasons is where I really like to spend my time. The porch is so huge it's like its own room."

"It certainly is. All these big and tall windows on the front really makes it nice."

"Right?! These windows have got to be at least eight feet tall. I know they almost hit the ceiling. That window over there…" Medallion pointed out the third window on the left. "It's one of the windows for the living room. The really crazy part about it is it uses the pulley system to open upwards and you can actually walk right through the open window! It's like a door. Auntie calls it a Windoor."

"Oh, how fascinating! I've never heard of anything like it! Oh, I'll have to come back in the spring just to experience it with a tart glass of homemade lemonade."

Medallion pulled the keys to the house out of her tote bag and put them in the lock opening the door for them to all enter. Nurse Jackie couldn't believe how beautiful the home opened up showcasing all its splendor.

"Oh, Medallion… this house… this home… I never dreamed for it to be so…"

On the ride up, Medallion talked about Glory and all of its magnificence, but the conversation did not prepare the nurse for such a sight. Standing at the front door, she was met with the central cantilevered staircase with its delicate "C" curve drawing her eye up to the ceiling. Looking over the openness of the foyer, a glimmer of dancing light up the staircase caught Nurse Jackie's eye. Investigating just a bit, she walked up the staircase to peek at what awaited noticing the refraction of light came from the Palladian window directly above the front door on the second level of the house.

"Mr. Martin, thank you for getting us here safely. You can set the baby in the parlor to the right. I'll be in there shortly."

Medallion reached back into her tote and handed the driver an envelope filled with a gracious tip.

"Thank you so much, ma'am. Whenever you need a ride back to the city, please feel free to call."

The driver headed out the front door closing it on his way out.

Medallion followed the driver to the door and locked it after he left. Turning her attention back to Nurse Jackie exploring Glory she saw her come back down the stairs.

"Isn't that window nice? Aunt Mary had it specially made infusing white and pink crystal into the window pane. She says since the house is old, the crystal will help free old souls that still feel tethered to the house and it will also repel the bad spirits since all souls like old places."

"I can see Mary's point. When people die at a place they lived, their soul instinctively does what the body did. Those crystals will catch their attention and help them move right along."

"Can you grab the baby in the front parlor on the right? This is the formal part of the house. We are going to go to the back where we can get comfortable."

"Sure. Let me go get that precious little guy."

Nurse Jackie continued to delight in all the old and new touches in the home as she went and got Isaiah and followed Medallion to the back of the house.

"Didn't I tell you it was beautiful? Aunt Mary just has a great eye for detail. I just love coming here. I can't wait for Waymen to arrive. He hasn't seen it since she finished renovating."

Medallion walked past Nurse Jackie who still had the baby in her arms while looking around and admiring the home.

"I keep asking Auntie to leave me this house in her will. She says it's an option, and I keep telling her it's her only option."

Making her way around the corner and through the kitchen, she found the crib her aunt had delivered sitting in the huge family room. She took Isaiah from Nurse Jackie and placed the baby in it before turning on the gas fireplace.

"It's getting a little cold don't you think?"

"I believe you are right. January is the right time for it. I heard there's a winter storm brewing off the coast of Virginia Beach. Says it's supposed to be here in a couple of days."

Following Medallion into the family room, Nurse Jackie found a place to rest her pocketbook on the couch. She looked around the room noticing in a space off the family room was a four season room made of the clearest glass windows she'd ever seen. Its entrance was a glass door that sat between the wall made of floor to ceiling windows allowing for an unobstructed view of the back of the property.

"I guess I should get started on dinner."

Nurse Jackie headed back into the kitchen to begin her prep work.

Medallion made her way into the kitchen as well; sitting down on the stool at the counter to watch Nurse Jackie work.

"Hey Mrs. Jackie…"

"Yes, baby. What's on your mind?"

"Well… I want to apologize."

She looked at Medallion from underneath her brow as she began chopping up vegetables for a stew.

"For what?"

"I mean… my attitude over the last couple of days wasn't that great. I want to apologize for being such a bitch."

Nurse Jackie laughed a little and continued to chop the vegetables without missing a beat.

"Think nothing of it. I know you didn't mean no harm by it. Now go in there and rest yourself. Dinner will be ready in about an hour or so. Go bond with your baby. The movers already put our things away so there's nothing for you to do but enjoy some quiet time with that son of yours."

Medallion smiled at her directive and headed back into the family room. *Ahh… if Waymen could see me now. He'd just love the sight of me being a mommy… doing mommy things.* Not wanting to miss the opportunity, she went over to Isaiah and scooped him out of his crib. She pulled her cell phone out of her back pocket and hit the camera icon. She held the phone upward and then tilted it down to capture her posed with full lips puckered and eyes dimmed seductively. Isaiah snuggled close to her chest, Medallion snapped a picture of them together capturing the picture, "Mommy and Son" before sending it to Waymen. Putting her phone back in her pocket, she put Isaiah back in the crib. *She* looked over at the little one once more in admiration. *He's so quiet in there. I bet you he's dreaming of me.* She kissed her two fingers and then placed them on the baby's cheek. She pulled her cell phone back out and checked for any unread text messages. *Hmmm… Waymen must be busy. He hasn't sent me a message since last night or said anything about my picture. Maybe it's just bad reception out here or something. I'll send him one more text. Her* fingers appeared to tap dance across the phone's face as she texted her message*:*

Hey babe. Checking on u. Wish u were here. Did you get our pic? Txt me 2 let me know when u r coming.

Just as she hit the send button on her phone, she heard the start of Isaiah crying in his crib.

"Aww… Don't cry. Mommy's here." *Wow. I like the sound of that… 'mommy'. And to think I was trying to avoid it at all cost.*

Picking Isaiah up from his crib, she began to rock him soothingly, but Isaiah's cry went from a whimper to uncontrollable screams— something Medallion was not prepared for.

"Mrs. Jackie! Mrs. Jackie! Can you come get him! Why is he crying like this?"

Nurse Jackie put the last of her chopped vegetables in the pot warming on the stove and then made her way to the family room.

"What's the matter Medallion? Is everything okay?"

"I don't know. He just started crying. What's wrong with him?"

The nurse took the baby from Medallion and gave him a look over. She squnched her nose at the smell permeating from the baby.

"Oh… he's fine. Just need a change. I'll take him for one and then you'll have him back with a clean booty."

Nurse Jackie headed up the stairs to the nursery with the baby in her arms. Medallion sighed a breath of relief as she'd never had to change a diaper before. Out of the corner of her eye, she saw the screen of her phone light up, and then it vibrated. *Text message. Must be Waymen.* Medallion picked up her phone and sucked her teeth "What the hell does Rodney want now…" She opened the text and saw the selfie of Rodney standing in the bathroom; his naked body dripping wet. Her eyes widened in delight and with shock at the visual. *Rodney ain't good for nothing but that massive piece between those muscular legs.*

The picture was tempting as it made her reminisce about the sexual heat she and he would create. Shaking her head to bring her back to reality and to wipe the lustful grin from her mouth, Medallion read the caption, "Wish you were here…"

"Yeah right." She rolled her eyes at the comment. But then her mind started to wonder if he really meant it. A sly smile crept into the corner of her lips and she hit the reply button to respond, but her phone chimed and then vibrated signifying the arrival of another text. Medallion lit up with delight as her thoughts went back to the tryst she and him shared. *Rodney playing little love games now. He must miss me. I bet he's texting me back wanting me to send him a nasty pic…*

She opened up the message and her mouth dropped in horror. Rodney in fact did send her another picture of him naked in the bathroom, but this time, there was a woman with him on her knees ready to satisfy him the way she used to. Medallion read the caption Rodney posted under the picture, "NOT!!" and saw the devious smile plastered across his face. Not wanting to indulge in whatever crazy game he wanted to play with her, Medallion angrily deleted the pictures and then threw the phone back on the couch.

Chapter 22

"There's a cold front coming in. They say we are going to have a deep freeze tonight, and the snow should start rolling in later tomorrow," Medallion said as she casually flipped through her Instagram page.

"I think they're lying about that deep freeze coming tonight." Nurse Jackie contemplated as she sat nestled in the chair closest to the fireplace in the living room while knitting a scarf. "I think the deep freeze is here now."

She chuckled a bit to herself and repeated the knit one pearl two pattern over and over again.

"I believe you are right about that." Medallion laughed as well.

She put her phone down feeling the baby squirm in her arms while he slept. She then stretched out on the couch with the baby on her chest so he could be more comfortable. She stroked Isaiah's hair as he continued to sleep soundly close to her heartbeat. It felt so right to have her son next to her along with a good friend to share the moment with. Watching Nurse Jackie knit in silence, she remembered how only a couple of days ago, she couldn't bear her intolerable meddling. Now, she was glad the nurse was with her and helping with Isaiah while Waymen was away. *Waymen...* Medallion sucked her teeth and rolled her eyes at the thought of him not being there and not sharing the peaceful moment with her. *Where are you?* Her body became tense with anger as thoughts raced around her head about him. She sat up and laid the baby in his crib and then carefully stood.

"Where are you off to?" Nurse Jackie peered at Medallion over the rim of her glasses.

"Huh... Oh. I'm going to make a phone call to Waymen. Just going to tell him about the storm that's coming."

She grabbed her phone before she left the living room, snatched a warm coat hanging on a hook near the back hallway, and headed for the door in the four seasons room that led outside. In the ice-cold air by the side of the house, she looked at her phone wondering what he was doing and hesitating to call. *It's Eight O'clock. He should be off work by now.* She dialed his number and listened to it ring a few times before he picked up.

"Hello."

"Waymen?" She felt his voice sounded weary, or more like he wasn't happy to hear her voice.

"Yeah."

"Ummm... How are you? You don't sound too enthused to hear from me. I mean— you haven't returned any of my texts or my phone calls in the last couple of days."

"Yeah... about that... I—"

"Oh, it's okay. I pretty much figured you were busy, and you'd get back to me as soon as you could. I just wanted to call and tell you about the big winter storm coming tomorrow. You should be on the plane here in a couple of days so that you don't run into it. Better yet, don't you think you should cut your trip short and come now?"

"Medallion..."

"You can always finish your project up here, and then you can relax with me and the baby."

"Medallion, I have—"

"Oh, and thanks for sending Mrs. Jackie with me. That's working out fine. She's a great help. She's been cooking and letting me rest by really pitching in with the baby. I also talked to Aunt Mary when we first got here. She asked about you too. We've got the house situated so all you have to do is come and relax and—"

"Medallion! Could you quit talking for a minute! I have something to tell you!"

Stunned by his outburst, she quieted down and prepared to listen.

"Okay. I'm listening…"

"I mean… this is hard enough to say, but I need to just say what I'm going to say without you talking all over me."

"Just say it, Waymen. What's wrong?"

"Well… it's like this… I'm not coming there. I'm staying in Richmond and when you get back, I'll be gone. I'm moving out."

"What! Waymen! Why are you leaving! I've been good! I've changed! I'm here with your son being a mom and waiting on you to come be a father and a husband! Don't leave me! Don't leave our family!" She began to cry uncontrollably as the words poured out of her mouth.

Listening to her sob, Waymen almost felt sorry for what he was doing, but then he pictured the test results. He clenched his fist to control the rage he now felt as the image of Rodney and his smug grin blurred his thoughts. He'd realized that he'd taken enough of the lies and the games.

"So, about the paternity of Isaiah. When were you going to tell me?"

Medallion's wailing cry stopped at the mention of the results.

"What do you mean? I umm, was going to tell you when you got here. I was going to surprise you and tell you that he's yours once you settled in at Glory. What… you are leaving me because I didn't tell you the test results at the condo?"

"You were going to surprise me with yet another lie and tell me Isaiah is my son!"

"What?! Who's been lying to you! Isaiah is your son! He's yours! Look at him, he's your SON!"

"Medallion, I know the truth! I saw the paternity test! I saw the results! He's not my son! He's your son! He's Rodney's son! He's NOT my SON!"

"But you said it didn't matter what the results were— that he'd be your son no matter what! That you wanted our marriage to work out and that you loved me more than any test result! What happened to you wanting to save our marriage!"

"Well, I guess I LIED! You know all about that don't you?"

Medallion fell silent. Waymen was silent. Neither could respond right away. The realization that he was leaving her was sinking in for the both of them.

"Waymen, don't do this to us. We've been through a lot—most because of my actions, but we made it through. We were getting back to a good place, and this was our shot at a second chance. Let's not waste it. Come here to Glory and let's talk about it. Come look at Isaiah and remember that love you started out to have for him. Remember the love you have for me and let's be one again. I love you, Waymen. I need you. I can't be a mom without you. There is no Rodney. It's just us."

"No Medallion. I'm not coming. This rollercoaster of a life you've had me on has come to an end. I don't want to be a part of your games anymore. You should have told me he wasn't mine. Had you been honest, we may have had a chance. I mean… I don't know. I really don't know if we may have had a chance because every time I close my eyes, I see you and Rodney. And every time I think of Isaiah growing up with a part of that man in his DNA and not me... it just does something to my heart. You've ruined me Medallion."

"Waymen we can fix this."

"No, we can't. It's unfixable."

"Waymen, don't—"

"Look, I got to go. I'm going to finish packing up my things and then I'm going to head out."

"Wait! You're still at the condo?! I can come meet you! I can leave the baby here with the nurse and I can come back to Richmond, and we can work things out! There's still hope!"

"Medallion, stay where you are. I'll be gone before you get here. I'll have the divorce papers drawn up in a couple of days and then I'll have them sent to you."

"Waymen! Don't go! We can fix this! I swear! Listen… I spoke to Rodney—"

"You what?! You are still in contact with this guy!"

"No! You got it all wrong! He called a couple of days ago, and I told him that the baby was his, but he didn't want him! He doesn't even want me! He sent me a picture of him and his new girlfriend! See! We don't even have to get a divorce! You don't have to worry about Rodney at all!"

"Medallion, all I heard is that Rodney contacted you, and that he knew the baby was his before I did! You just don't get what you've done and are doing to me! I truly believe that divorcing you is the right thing to do."

"Waymen! No! We still belong together! How about this… How about I just give Isaiah up for adoption? It'll be like he never happened. We can start over and have our own kids… together."

"Are you serious?! You are going to give a child away because you didn't pick the right man to be his father?! Medallion, you have really lost it. I don't know why I didn't see it before, but you have a lot of issues you need to work out."

"Waymen, please don't leave me! I love you! I had the baby for you! I don't love that child as much as I love you! You mean more to me than him! Let me come to Richmond! Please let me fix you and me!"

"Goodbye, Medallion. Please work on yourself. Focus on learning to love your son."

"WAYMEN! DON'T GO!" Medallion shrieked the words into the phone, but it was no use. The phone flashed, "CALL ENDED" before she could say anything else.

She redialed his number, but was sent straight to voicemail. In a panic, she switched the phone to text mode and typed in "call bk! I luv u! U luv me 2! We have to fix this!" She hit the send button and let out a loud scream of frustration as she turned to walk back to the house.

"I heard what you said about that boy."

Medallion looked up startled to see Nurse Jackie standing in the doorway of the Four Seasons room.

"Why are you spying on me! I was having a private conversation with my husband!"

"It's a shame you would give your son up just to be with a man. A good man you cheated on but a man just the same."

"It's none of your business what I plan to do with my son."

"You are right. It is none of my business, but it seems to me that if you choosing to give up yet another person who loves you unconditionally, someone will willingly give them both the love you have sincerely squandered."

"No one asked you to be vocal about my life." Medallion pushed passed Nurse Jackie and made her way to the kitchen in search of a bottle of wine and a glass.

"In all my years, I've never met such a bitch as you."

"What did you just call me?!" Medallion turned around to face the nurse, appalled at her words.

"Yeah, I said it. I call it like I see it, and you are a true bitch. I'm going to make my way to bed, but I'll be leaving come morning. I've decided I'm resigning my position. Your aunt will send another nurse I'm sure."

She grabbed her knitting from the living room and headed up the steps to turn in for the night.

Chapter 23

Nurse Jackie's chest heaved with fury as she made her up the stairs.

"I can't with this girl. She makes my blood boil."

She went to her guest room and sat on the bed to take off her shoes. Looking out of the bedroom window, saw the shimmer of the lake in the distance. The scene looked extremely calm to her and in contrast to the emotions she felt. *I'm so riled up right now, wouldn't be able to sleep if I tried. Probably would be better for me to go take a walk before I turn in.* She grabbed her warmest coat to head back down the steps.

As she made her way to the top of the stairs, she heard the water running from the master bedroom. She crept into the room and checked around. *She must be about to take a shower.* She peeked into the bathroom right as Medallion sat down in the tub with a bottle of wine right beside her. Nurse Jackie shook her head in disgrace. *Now, she know she is not supposed to be drinking and she breastfeeding…* She quietly shut the door, peeked into the baby's room where she saw Isaiah nestled snug in his bed before heading down the steps and on her way out of the Four Seasons room's back door.

***

Oh my god. I have really fucked up my life. I don't know why I thought having this baby would make things better. No matter what I've done, Waymen is still my husband and I have got to find a way to get him to love me again. Medallion leaned out of the tub and filled her glass with the red Moscato she'd brought from the kitchen. The warm water and the bath's tickling bubbles popping against her skin began to relax her while mulling over her dilemma.

How did that love spell go again? She sipped on her wine as she let her thoughts take her away. *Or is it a spell? I could just hit him with one of those love spells Auntie taught me...* The luxurious master bathroom was not only equipped with an extra deep soaking tub but also a radio with surround sound. Medallion hit the audio button on the entertainment panel nestled on the ledge of the tub. The soothing sounds of easy listening jazz floated from the speakers and filled the room with its melody.

Crushed raspberries, lemon and lime juice, and some type of oil... Medallion relaxed a little more as she took more sips of her glass of wine. *Was it castor oil? Baby oil? I can't remember.* She raised her hand to the control panel once more and pressed the light dimmer button creating an ambiance for destressing. She let a small giggle escape her lips as the vision of the red sex candle for those types of rituals which was shaped as a massive penis with a small woman's bare body hugging it affectionately encase her pure thoughts.

Might as well forget using the love spell. I know auntie would NEVER *have that thing in the house.* Medallion burst into laughter at the thought of such an obscene tool of the craft. She took another sip of her wine and sunk deeper into her tub while going deeper in thought.

And even if I had that ridiculous candle, I'd have to get Waymen to sleep with me to even finish the spell. The preprogrammed jet action for the tub turned on automatically. Medallion positioned her lower back in front of one of the jets to ease some of the tension she'd brought upon herself. *If I have to stress out about Waymen leaving me, this is the best way to do it.* She set the alarm for the house assuming her and Nurse Jackie were in for the night. She turned the music up a little more and allowed her eyes close.

Chapter 24

The cold crisp air felt good on her skin as she made her way to the lake. She was glad that it was located on the property, as she felt safe enough to take a walk at night. While strolling, she thought about what she heard Medallion saying to Waymen over the phone. She could only pity him for having picked such a selfish and heartless young woman to marry. She pulled her jacket tighter around her as the wind chilled the air a bit more. She finally made it to the lake and saw a black metal ornate bench under the willow tree. She sat down and watched how the reflections from the stars above danced on the lake's ripples. The moment at the water began to heal her from the turmoil created within her.

As Medallion lay still in the tub drinking her wine, the blaring sound of the home alarm jolted her out of her sleep. Panic set in as visions of an attacker lurking around in the dark ready to kill filled her mind. She silenced the noise from the alarm by entering its passcode from the entertainment panel and then got out of the tub; grabbing her towel as she made her way out of the bathroom. As she passed the king size bed on her way out of the room, she grabbed and put on the pants and night shirt laying across it. Once out in the hall, she stood in silence listening for unfamiliar sounds. There was a distant clink heard that sounded like it came from down the hall. Nervous, she slowly walked towards the noise hoping she'd catch the intruder before they caught her.

"Mrs. Jackie…" Medallion spoke in a slightly elevated tone. "Did you trip the alarm?"

She nervously waited for a response but there was no answer.

"Mrs. Jackie…" Medallion walked towards Nurse Jackie's door and opened it slowly. *She's not here.* "Mrs. Jackie are you here?"

She continued towards the baby's room whispering, "Mrs. Jackie, are you in here?"

Still no answer. Standing with her head in the door of the baby's room, she heard the door downstairs creek and moan once more, and then there was a loud slam. Fearing eminent danger for her, the baby, and the nurse, Medallion jumped at the sound of the clanking door. Her body trembled in panic. *Nurse Jackie isn't answering and there is someone in the house! They must have gotten her first!* Medallion closed the door to the baby's room assured that he was safe and made her way down the stairs. At the bottom of the staircase stood a table, and on it stood a bronzed candelabra. When Medallion grabbed it, she felt all of its weight in her hand determining it was heavy enough to cause bodily harm.

With her weapon hoisted high like a baseball bat, she crept towards the kitchen keeping close to the wall.

"Mrs. Jackie, are you down here!" She whispered harshly. "I've got a weapon in my hand that's going to hurt you pretty bad if I hit you with it. Please say something to let me know you are down here!"

As she continued by the living room, she saw the shadow of a person walking past the window outside of the house. Medallion began to tremble in fear. She gripped the candle holder tighter and continued towards the kitchen. *Oh God! Don't let me die here! Please don't let me die here!* Then she heard the door creak once again and shut. Creak open again and then bang shut. *It's the door in the Four Seasons room...* Medallion ran towards it, shut the door closed, and then locked it tightly hoping she beat the shadowy figure lurking outside the windows from entering before she had a chance to close it.

"Nurse Jackie… are you down here?"

Medallion walked back into the kitchen, and as she made her way towards the back staircase, she saw the figure of a tall man standing before her. She let out a horrible scream swinging the weapon across her body where it made contact with the shadow's mid-section. The darkened figure let out a groan as it went down to the floor. Medallion lifted the candle holder above her head to bring it down with all her might on the groaning man when she heard the front door's doorbell ring.

"Open up! It's the police!"

Medallion dropped the candelabra and rushed to the front door.

"Help! Help! There's a man in my house!"

She opened the door to see an officer standing with his badge flashing in the palm of his hand.

"Come in officer! He's there! Lying on the floor! He attacked my nurse, and he was about to attack me!"

The officer rushed in and made his way to the man still groaning and rolling in agony on the floor. Medallion finally turned on the lights as she stood behind the police officer.

"Arrest this man, officer! He's killed my nurse!"

"George, are you okay!" The officer checked over the man writhing in pain on the floor.

"Yeah, she hit me pretty hard there. I'm a little winded, but I'll live."

"Officer, you know this man?"

"Yes, this is Officer George Frazier, and I am Officer Chase Richardson."

Officer Richardson helped his partner from the floor. Once upright, Officer Frazier flashed Medallion his badge.

Medallion cupped her hands over her mouth in shock. She looked at the candle holder and looked at Officer Frazier imagining had she hit him over the head like she'd planned to, she would have caused major damage.

"Officer Frazier, I am so sorry. I didn't mean to hit you. I thought you were an intruder."

"No worries ma'am." he said while continuing to rub the side of his body.

"We're responding to the notification from your alarm system. We got a call from the automatic system saying there was a break in." Officer Richardson walked over to the alarm's main console and keyed in a few numbers. "There. Now the silent alarm will stop at the police station since I put the police code in."

"We were going to ignore the call since Mrs. Mary called us about a couple of days ago and told us there would be family on the property for a while and not to worry. But it's so late at night for folks to be setting off alarms on accident. We figured we'd come and check on the place just to make sure you were actually here and not a group of teenagers looking for a place to make-out."

"Yeah, we've been getting calls about teen break-ins lately. Actually, this house has been targeted several times. Lucky for Mrs. Mary she has this alarm, and now she's even luckier 'cause you're going to be here for a while. It's good to have people living in it so it won't look so vacant all the time."

"Is everything okay in here?"

Medallion and the two officers turned towards the front door and saw Nurse Jackie timidly standing there.

"Nurse Jackie! You're okay!" Medallion rushed over and put her arms around her. "I thought something had happened to you. The alarm went off and you weren't in your room."

"No need to worry. I went for a walk around the lake. What made the alarm go off?" Nurse Jackie walked into the house and put her coat down. "And what happened to this young man?"

She looked at Officer Frazier as he continued to rub his bruise.

"Well, I heard the door in the Four Seasons room slamming open and close and after I came back from locking it, he was standing in the foyer in the dark. I thought he'd done something with you and was about to attack me. I hit him with the candelabra laying over there on the floor."

"Yeah, it was a pretty good swing too. Got me right in the gut."

Officer Frazier began to laugh but decided not to continue as the pain from the blow was still prevalent.

"Mrs. Foster, if you would allow me to check the home before we leave just to make sure all things are clear. We'll be on our way once we're done."

Medallion welcomed them to do their search.

"I must not have shut the door very well when I left for my walk." Nurse Jackie fidgeted in shame not wanting to believe her blunder.

"Yeah… you have to be careful with that door. If you don't pull it tight enough, it will eventually open on its own. It's funny, with all of Aunt Mary's money, you'd think that would have been the first thing she would have fixed on this house."

Nurse Jackie gave a strained closed-lipped smile at the comment and then made her way back upstairs.

"Well, I'm headed up for bed. I'll be leaving in the morning. Ain't trying to stay another moment in this house with you and your nasty ways."

Medallion rolled her eyes and sucked her teeth. "Whatever Mrs. Jackie. It'll be good for you to go. I didn't need you anyway."

"That's fine too 'cause your baby crying, and since I'm not needed, you can handle him by yourself." Nurse Jackie opened the door to her room, went in, and closed the door behind her.

Meddling old wench… Back in the nursery, Medallion gathered her son and allowed his head to rest on her shoulders. His crying calmed down to a few whimpers once he felt the warmth of his mother.

"Ma'am… we're all done." Officer Frazier hollered up the stairs. "The house looks free and clear."

Medallion made her way to the door and let the police officers out.

"Thank you for checking on things. The alarm must have gone off when Mrs. Jackie left out the back door to take a walk around the lake. I told her that door is tricky sometimes."

"Well, we're glad there wasn't anything truly wrong."

"Me too." Medallion shook both of their hands. "Thank you for coming on out and checking on us."

"Not a problem ma'am. Have a good night."

"You too." Medallion watched as they got back in their cars and headed back down the driveway. "Now as for you". Looking down at Isaiah who she'd grabbed out of his crib right before the police left. "I guess you must be hungry…" She glanced down at him. He was now calm and had gone back to sleep. "Well, I guess you were sleepy."

She went back up the steps and instead of putting him back in his bed, she took him with her and put him in the bed with her.

As he laid soundly beside her, she watched him quietly for a long moment.

"You're the cause of all my problems. Waymen doesn't want me because of you, and Rodney doesn't want me because of you."

She watched him sleep soundly a bit more and then went to the bathroom to get her wine glass and bottle. She poured herself a drink and laid beside him in the bed. Resting on the bedside table was her phone. She picked it up and dialed Waymen's number. It rang once before going to voicemail so she decided to leave him a message.

"Waymen, listen to me. We love each other. I had a scare tonight where I thought I was going to die. To make a long story short there was an intruder tonight, and had I not thought fast, we would have all been dead. You should have been here with us, Waymen. You could have kept us safe. Please come here, Waymen. We can work it out. I won't give the baby away if you come back. Just come back." Medallion ended the call and then poured herself another glass of wine and then laid down beside her son.

Chapter 25

"Mrs. Medallion… Mrs. Medallion… Wake up." Nurse Jackie shook Medallion hoping to rouse her. "Mrs. Medallion... Wakc up, Mrs. Medallion. Where is the baby?"

"Hmmmm…"

"Mrs. Medallion, WAKE UP. The baby, where is the baby?" Nurse Jackie continued to shake Medallion.

"Leave me alone, he's in the bed with me."

Nurse Jackie looked around the bed and on the floor, but she didn't see the baby. She shook her head 'no' in frustration and began to shake Medallion once again.

"Mrs. Medallion, he isn't on the bed or around it. He's not here or in his room. Wake up, we have to find him."

"He's on the bed with me, woman!"

With her face still semi-buried in her pillow, she flopped her arm across the bed but didn't feel his soft little warm body. She opened her eyes to look in the direction of her arm.

"He was right here beside me…"

And then a horrific image of a small arm peeping from underneath her body flashed in her head, *Oh my goodness... I didn't!* Medallion lifted herself from the mattress and saw that she'd rolled over her son where he initially laid between her back and the pillow.

"Medallion, you didn't!" Nurse Jackie cried out.

She picked up the baby and felt for his heartbeat. The color in his complexion was fading fast. She checked him for breath.

"I can't tell if he's still alive!"

"Save him Mrs. Jackie! Save my baby!" Medallion's tears began to flow as she thought of the moment's ramifications.

Using CPR, Nurse Jackie began to pump air into his little chest. "Come on baby, come on..." She said as she worked hard to get Isaiah to breathe...

***

Sunta sat up as she heard the small, faint sound of a baby crying.

"Is that him? Is that my baby coming back?"

She looked into The White and saw an angel floating towards her with a bundle wrapped in her arms.

"It's him... I know it's him."

As the angel got closer, Sunta could see the bundle's shape forming into a child.

"He's here! My baby's coming to me!"

As she stood up to meet the crying baby, she saw a light appear behind her. Sunta turned to look and saw two angels appear. She smiled at them.

"It's time. My baby is finally here. Once the angel hands me my baby, I can go with you. I'll be ready to go with you when my baby gets in my arms."

The two angels stood one on each side of the bright light that pierced through The White. They stood stoically not saying a word. Sunta turned back to the direction from where the baby was coming and began to walk towards them.

"Mama been waiting on you, son…"

As she proceeded towards the baby and the angel, the guardian angles who stood by the bright light appeared beside Sunta pushing her out of the way.

"No… you can't have him! He's mine!"

A loud boom of a voice came from where the angels stood and said, "Do not interfere with the work that has to be done." Sunta's legs trembled— almost buckling under her as the voice vibrated through her body.

"This child does not belong to you. Do not interfere, 'fore he has a chance to come with us or go back."

"What you mean go back?! He's my baby!" Sunta pushed through the angels and reached for the child. "He's my son, and he belongs with me!"

***

"Call an ambulance Medallion, we are going to have to get him to a hospital!"

Nurse Jackie breathed into his mouth and began to use her two fingers to pump on his chest once again.

"One, two, three, four, five, six" She counted the little pumps she performed on his chest.

"I don't think he's going to make it…" Medallion's tears were bountiful as she thought about all the horrible things she said about her son. "I didn't mean it, Isaiah. I want you to stay with me."

Nurse Jackie continued to pump his chest pressing in a steady rhythmic motion. Medallion watched the nurse in agony but out of the corner of her eye, she saw the paintings of the elders hung on the wall twitch and jump in synch with the nurse's pumps. She curiously turned her head to the paintings noticing a panic in their eyes she'd never seen before. She quickly looked back at Nurse Jackie who continued to do the work of bringing her baby back. The nurse breathed into his tiny mouth once again and began pumping once more.

Jackie's usually calm demeanor was replaced with urgency when she briefly turned her attention to Medallion. “Medallion I said call the ambulance!”

But Medallion could not head the nurse’s calling. She was struck with awe as the elders within their frames began to move ever so slightly as if shifting... creating a current that allowed the house to breath and move along with the nurse. *Their energy... their sending it to him...* Medallion began to feel the weight of the air around her move slowly to the lifeless child, whose skin was no longer the shining color of a polished onyx but a dulling grey. She went over and kneeled by the child.

“Didn’t you hear me girl! Get the ambulance!”

The house began to shake and tremble. Medallion looked all around the room and once again at the elders on the wall with an urge to pray. “To the elders who are here, I thank you in this moment. Please save my baby!” The floors vibrated underneath their feet as if Medallion’s cries were heard. Nurse Jackie continued her mission to return Isaiah to his mother, and then without warning, the lights flickered and went out leaving the house in total darkness.

***

“He’s my baby, my baby, my baby, my baby!” Sunta held on tight to the young child. She held him firmly as the angles made their way over to her.

“DO NOT INTERFERE!” Their voices louder than before.

Sunta began to run with the baby in her arms as The White began to shake all around her. An angle grabbed her arm to pull her grip loose from the child, but it was too late. She felt herself lifted as if in a strong wind. Then, a fiery heat encased her and the child as they passed through the blinding light from where he came.

***

“One, two, three, four, five, six. Come on, Isaiah, you can make it. Come on baby…”

In the darkness of the house, Medallion waited in anticipation for her son to show some life. “Little one... I’m so sorry

I did this to you. Mommy loves you so much. Give me one more chance to make this right..." Medallion began to weep.

"Come on baby..." Still in the darkness, Nurse Jackie continued to give him her breath as she pumped his tiny chest. "We not letting you go." Her fingers near his tiny sternum, she stayed focused on his life. "One, two, three, four, five, si—" Then, she heard his little cough; breaking the intense fear that covered the room.

"He's back!" Nurse Jackie exclaimed in a gasp as Isaiah began to cry.

"ISAIAH!!" Medallion screamed.

With an electric hum in the air, the lights flickered back on as she scooped up her son. Medallion cried tears of joy. She raised Isaiah to the paintings on the wall of the elders who were now still and at rest. "Thank you! He's here! He's with us!"

Sunta saw the scene while hovering from above unseen by the human eye. She looked around the room, not knowing where she was but very aware she was in a place other than The White. She looked on as the two women hugged her son Elijah in relief of his return. Her temper boiled at the site. Her anger fueled her energy making it strong enough to express herself. She looked towards the ceramic vase on the tall dresser and knocked it over with all of her force causing the women to jump as it crashed to the floor startling them. *That's my son.* She said as she began to fade further away.

Chapter 26

"Good morning."

Nurse Jackie walked into the kitchen with her bags in tow. She was surprised to see Medallion sitting at the kitchen counter hovering over a cup of coffee.

"Morning," Medallion said in a tired weary voice.

She stared out of one of the kitchen's massive floor to ceiling windows as she contemplated how the night before was full of fear and regret leaving her tired and barely able to get out of the bed.

"I fed the baby on my own."

"Good. You'll need to get used to that."

Nurse Jackie headed for the counter and grabbed an available coffee mug to pour herself a cup.

Medallion noticed Nurse Jackie ease onto a stool next to her as she continued to sip her coffee.

"So, you're really leaving huh?"

"Yes ma'am. I can see you don't need or want me here." Nurse Jackie took another sip of the brew.

"I may not want you here, but by the way you handled things last night, I sure do need you here. Could you please reconsider staying— just until I can convince Waymen to come?"

"Chile, please. You couldn't get me to stay if this was the last place on earth."

She took another sip of her coffee.

"Mrs. Jackie… don't be like that." Medallion looked down at her phone as it lit up. "Oh God… It's Auntie."

She bit her bottom lip in worry before answering the phone. "Hey Auntie…"

"So, I got a call from the security company about an alarm last night? What's going on?"

"Oh, nothing much… just that dang door in the Four Season's room. Geesh Auntie, you really should have shelled out a few more dollars to get it fixed."

"I should, shouldn't I? I'll call the contractor to come out after the storm and fix it up."

Aunt Mary sensed more was left being unsaid. Something in Medallion's voice gave her spirit a stir.

"So, how's everything else going so far? You and Nurse Jackie getting along?"

"Well…"

"Well, what? Don't tell me you are fighting with Nurse Jackie."

"Um… well, see…"

"No excuses, Medda! You are NOT going to run her off! Whatever is going on between the two of you, you better fix it. Lawd, chile! What's gotten into you?!"

"No Auntie… you got it all wrong. I was going to tell you that she's been wonderful and umm... well, something happened to Isaiah last night and she was there to help me and him."

"Isaiah! What's wrong with him?"

"Oh, nothing major. Isaiah is fine. He just scared us a little bit. He wasn't breathing after I rolled over him by accident, but he's fine now. Got his color back and everything."

"Rolled over him?! Not breathing?! Medallion!!"

"No Auntie! Don't over-react. Nurse Jackie was here and did CPR. He's fine."

"Oh Medallion… you got my nerves all riled up! What is WRONG with you!"

Anxious tears rolled swiftly down Mary's cheeks at the thought of losing little Isaiah.

"It's okay, Auntie. Everything is fine now. Isaiah's fine. I'm fine. Nurse Jackie is here."

"Not for long..." the nurse mumbled under her breath as she continued to drink her coffee all while listening to Medallion's side of the conversation with her aunt.

"Listen, Medda. This is too much for me to take in right now. You can NOT be so reckless with your child. He is your charge. You opted to have him and it is your responsibility as a mom to keep him protected. You cannot FAIL in this job you have. You have GOT to take it more seriously!"

"I know, Auntie. Last night scared me. I promise to do better."

"You can't promise to, you have to, Medda. It's important."

There was a short pause in the conversation while Mary collected her thoughts. Medallion waited patiently for her aunt to speak once more after she finished absorbing all she'd heard.

"Medda, once you get off this phone, I need you to go to the pantry and pull out some dried tulip petals. Get a handful of Himalayan pink salt, and some mineral oil. Draw that baby a bath in the sink and put all that in there, then I need you to burn some sage all around him as he soaks in that bath while one of those white candles burns. Let him soak in that for about five minutes. While you doing that, close your eyes and imagine your mama and daddy. See them as your eyes are closed and thank them for bringing him back to you. After that I—"

"Auntie, let me call you back."

"Wait Medda, I'm not done telling you what to do. You gotta do this or—"

"I know, but let me call you back. Love you."

Distracted by what she saw out of her kitchen window, Medallion ended the call before her aunt could say another word. From the woods at the edge of the property, a woman emerged from them. "I wonder who that could be?"

Nurse Jackie looked up from her coffee to see the young woman walking towards the house. *Strange… she* thought to herself.

"Why isn't that child wearing a coat? It's got to be twenty degrees outside."

Both Medallion and Nurse Jackie got up from their stool in the kitchen and headed for the back door of the Four Seasons room to greet the young woman.

"Yes, may I help you?" Medallion stared at the girl whose looks were mesmerizing.

Her coal black hair showcased individual coils that sprouted from the root of her head and then rested delicately on her shoulders. Her eyes were dark pools of black that anyone could drown in. Her skin was the warmest shade of brown, and the cold weather gave her cheeks a rosy flush. Her height was as impressive as her looks. She was tall and lean, and Medallion noticed that as tall as she was, the young woman was at least an inch or two taller.

As breathtaking as the girl was, there was something different about her and Nurse Jackie sensed the difference in her right away. She discretely grabbed Medallion's hand squeezing it slightly; narrowing her eyes at the young woman standing before them.

***

Sunta presented a tiny smile at the two women hoping they didn't see that she was not entirely solid. She'd used most of her strength to materialize, and her powers had been enough, but there was an unmistakable glow that shown off her skin. She could have waited a day or so until she was strong enough to reveal herself, but she couldn't wait. She had to see him— touch him, know that he was here, and then prepare him to go by the new moon's light.

When Sunta entered the house the night before, she watched them holding him. Elijah was beautiful and all that she remembered. That night, she flew around them unseen. Her presence invisible to the naked eye... She breathed in his air, remembering his smell, and wanting to hold him. She followed them to his room and watched them as they laid him in his crib. She whispered a kiss on his cheek and rested by his side; absorbing some of his energy to help her come to him as she stood before them.

When the women opened the door to meet her in the yard, she remembered their faces as the women who cried over her son, Elijah. *The young one held my son, s*he thought to herself as she stared deeply at the beautiful woman. She looked at the older one, and her smile waivered. *She stares at me like she knows…* She looked away from her questioning glare and focused on the younger.

"Yes. I's come from down the way and I um… saw you yesterday."

"Oh, you saw us move in yesterday? You must be from the neighbor's farm." Medallion stuck out her hand to shake the young woman's. "My name is Medallion, and this is Mrs. Jackie. My Aunt Mary owns this place and Mrs. Jackie and I are just visiting. Would you like to come in for a minute to get the chill off of you?"

She looked down at her arms and down towards her feet aware she had on only a white long-sleeved gown and nothing to cover her feet— far from appropriate attire for the cold weather season.

"Yes, I'd like to come in and visit if y'all don't mind."

Medallion and Mrs. Jackie stepped aside and let their guest walk in. She looked around in awe at how much the big house from her past had changed. She took a deep breath in and could faintly make out the smell of some of the scents from her time spent there cooking and cleaning for the family. *I'm home…* She thought as she let her fingers graze the wall in remembrance.

"So, you notice the renovation work my Auntie has done? You must not have been here since she finished the reno. Why, the way she talked about how everyone loved the redesign and décor, I would have assumed the whole county came by to give their glorifying opinions."

Medallion belted out a welcoming laugh and followed the young lady who aimlessly wandered into the kitchen.

"No ma'am. I ain't been here in a long time. I been away a while."

"I'm sure you have since Auntie never mentioned younger neighbors. How old are you by the way?"

"Oh, I be about 16— 17 or so. I lose track."

She walked around the kitchen marveling at the gadgets on the counter-top and barely paying attention to Medallion or her questions.

"Well, where are you from, dear?"

Nurse Jackie watched as the curious young lady found a stool at the kitchen counter and sat on it. *Something just isn't right about her…*

I'm from 'nother side of the county— real small part. I'm hear visiting and then I got to get back."

"Who are you visiting? Anyone my Aunt would know?"

"Oh, just some family. Can't say if your Aunt knows them or not. They ain't never mentioned her to me."

Medallion pulled out a coffee mug and placed it in front of the young woman and began pouring from the warm pot.

"Coffee?"

She breathed in the warm aroma and smiled with her eyes closed.

"That smell good."

She picked the warm mug up with both hands; placing the cup to her lips. The steam from the mug could be seen rising in front of her eyes filling her with delight about the warmth she was about to consume. She began to drink the coffee in gulps without thinking about how hot it was.

Nurse Jackie flinched while watching the girl swiftly drink the hot coffee.

"Baby, don't that burn your whole mouth and throat drinking it that fast?"

She put the cup back down and wiped her mouth with the back of her hand.

"Guess it didn't bother me. I was real thirsty."

Nurse Jackie's suspicion about the young woman were heightened. Her instinct told her to be beware. A streak of goose bumps went up the front of her arm, and a chill went through her as she continued to watch the young woman with inquiry.

"Medallion, can I see you in the other room for a bit?"

Nurse Jackie eyed Medallion and raised her brow at her as she motioned her head towards the foyer for a private moment.

"Excuse me for a sec. Feel free to pour yourself another cup of coffee, and we'll be right back."

Medallion followed Nurse Jackie towards the front where she stood impatiently with her arms folded.

"You see that in there? You saw how she drank all that coffee and it didn't bother her that it was steaming hot?"

"I mean… she said she was thirsty. Maybe it wasn't that hot to her."

"No. What we saw in there won't right. Something is different about that girl."

Medallion chuckled at Nurse Jackie's frivolous suspicions. "There's nothing wrong with her. She looks perfectly fine to me."

"You mean to tell me you find it perfectly fine to see a young woman coming out of the woods, in the early morning, wearing a whisper of a gown, no shoes, and then gulp down a cup of hot coffee?"

"Okay, she comes off a little eccentric, but nothing too unusual. I see my aunt in the garden with no shoes on all the time 'cause she likes the dirt and the mud between her toes. That girl in the kitchen is harmless I bet."

Nurse Jackie shook her head 'no' to Medallion's reasoning.

"No. Everything about her is sending off red flags. I'm telling you, you need to send her on her way. I got a feeling she means you no good."

"Wait— why you keep saying *I* have to send her away, and she means to harm *me*? What makes you think she wants to hurt me?"

Medallion thought about it for a moment and then frowned.

"So what… you think she's stalking me? You think she trying to get me out of the way so she can be with Waymen or something? Oh hell nah! She can't have my man!"

Medallion pushed the sleeves of her shirt up her arms as she started to rush back into the kitchen and confront the young woman, but Nurse Jackie grabbed her arm and pulled her back into the foyer before she could get away.

"Would you calm down!" Nurse Jackie commanded in a hushed voice. "What I'm feeling is deeper than that foolishness you playing with your husband. Listen to me when I say her presence comes with an evil desire. Now, get her out of your house."

Medallion looked at Nurse Jackie and saw the seriousness she'd been trying to portray. She regained her composure and agreed with the nurse.

"Alright. I'll send her away."

"Good."

Nurse Jackie followed behind Medallion as they made their way back to the kitchen.

"Have you finished your coffee?" Medallion said as she entered the kitchen.

The girl was not sitting at the counter where they left her. Medallion looked at the nurse with curiosity.

"Well, where did she go?"

The nurse shrugged her shoulders and walked past Medallion to grab her bags.

"Maybe she left on her own."

"Well good. I didn't want to be rude to that girl by throwing her out. She probably heard us talking and took offense, and now she really won't be back."

"Nah. It don't feel right. Just be careful." Nurse Jackie looked down at her feet; now hesitant to leave Medallion and the baby. "Well… I guess this is it. My cab should be here shortly."

Medallion picked at her fingernails trying her best to end things with the nurse on a more pleasurable note.

"I understand. Hey. If you gotta go, you gotta go. Don't worry about me. I'll figure out something to tell my aunt on why you had to leave." She looked up as she remembered one last gesture of kindness. "Oh, let me go get the baby so you can say goodbye. He's probably up anyway."

Nurse Jackie nodded in agreement and watched as Medallion raced up the stairs. As she waited, she stared out the kitchen window and out at the woods that lined the property. Even in the daylight, they looked dark and dense. The chill of the season had taken the leaves from the branches of the trees and they all laid on the ground looking as if they would crunch if you walked on them. *What's on the other side of those woods? I can't imagine anyone walking through them for any reason.* As Nurse Jackie contemplated the possibilities, her thoughts were interrupted by Medallion's scream, and then her feet fumbling down the stairs. "He's missing! He wasn't in his bed!"

"What do you mean? The baby is gone?"

"Yes! That girl must have taken him!"

"Chile, I told you she was evil! I don't know why you don't listen to me!"

They both took off in different directions and began searching the big house. Nurse Jackie rushed into the dining room looking under the tables, chairs and in the tall china press by the wall. Medallion ran into the den and began pulling out the seat covers of the sofa. She opened the drawers of the entertainment center with no sign of the baby being there. Finally, they ended up charging back up the stairs and began to check the upstairs bedrooms. Medallion burst through the master bedroom door but neither the baby nor the girl were there.

She checked the closet and then headed to the bathroom. Out of the corner of her eye, she caught something move out of the window. She went back to the window and saw the girl walking around the yard with the baby in her arms. *Isaiah!* Medallion banged on the window to get the girls attention but to no avail. The young woman continued to walk in circles as she patted Isaiah on his back. Medallion could see that the young woman moving her lips as if she were talking. *What is she doing to my son!* Medallion quickly left the bathroom and bolted down the stairs and out of the front door.

***

"Baby, oh baby, you are mine forever. Baby, oh baby, you are mine forever. I've finally found you. We belong together."

Sunta recited the words to the little boy as she hugged him closely to her. When she was in the kitchen waiting on the two women to come back, she heard the baby coo in the little white box sitting on the counter. The sound of his voice startled her, but it was unmistakable. She'd heard it when he was crossing over, and his voice became embedded in her soul.

When she heard it in the little box, she tapped the white square contraption that held his voice, and suddenly, a bigger flatter box on the wall lit up and the baby was there. Sunta stared at him in amazement. It was like he was a live picture on the wall. She walked over and touched the moving picture and noticed the words "NURSERY" in the corner.

Sunta didn't know how to find him, but she remembered last night how the woman laid him in his crib within a room that looked like it was made just for him. *He's in this house somewhere. This moving picture is telling me where he is.* Sunta remembered the staircase on the other side of her master's old smoking room being another way to the second floor.

She snuck out of the kitchen, through the great room, and ended up in a room that smelled a hint like Master's favorite cigar. She was in Master's den, but the room was now full of decorative furniture of a woman's touch and another moving picture hanging on the wall. Diagonal from where she stood, she could see the back staircase that led upstairs. She quietly crept up the rugged steps and began her journey down the second floor hallway. She looked into every room until she found him lying in the bed just like she saw on the moving picture.

"I found you…" She said to the little baby as she smiled at him.

She picked him out of the bed and breathed in his air once more.

"You smell like mine."

She let his cheek rest on her cheek. "You feel like mine."

She looked into his eyes and saw within him the same child she held so long ago. In that moment their souls connected and Sunta saw him for who he truly was. "You look just like mine."

She sat in the rocking chair by the window with him and began to hum a song she'd always wanted to sing to her baby boy.

"Baby boy, baby boy, my world of joy is my baby boy."

As she remembered those last moments with her son so long ago, her breast began to ache. She touched them noticing how tender they had become. She smiled.

"It's time to nurse, baby…"

She led his mouth to her chest and then closed her eyes in soothing relief as he began to suckle. While he nursed from her, she hummed softly to herself as Isaiah fed effortlessly from her.

***

"What are you doing with my son!" Medallion ran up to the young woman and spun her around with the pull of her shoulder.

"Wha… what's wrong…"

Sunta looked at the young woman in confusion and then noticed her surroundings. She was outside. The baby still in her arms. *How did I end up here?* The last she could remember was her sitting in the rocking chair feeding her Elijah.

Medallion took Isaiah from the woman and stepped back. "What are you doing with my son out here in the cold weather?"

Sunta saw the anger in the woman's face. She saw the baby in the woman's arms and her soul cried out. She couldn't lose him again. She thought of a quick excuse.

"Well. Um… while y'all was umm… talking I… uh… heard the babe on that thing in the kitchen. I just uh… took it upon myself to calm him is all. They say the cold in the air soothe a crying baby the quickest."

Sunta reached out longingly and stroked a finger down the baby's cheek. Medallion quickly jerked the baby away; not wanting the girl to touch her son. Sunta smiled sweetly.

"See, look how quiet he is."

"Well, you could have said something, and I would have gone and got him." Medallion said with anger behind every word.

"I would of, but you two were talking. Then I heard that other one say something about don't trust me."

Medallion lowered her eyes in shame at what the young girl said.

"I don't want you to think I'm some type of monster going around hurtin' folks, so I went up and got the baby and calm him so you know I can be trusted. 'Cause you know if a baby can't trust you, then it's got to be something wrong with ya."

"But you should have let me know he was crying. You can't go picking up other people's kids."

"I'm sorry. I didn't mean it like that."

"It's fine. No harm came to him. Come on back to the house. I'll fix you something to eat, and maybe we can find you a coat and some shoes to wear back home. You shouldn't be walking around like that." Medallion grabbed the young girl's hand while heading back to the house. "By the way, you never told me your name."

"Oh, it's Sunta."

Chapter 27

"Wha--!" Nurse Jackie woke from her sleep in a fright as the nightmare was too real. Still groggy, she placed her head in her hand to rub her eyes from the sleep. She needed clarity from such horrible visions, but as she closed her eyes to readjust, she saw flashes of a woman sweating while in agony on a dirty wooden floor. The high pitched screams the woman in her dreams made, continued to echo in her head. The woman she dreamt of was in pain and the panic in her eyes worried Nurse Jackie as she wrestled with herself to wake up.

She opened her eyes quickly once again not wanting to see any more of the gruesome scene. There was blood all around the woman in her dreams. She saw a knife there on a table; it all looked like a torture scene. *Why did I dream something so horrible?* The nightmare took a toll on the nurse. She felt the pain the woman went through, and she had the urge to cry for her. *It was too real…*

Nurse Jackie sat up in her bed and took a sip of water from the glass on the nightstand beside her bed. She looked around the room. She was still here. Still in the room. Still in the house. *I should have left when I said I was.* She shook her head at her bad decision to stay with Medallion. *I'm probably having nightmares because I regret that I agreed to stay.*

Earlier, when she finally made her way to the backyard as they were looking for the baby, she was shocked to see Medallion and the strange woman walking back to the house together while she held Isaiah. Both Medallion and Sunta smiled and giggled as they walked past Nurse Jackie and back into the kitchen. She put her hand on her hip with contrary belief as she watched them become fast friends.

"What just happened? Didn't she just try to kidnap your baby, and now she's a welcomed guest in your Aunt's home?"

Medallion sucked her teeth and rolled her eyes at the nurse's comment.

"Oh, calm down. It was a total misunderstanding"

Sunta nodded in agreement.

"I'm going to put the baby back in his bed now that he's calm."

Nurse Jackie watched Sunta in silence until the girl was out of sight and earshot before chastising Medallion for being naive.

"You can't be serious?! That girl tried to kidnap your baby and you let her back in the house! You obviously meant what you said about giving your son up. What, did she agree to take him off your hands so you can go play more silly games with your husband?"

"Would you just stop it? I'm not giving my son up. She was trying to calm the baby down because he was crying while we were talking about her. And yes, she heard every word we said. She thought the fresh air would do him some good is all."

"I'm a nurse, and I've never heard of anyone taking a baby outside in the freezing cold to calm it down." Nurse Jackie folded her arms in anger. "I can't believe how cavalier you're being about this stranger in your home. You are going to end up regretting this woman."

"Listen, Mrs. Jackie. I know you are upset with me for the things I've said and done. I can see that I'm not one of your favorite persons and that's my fault. After last night's scare, it made me realize how childish I was being and that I need to own up to all that I've done to ruin my relationship with my husband and how I haven't been the best mom to my son."

Nurse Jackie unfolded her arms and her demeanor softened as she listened to Medallion's heartfelt acknowledgement of her bad behavior.

"Come here, baby." Nurse Jackie stretched out her arms, and Medallion walked into her embrace. "You going to get it right one day. You just have to think about others before you think of yourself. The people that care about you matter. Their feelings matter and your actions do hurt them."

Medallion lingered in her the reassuring hug. The warmth from Nurse Jackie's body made her feel secure. *I wish Aunt Mary were here.* Medallion hugged Nurse Jackie back and they both finally let go.

"So, what I'm trying to say is, Mrs. Jackie, don't go yet. I don't want to be in this big house alone."

The nurse smiled humbly. "I understand. Well maybe I should stay."

"Could you? We could give it another try. Maybe become real friends? Aunt Mary chose you for a reason. Honestly, I don't think I could face her if she ever found out you and I didn't get along and you left me here because of my attitude."

Nurse Jackie laughed at the thought. "Well then, this fiasco will be our little secret."

Medallion gave Nurse Jackie a quick cuddle and grabbed her bags. "I'll put these back in your room for you."

"Well, I'll get started on another pot of coffee and then start getting breakfast ready."

Medallion smiled at the new opportunity to make things right and then headed for the steps that led to the rooms upstairs.

As Medallion left, she used the back staircase and crept quietly into the kitchen. Once there, she watched the plump little old woman crack a few eggs into a warming pan without being noticed. The woman then bustled her way over to the cold closet, grabbed some other things, and turned around to lay them on the counter. Sunta closed her eyes. She slowly evaporated and materialized behind the busy little woman; close enough to her that the cold chill of her breath sent a shock down Nurse Jackie's spine making her drop everything in her hands. Startled, she turned around to see Sunta staring at her with those darker than brown eyes. The young girl's glare was almost menacing, and Nurse Jackie felt the cold chill take over her whole body.

Nervous but not wanting to show fear, she hurriedly gathered up the things she'd dropped on the floor and set them on the counter.

"Chile, you scared me out of my wits. Why are you standing so close to me watching me all quiet? Don't you know it's rude to sneak up on people?" She tried not to sound nervous around the young girl, but her mystique bothered her soul.

"Can't be no ruder than you staring at me like you know something."

Nurse Jackie pushed passed the girl and made her way to the eggs frying in the pan; pausing for a moment to absorb what Sunta said.

"Yeah. You feel it don't you. You and me. We's almost the same."

Sunta rolled her eyes into the back of her head exposing the white around her pupils. The room grew dim, and the chill Nurse Jackie felt when Sunta startled her did not compare to what she felt in that moment. The room had grown colder. The draft around her had a dampness that made it feel like small ice crystals were in the air. Nurse Jackie turned away from the stove and was face to face with the mysterious young girl. Neither uttered a word. Sunta finally breathed in deeply, sucking up the air between them. Nurse Jackie began to choke.

Suffocating, she felt her throat tightening to a close, and her head became light making her dizzy. She held on to the counter for support as she began sliding slowly to the floor. Sunta gripped the nurse's forearm forbidding her to fall. Then, as if it never happened, Nurse Jackie was able to breathe again. Her head became clear and she straightened herself from the descent to the floor. She gasped and coughed while struggling to breathe in the air she was deprived. Once she was better, Sunta's darker than brown eyes returned from the white glossed over marble-like pupils they once were.

Sunta leaned in close to Nurse Jackie and whispered, "I know you know what I am. It won't be long before you know what I want. Leave this house now, and I won't take your life as a parting gift."

"Is everything okay?" Medallion walked into the kitchen in time to see Sunta bent over Nurse Jackie seeming to help her up.

"Everything fine in here Mrs. I was helping Nurse Jackie. She seem to have lost her footing a little. Maybe on some of dis grease popping from da pan."

Sunta flashed Nurse Jackie a warning look as she walked towards the backdoor.

"You don't have to go, Sunta. Mrs. Jackie is cooking breakfast. I'm sure there'll be enough to share with you."

The nurse's eyes widened in fear and her hands began to tremble as she continued to prepare breakfast.

"No ma'am. I've intruded enough this mor'nan. I'll come back some other time and chit-chat. Y'all enjoy your breakfast. I'm a lil' tired anyway. I had a long night."

With a wave of her hand, Sunta was out the back door.

"You alright?" Medallion asked the nurse.

After Medallion waved goodbye to Sunta, she turned and looked at Nurse Jackie who appeared to be in a daze, and Medallion could smell the burnt eggs in the pan.

"Looks like you over-cooked that. You want me to make breakfast? I do know my way around the kitchen a little bit."

She picked up the pan from the stove's eye and allowed the burnt breakfast to be destroyed by the garbage disposal.

"I… I think I may need to go lay down".

Sunta was right… Nurse Jackie knew there was something wrong with the young girl who'd appeared through the woods. *But she was wrong about me leaving. I'm not going anywhere.*

Chapter 28

The morning scare kept Nurse Jackie in her bed for the rest of the day. The terrifying dream she'd experienced earlier in the night kept her from falling into the deeper sleep she desperately desired. As she rolled over to get more comfortable, she heard a thump come from outside of her closed door. Looking out of her bedroom window, she realized she inadvertently slept the day away. She noticed the time on the clock sitting on her nightstand.

"Oh my… It's midnight. How did I sleep that long?"

As she struggled to remember any part of the day she missed, the thump that woke her from her sleep could be heard once more; startling her back into the present. She called out from her bed, "Medallion, are you up?"

She didn't receive an answer. *Must have been nothing...* She wiggled back down and underneath the covers assuring herself that the rest she received was much needed.

Just as she was about to drift off, she heard the thump outside her door once again. This time it was louder, and she could no longer ignore the noise coming from the hall. She got out of the bed and grabbed her robe. She placed her arms in the garment and then tied a knot with the belt around her waist. Suddenly and without warning, her bedroom door began to rattle violently. Nurse Jackie jumped back in surprise. *What in the world is going on!* She felt her heart pulsating in her throat as fear of the unknown rose within her.

The door shook as if someone on the other side were trying to force their way in. She gripped the collar of her robe together as tightly as she could praying the intruder on the other side of her door couldn't make it within her room. Cautiously she walked towards the door terrified of what could be on the other end, but the shaking door abruptly went silent. She stopped walking and waited not knowing what to expect. Then, in the quiet of the room, she heard the soft cry of the baby from the nursery down the hall.

Nurse Jackie's chest rose high with each breath while she stood still in fright not knowing what to do next, but the baby's voice called to her with his soft cries. And to make matters worse, Medallion still hadn't responded. *What if they are in trouble… Oh God. I have to do something to help…*

Again, Nurse Jackie began to slowly walk towards the closed bedroom door and then opened it slowly. As she did, it loudly creaked; exposing her to the dark abyss of the hallway. Courageously but apprehensively, she began her trek towards the baby's room through the dark black hallway while his cries grew louder and more desperate. Then she saw a sliver of light come from his room.

She paused her steps as she watched the sliver of light shine through the crack lulling her into a sense of security. *Medallion must have heard him too.* She relaxed her stance figuring things were okay with the baby now quiet.

Relieved, Nurse Jackie began to turn and walk back to her room, but the door of the nursery flew open. The sliver of light was now illuminating the once darkened hall. A shadowy figure came through the light. Nurse Jackie gasped as she watched Sunta walk out of the room with the baby in her arms. *What is she doing?*

"Baby. My baby. Baby. My baby." Sunta sang in a light and airy voice appearing not to notice Nurse Jackie standing by the nursery's door.

The icy chill from the kitchen came back while Nurse Jackie watched in fright as the young girl walked down the steps. Once she thought Sunta was at the bottom, she walked trembling with dread to the top of the staircase. With eyes straining in the dark, she peered through the rungs of the railings of the staircase but Sunta could not be seen. Nurse Jackie contemplated her next move. *Maybe if Sunta moved... or if the baby cried, I'd know what I should do...* The house was deathly quiet, and the nurse continued to keep still; trying to hide in the shadows while waiting on Sunta to do something which would help her make a decision on which action to take. *I have to go tell Medallion what that girl is before something bad happens.*

Turning around to head towards Medallion's bedroom, Sunta stood before her. Her face was full of anger.

"You were just down the stairs… How did you get up here so fast? Where's the baby?" Nurse Jackie exasperatedly questioned.

As they stood face-to-face, Nurse Jackie watched a change in the young woman's face. Sunta's skin grew pale, and her cheeks became jaunt. The pupils of her eyes dilated until her sockets were pools of darkness. Her mouth slinked opened into the shape of a long, dark, and hollow oval.

"Lord, chile... this ain't right... You are a lost soul for sure... Lost ones don't belong here... I... bind you... in the name of..." Nurse Jackie's eyes begin to fill with tears and panic as she forced her words through Sunta's tightening group. "God... keep the baby here..."

Sunta let out a low and slow moan sending a cold chill down Nurse Jackie's spine along with a vibration through her body. Sunta then grabbed the nurse by her neck raising her up just enough to hover her over the staircase's first step.

Nurse Jackie opened her mouth to scream for help, but the grip Sunta had on her neck silenced her. Fearing death was near, she arched her feet hoping her toes would touch the ground as she struggled to find her footing on the steps. She grabbed at Sunta's arm hoping for stability, but the pale grey arm began to flake and peel; almost crumbling underneath the old woman's touch. The ghostly woman tilted her head slowly while looking strangely at Nurse Jackie. Sunta's bellowing moan ceased as she spoke her next haunting words.

"My baby. *My* baby," She emphasized before she flung the scared old woman down the steps.

Chapter 29

"Ohhh…"

Slowly, Nurse Jackie placed her hand on the side of her head to touch the knot that had already begun to form.

"Ouch!"

The knot exploded in pain when she touched it. She opened her eyes to see the foyer chandelier hanging from the ceiling from where she laid on the cold marble floor. *What happened last night?*

As she tried to roll over on her side, a sharp pains ran up and down her spine. Her muscles began to ache with every attempt to help herself. She winched in pain struggling to move around until she was finally able to sit up on her bottom. She grabbed the railing of the banister in an attempt to pull herself up the rest of the way.

"Ow! My leg!"

Nurse Jackie raised the hem of her night gown exposing black and blue bruises down the side of her leg. She looked up the stairway remembering what she experienced the night before. *Sunta did this to me.*

She recalled how Sunta threw her down the stairs. Then a revelation came to her like it been anxiously waiting in the recesses of her mind. *Sunta's the woman in my dreams from last night!* And like the switch for a light being turned on, she began to see flashes of the nightmare of the woman crying and screaming with blood all around her.

As she sat at the bottom of the steps in pain, the horrific visions began to fill her thoughts. *Sunta was there… screaming. Blood all over splintered wooden floors… Baby crying just like last night...* More revelations from the vision showed other women in the room chanting words Nurse Jackie had never heard. Then in another flash, a baby boy's face sprang into view. His eyes were a clear blue. His skin was the darkest shade of brown. He was being held by one foot while being placed on a table. The more Nurse Jackie tried to remember the dream, the hazier it became. *What does she want? She kept saying 'My baby. My baby.' What does she want?*

Her headache began to intensify as she pondered the question. *I can't think about it anymore. Too much pain.* Nurse Jackie looked out the long panel window beside the front door. It was morning. *I've been lying here all night.* She looked back up the stairs and hollered, "Medallion! Medallion! Help me!"

Behind the closed door of the master suite, Medallion was already up. Her night was restless; filled with visions of women chanting, a baby, and another woman lying screaming on the floor. She couldn't figure out what her dream meant even though she felt as if she knew the woman. There was a feeling of connection and a sense of protection between all of them. The dream was so compelling she'd gotten up out of her bed that morning to sit and think about it more. None of the scenes made sense to her but in some way it all felt real.

Medallion reached over to the nightstand and picked up her cell phone to dial her Aunt Mary and talk with her about all she'd dreamed, but she paused when she heard the faint sound of someone yelling her name. She put the phone back on her nightstand and opened the bedroom doors.

"Medallion! Medallion! I need your help!"

She walked down the hall and stopped at the stairs. She looked down the staircase and saw Nurse Jackie sitting at the bottom of them.

"What are you doing down there?"

"I um… fell this morning."

Choosing to keep the horrific details to herself, she kept quiet about what really happened until she could figure out what Sunta wanted.

"My goodness! Are you okay?" Medallion quickly went down the stairs to help the nurse.

"Yeah. I lost my footing on my way to the kitchen."

"Well, I must have been distracted because I never heard you fall."

Medallion braced herself as Nurse Jackie bore her weight against her and they both headed to the front parlor to allow Nurse Jackie to lay on the couch.

"I believe my leg is broken pretty bad, and I think I've messed up my hip."

"With a fall like that, I can believe it." Medallion headed for the kitchen. "I'm going to grab you a glass of water and some pain pills."

While in the kitchen and headed to the faucet with a glass to fill, she saw Sunta approaching from outside. She set the glass on the counter and opened the kitchen sliding door to greet her.

"Good morning Sunta. You are here just in the nick-of-time.'

"How so?"

Sunta walked into the kitchen and looked around. She was stronger than she was the day before. The home's vibrations from the past mixed with the present created a sensation that fueled her being. With her new energy, she was allowed to absorb the force and become more solid. Her body now warm from the inside out no longer glowed as it did the day before.

"Well, the baby is about to wake up, and Mrs. Jackie fell down the steps this morning. I think she broke her leg and probably her hip."

"You want me to get the baby?"

"If you don't mind? I'm going to get Mrs. Jackie taken care of."

Sunta obliged and happily made her way to the nursery. There, she found Isaiah in his crib still asleep. As his chest rose and fell in his circadian rhythm, Sunta smiled proud and deeply.

"My baby boy."

She scooped him up and laid him on her bosom. In her arms she felt the weight of his body as he laid within them.

"I missed holding you."

She stroked his thick cold black curls away from his face and then kissed his cherub-like cheeks. His skin was soft on her lips and she brushed them back and forth against the curve of his face.

"You so soft… just like I imagined."

As she whispered in his ear, he began to stir and his eyes began to flutter. Isaiah let out a little refreshing yawn and looked at Sunta with his big grey eyes. Sunta smiled at him.

"Hi my baby" she said in a sing-song like voice. She rocked him in her arms as she walked around the room.

One corner of Isaiah's small mouth creeped up giving the appearance of a slightly crooked smile. She laughed with enjoyment.

"I knew you would know who I was. I'm your mama." She gave him another kiss on his other cheek while taking in his delightful baby smell. "I can't stay long in this world, so Im'ma take you back wit' me to mine when the time right."

Isaiah squirmed and cooed while Sunta continued their conversation.

"Oh we can't go right now, my baby. We gotta prepare. It's gonna take some time, but we gonna leave this place. And we'll be together forever."

Sunta dug into her pocket and pulled out a small satchel. Earlier that morning, she had gathered enough ingredients from her walk to Glory for a connection spell to place in the baby's food. She emptied the ingredients of her pouch into the baby's breakfast milk which was already prepared in a bottle on the dresser. She shook the bottle to mix the ingredients with the milk and then fed him the concoction.

"All you need is a little every day to make you love me more."

Isaiah drank the milk as she rocked him in the rocker beside the window. She stared down at him and smiled. His eye color appeared to change to ice blue as he drank.

"See it's starting to work already."

Chapter 30

"Okay. Thank you, doctor."

Medallion nodded her head in acknowledgement as she listened to Doctor Nann on the other end of the phone.

"Yes. We have the leg propped up, and she's holding an icepack." She wrote down some notes on a pad by the couch and continued to listen. "Yes. I'll make sure to do that. Have a great day. We'll be on the lookout for the ambulance."

Medallion hung up her phone and wrote down the doctor's final instructions.

"Well, what did he say?"

"He said you probably broke your leg and bruised your hip just like you said, or it could be just a sprain. He'll know for sure once you get to the hospital."

Nurse Jackie slumped down in disappointment.

"So, it sounds like I won't be of any help to you now."

"Sounds like it."

Medallion handed Nurse Jackie the notes.

"Here's the doctor's instructions he wanted me to give them to you. He said you need to go to the hospital, and that these prescriptions should be waiting for you when you get there. You'll be on bed rest for a long while, so he wanted you to either start making arrangements to go back home or to stay in the hospital here."

"Well, wouldn't it be easier if I stayed here with you after they fit me for my cast? Don't you need some company?"

"Me? No. I'm pretty sure Waymen will be here in a couple of days. He just has to calm down from the fight we had."

Nurse Jackie looked dumbfounded by Medallion's reasoning. Even though she heard one side of the argument, she was positive Waymen was not going to come back to her ever.

"Do you seriously think Waymen is going to forgive you and come be with you after everything you put him through?"

"Of course! I am his wife. For better or worse, through sickness and in health. We took those vows and he has to honor them whether he likes it or not. Waymen will come around. We've gone through this before— well not exactly this, but more or less the same."

Nurse Jackie shook her head in disbelief before she continued. "Honey, you are delusional if you think a man is going to shovel the shit you give, but hey. You know him better than me. If you think that man is coming back, then keep hope alive."

Medallion laughed.

"Mrs. Jackie, you don't know anything about this new kind of love. You are old school. Guys nowadays like all this drama. Waymen is better than most men in a lot of ways, but for real... he ain't no different."

"But honestly, honey, all this fussing and fighting y'all doing ain't healthy. It's gotta stop."

Medallion chuckled at the sound advice Nurse Jackie gave.

"You looking at it all wrong. That's passion you see when him and I are fighting. Passion keeps the love strong. He's coming here and when he does, we'll make up... If you know what I mean. I'll just be here for a couple of days by myself is all."

Medallion instinctively picked up her phone and checked her text messages and missed call logs for a small sign that Waymen was thinking about her. She wanted to assure herself and Nurse Jackie that he was in fact going to meet her at Glory. *I hope I'm right this time. I screwed up big with the baby not being his. Hopefully he does honor our vows.* There were no notifications from Waymen on her phone.

Chapter 31

Just like in my dream! Nurse Jackie gasped in fear when she saw Sunta walk down the steps with Isaiah.

Medallion saw the shock in Nurse Jackie's eyes and turned to look in the direction she was staring. Medallion sucked her teeth at the old woman's reaction to Sunta.

"Mrs. Jackie… Stop acting like that. I invited her in when I saw her walking up from the woods this morning."

The nurse grabbed Medallion's arm in a panic. Sunta glared at Nurse Jackie and then gave her a sneaky smile before she headed into the kitchen with Isaiah cradled in her arms. Nurse Jackie pulled Medallion closer to the couch with anxiousness all over her.

"What's wrong with you, woman? You act like you've seen a ghost?" Medallion looked at her curiously as she wondered what could possibly be wrong.

"Medallion, listen to me. That girl in there— Sunta. She's not who she says she is. You've got to get away from here or she's going to hurt you and your son."

She was shocked to hear Nurse Jackie speak like that, especially since they'd had the same conversation the day before. She hadn't known the old woman long, but she felt that Nurse Jackie was as real as they come. It was surprising to hear a woman like that talk so insanely about a harmless young lady.

Medallion patted Nurse Jackie on the shoulder and pulled away from her spot beside her on the couch.

"Mrs. Jackie, that girl isn't going to hurt anyone. She's a young girl, and Isaiah looks to be very happy with her. I think you bumped your head a bit hard when you fell down the steps this morning."

"No, Medallion," she said sharply. Listen to me! I had a dream last night— more like a nightmare. She was in it!"

As Medallion made her way out of the room, she paused at Nurse Jackie's words. *Nightmare… I had one too last night.* She turned and looked at her inquisitively.

"Medallion, she was in my dreams and she—"

"Hold that thought Mrs. Jackie. I think that's the EMT Techs at the door." Medallion walked to the foyer and opened the door. "Thanks for coming. She's this way."

She led the EMT team to the parlor where Nurse Jackie lay on the couch and then stepped out of their way. She watched patiently as they slowly but carefully lifted Nurse Jackie onto the stretcher and then gathered her bags on their way out the door. Medallion walked behind the emergency team and when they got Nurse Jackie into the ambulance, she made her way to the worried looking woman to say her goodbyes.

"Lady, I hope you feel better soon. When you get to the hospital, give me a call to let me know you are okay and we'll talk about your dream. I want to know more because I had a crazy dream last night too."

"Yes! The dreams! They are connected and you need to listen to me. That girl... Sunta. She's evil and you need to leave this place. You need to—"

Medallion shook her head implying she was not going to listen to the nurse's rude comments about Sunta any longer. "Don't worry Mrs. Jackie. She's harmless. Just get better and call me when you get settled in."

Medallion shut the door of the ambulance and watched as it drove off. She turned and walked back to the house and saw Sunta standing on the porch with the baby still in her arms.

"You know you can put him back in his crib." Medallion said nonchalantly passing them both in the doorway.

"I'm fine holding him. I like it."

Sunta gave Isaiah a kiss on his cheek and followed Medallion back to the kitchen.

Once there, Medallion reached into a cabinet, pulled out a coffee mug, and turned on the coffee pot.

"So, what was that ol' lady scared about?"

Medallion thought on Sunta's question for a moment and decided against telling her about the nurse's ramblings.

"Oh, it was nothing. She just didn't want to leave."

"Oh. Well, looks like she took a nasty fall. Where they take her?"

"Just to the local hospital."

"Well, she needed to go after all that."

"Yeah. She'll be fine in about a month I guess."

Medallion watched Sunta who had already tuned out of their conversation and was cooing and tickling Isaiah. Both she and her son looked like they were enjoying their time together. Sunta caught Medallion's stare and smiled back.

"I'm sorry. Would you like to hold him?" Sunta walked over to Medallion and held the baby out for her to take.

Feeling the urge of motherhood tugging at her gut, she smiled while holding her hands out for the baby. Sunta placed Isaiah in the crook of Medallion's arm.

"Well, good morning." Medallion felt the baby's body tense into the beginning of a cry. "Oh, don't cry little one."

Isaiah's lip trembled and turned into a frown before he began to wail.

"Sunta, did you feed him his bottle on the dresser upstairs? He's crying like he's hungry."

"I gave him what was there. Maybe he need more."

"You might be right..." Medallion made her way to the couch in the living room and opened her blouse. "Come on son, go ahead and nurse...."

Isaiah squirmed and shook turning down his mother's offer of her milk.

"Here, I made him a little sugar tit."

Sunta scooped the baby out of Medallion's arms and placed the bottle's nipple into his mouth. Suckling the sweet taste, Isaiah calmed down and snuggled into her.

"A sugar what?"

Sunta giggled as she watched the baby drink the bottle.

"Ain't nothing but some sugar and water and a bit of honey... a sugar tit. My ma'am used it on me and my sisters when there won't no milk, or if we cried for something else."

"Well, whatever it is, he seems to like it. Wonder why he didn't want to nurse?"

"Never can tell with babies sometimes. Every day is a new day with 'em."

"Yeah, I guess you're right".

Medallion watched Sunta methodically walk around the family room with the baby drinking from a bottle. Her son so at peace and Sunta the same. Sunta's slow walk led her to the big window in the corner of the family room. She instinctively stopped in the middle a sunbeam that flooded the floor. Medallion couldn't help but marvel at Sunta's beauty. She was such a vision to behold.

"My goodness… you want him back? He seems pretty settled now."

Sunta walked back over with the baby and lifted him towards Medallion.

"Oh, no. You can hold him. I've got some things I have to work on." Isaiah's eyes opened with a flutter catching Medallion's attention. "Auntie said they would change but I didn't think it would happen that fast..."

"What changed?" Sunta asked.

"His eyes... I could have sworn they were grey and now they are blue."

"Umm... well ain't that something?"

Medallion stared into his eyes a moment longer before walking back to the back stairs.

"Hey. Why don't you stay for the day and watch him for me?"

"I don't know… looks and smells like snow is going to roll in soon. I might have to get back." Sunta didn't want to seem too eager to stay and allowed Medallion to extend the invitation.

"Oh yeah. I forgot about the snow storm coming. Well, why don't you stay, and then when the storm is over, I'll get an Uber to take you home? I could use the company until my husband gets here."

Sunta smiled politely and looked down at Isaiah. *Soon my baby. Soon it will be me and you.*

"Sure ma'am. I can stay for a spell or two."

Chapter 32

"Waymen, I know you are still mad with me, but you have got to get over this. I've made up my mind to come home in a couple of days. I'll send the baby to my Aunt's and you and I can work things out— you know what I mean.... I can wear that red see-through lingerie you like with the thigh-high shear stockings. I'll cook you your favorite meal and we can sit down to talk things through. We don't have to end our marriage this way."

She paused as she thought on her last words.

"I've been a fool, Waymen. A fool for you, and foolish because of you. Had you been the man that I needed, I would have never slept with Rodney and we would never be getting a divorce."

She hit the send button and regretted it instantly and sent another.

"Scratch that last part Waymen. I'm just mad. I love you. Call me back."

Medallion hit the send button on her text message app and then flung the phone across the bed as she flopped back on her pillow. This was the third text message she had left him begging for his forgiveness and it was only mid-afternoon. After Nurse Jackie was taken away by the ambulance, the only thing on her mind was refocusing on her marriage and getting Waymen to talk to her.

Since Sunta was now taking over Nurse Jackie's duties, she wanted to put every effort into getting Waymen to come back to her. However, he hadn't returned any of the messages she'd already left. Lying in the bed and wondering what to do, Medallion became restless. Consuming thoughts of her husband and their divorce began to overtake her mind; making her feel out of control. *I've got to do something to distract me from all of this. She* grabbed the remote control and turned on the television.

"... And as you can see, the winter storm is headed for the southern part of Virginia tonight."

The slender, long haired meteorologist flung her hand and pointed to areas that marked the location of small counties on the digital map behind her.

"People in this area can expect about 1-3 feet of snow along with frozen rain and extremely cold temperatures."

The meteorologist clicked the button in her hand and a summary of the week's weather appeared where the digital map once was, showing temperatures in the upper teens and low twenties.

"This winter storm is going to hit hard people. The next couple of days for you will be a cold one— colder than we've had in years. Be prepared to stay indoors, and if you don't have to be anywhere, stay off the roads. It's going to be pretty dangerous to travel."

Still restless, Medallion flicked off the television and aimlessly looked around the room. A glimmer of something shiny in Aunt Mary's closet caught her eye and she smiled. *Aunt Mary's pretty dresses.*

As a child, Medallion would spend hours in her aunt's closet adoring her elaborate wardrobe. In her earlier years, Aunt Mary would be invited to all types of society parties. Her closets hosted an accumulation of astounding garbs that saw the light of day maybe only once. Even though Aunt Mary chose to retreat to the confounds of her little chateau in the quiet part of Southside Richmond, she never parted ways with her lovely dresses.

Medallion would always ask if she could have some of them since she wasn't wearing them anymore, but Aunt Mary always declined the offer. The dresses were her memories of an illustrious past that she fondly enjoyed.

"One day when I'm dead and gone, you can have them all. But for right now, let me enjoy them as they are."

It had been a while since Medallion rummaged through her aunt's dress closest. Since the house was only newly renovated, visits were cut to just maintenance checks and upkeep. But now that she was here for a couple of months, she was eager to take a walk down memory lane in the closet.

Medallion flicked on the light of the gigantic closet which was more like a dressing room of a fancy department store. Expensive shoes filled the wall opposite of the closet door and spotlights were strategically placed above and beneath the shoes showcasing how magnificent they were. To her left was the rotating curio cabinet for her jewelry which dazzled, sparkled, and shined when the light from the window refracted off of it.

Medallion smiled to herself realizing the shimmer from the diamonds that were prominently placed in the display case definitely lured her in. And then, to the right of her were the wonderful party dresses- all hung in order by color and then length. There was a tag on each dress that stated the date and the festive occasion it was worn. She saw a purple floor-length chiffon gown and pulled it out of its lineup. She held it up to her and turned towards the three-way angled mirror.

"This is so pretty…"

The dark plum dress complimented her skin tone nicely. The diamond straps lent the dress an heir of elegance that could only be pulled off by someone as stylish as Aunt Mary. Medallion could not even imagine where her aunt would have worn the dress, but she imagined herself wearing it to meet Waymen just like in a romance novel about desperate love.

As she continued to daze about all the wonderful places she could wear the dress, she thought of how enchanting her aunt must have looked wearing the gown. Unfortunately, there were rarely any pictures of her with people outside of the family; Medallion believing it had to do with the specialized service she provided. Medallion grabbed the delicate tag that hung from the side of the purple diamond strapped dress and read it. *Spring, 1947. Alter Ball. D.W.* Medallion didn't know what the "Alter Ball" was as the highest of society never advertised their events, but she knew the initials "D.W." had to have been her date for that particular occasion.

Over the years of playing in her aunt's closet, she'd mostly cracked the code on how to read the tags. When she got older, she'd written down the event names and googled them for a glimpse into her aunt's past. Most of the time, she found old pictures online of the events with some of the people in attendance. Medallion would look closely at the pictures hoping to see her Aunt in one of them laughing gaily or purposefully posed for the camera. Unfortunately, she never stumbled on such a jewel.

"D.W." Medallion said to herself. Those initials appeared on most of the tags starting from the 1930's up until the late 1950's. She could only deduce that D.W. was Aunt Mary's lover. She'd tried to ask her about the initials several times, but Aunt Mary never gave a real answer.

"Oh… we were just really great friends." Or she'd say, "No one in particular. Just someone I knew."

Unfortunately, Medallion couldn't do an internet search on just 'D.W.' and get a hit on who it could have been. She could only imagine that D.W. was a great love lost. Sometimes she even thought D.W. could have been her uncle... if her aunt ever even married, but there was no one to confirm her theory. Her Great Aunt Mary was the only sibling alive out of seven children— girls as a matter of fact. She was the one that never married, and she never had any little ones.

As Medallion put the dress back on its satin hanger, she spotted an old hat box. It wasn't like the other things in the closet that were well kept like new and shiny. The box was very old looking, had old dried out brown water stains on it, and it appeared as if on any given day it could topple over from years of wear and tear. She had never seen the box before and she was happy to have discovered a new treasure in the closet. *Maybe the decorators found it during the renovation and placed it here.*

Curious, Medallion took the box from the shelf and shook it just a little. The things contained within the box jolted around and made muffled thrashing sounds. She headed out of the closet with her newfound treasure and closed the closet doors behind her. She plopped down on the floor in front of the bed and read the word "Memories" on the top of it. She pressed the lock on the box and the top unlatched. She opened the hood of the box where she found news clippings, pictures and books stacked high.

Medallion picked up a few of the news clippings. One of them showed Aunt Mary smiling joyfully. The article read, "Local Negro Woman Buys Plantation". Medallion beamed with pride as she read the article's account of how her aunt bought the plantation home her family came from. The article mentioned how she was the first known Negro to have achieved such feats. Medallion set the article aside and picked up another.

This time it was the clipping of her parent's obituary and how they died in a terrible accident. The year was 1989. Medallion was seven at the time. The accident happened at night. There was a heavy summer rain that flooded the whole area. And the next morning, as she sat on her Aunt's breakfast table, she was told she would never see her parents again. The article made her relive that sad moment, and a tear of remembrance landed on the news clipping when it fell from her sorrowful eyes.

Not wanting to rummage through any more of the clippings, she gathered them up and placed them in a pile right beside her. She reached back in the box and picked up a handful of the pictures. She looked at a few of them and laughed at some of the familiar faces that were now only recollections. There was cousin Tab laughing at something off camera while standing over the grill at a family reunion from many years ago. In the backdrop was the family plantation in all its grandeur.

Flipping through some more pictures, she spotted Aunt Mary in one of the pretty dresses from the closet. She was on the dance floor in the arms of a tall stranger (as his face was turned away from the camera) and surrounded by a sea of onlookers. In the picture, Aunt Mary smiled as her partner delicately dipped her at the curve of her waist. Her arm stretched above her head while she skimmed the floor with her fingertips. Her aunt's eyes were lowered as she held the dance pose, but her smile told the tale of a wonderful event. The caption read, "D.W. and Mary. 30th birthday."

Medallion dropped her jaw. *The infamous D.W.!* She couldn't believe she was finally looking at somewhat of a picture of him. Had the camera and their movements been timed just right, she would have seen the man that her aunt shared a lot of special moments with.

Medallion placed the picture aside and went to the next where she saw a picture of her and her childhood best friend TiTi sitting on the porch with a bowl of fruit in between the two to share. She hadn't seen TiTi in ages. For a time, they were inseparable, and her parents allowed her to come along with Medallion to the plantation when Aunt Mary would take her yearly trips. *I'll have to call TiTi when I get back to Richmond. I'm sure she's still around. I should have never been that mad and ended our friendship over something as stupid as gossip.*

The further Medallion went down the stack, the older the pictures became. And soon, the faces in them became unfamiliar. When she got to the last picture, she read the date, 1858. The photo caption read, "Slave women owned by Master Johnson". Medallion looked at the aged and worn black and white picture of the seven women. They stood proud as if they were not ones to be owned. Their faces were stoic; not a smile to be seen amongst the group.

She studied the seven pair of eyes staring back at her and saw the strength in each set. These women looked determined. She'd never seen a picture of a slave, and then she realized that if their picture was in the box, they had to be family as well.

"Egungun..." She took her time to look at each one of the women wanting to see a glimpse of familiarity in their faces. *Maybe one of these ladies looks like mom or Aunt Mary or anyone in my family for that matter.* Woman number three in the picture wore a head scarf, and underneath it her hair flowed in waves to her shoulder. Her chin had a small dimple, and her cheek bones were pronounced under her full round face. She was a shade or two darker than the others, but she undeniably looked like her mother. Her eyes passed over woman number four in the picture, but they stopped at woman number five who had Aunt Mary's big round eyes and the distinct curve of her aunt's lips.

Beside the fifth woman in the picture, was a younger lady. She stood as strong as the others, but Medallion could see that she lacked a certain heir the others had. Medallion wondered about her. She was beautiful. She was taller and slenderer than the others, but her belly was full with child. Her neck bowed back slightly as she looked up to the camera's lens while the others stared straight ahead at it. Her head wrap was raveled high, and her whole look gave a bit of mysticism. *Who is this woman*? Wanting to know more about her, Medallion placed the picture beside her on the floor before placing everything else back in the box. *I'm going to call Aunt Mary and ask. I'm sure she knows.*

She got up from her spot on the floor and closed the memory box. As she reached for her phone, she was startled to see Sunta standing in the doorway of the master bedroom blankly staring at her.

"Oh! You startled me." Medallion giggled at her absurd response to Sunta standing there. "Did you need anything? "Where's the baby?"

"Everything fine ma'am. I was just checking out the house. I never seen it so pretty before."

"Oh, so you must have seen it before the renovations?"

"Yeah. I seen it before. What you got in your hand?" Sunta pointed to the picture in Medallion's hand.

"Oh this?" Medallion held up the picture so Sunta could see it. "It's a picture I just found. I'm going to call my aunt and ask her who the ladies are in the picture."

Medallion looked at the picture and then looked at Sunta, and then at the picture once more.

"You know, Sunta… this lady right here... the pregnant one... It looks like you."

Sunta stared at the picture remembering exactly when it was taken. Master Johnson took it a couple of days before they were to be put up for sale at the farmer's market in Richmond since buyers there always paid more than the buyers that were local to their county. He was going to have the picture posted in town and the newspaper to draw in buyers. It was no secret that the estate of the plantation was in debt and was not turning a profit. Master Johnson was selling any and everything that was not tied down at the time.

Sunta and her sisters knew if they were to be sold at the Farmer's Market, then they would be separated and would never see each other again. They'd made plans to run away before they were to travel to the market. The night of their escape, Sunta went into labor and lost her life. She ran her finger down the side of the picture as she mourned her life and ached with longing for her sisters.

"Bettye…" she whispered underneath her breath to herself.

Bettye tried to save her life that night, but it was no use. With strong hesitation, Bettye and the other sisters did the next best thing. They saved her newborn son from dying along with her. They performed the Chant of Forever over her soul to make sure the baby had a safe pathway into this world.

Unfortunately, no one knew what happened to the soul after it left the body if the chant is performed on the dying. The chant doesn't prolong the life of a dying person like it would the living. Sunta was sure her soul could neither enter Heaven nor Hell because of the ritual. She was stuck in The White forever. No one could help her there since she was there alone. Seeing Isaiah appear in The White was her time to react to the sentence in that prison.

Her eyes widened at Medallion's comment in hopes that she was not found out.

"She does look like me a little bit I think. Maybe it's just coincidence."

She turned away from the picture to wipe her tears which had begun to form.

"Maybe you are right. But this area is small. It may be that we are related and don't even know it."

Medallion reached for her phone to make the call, but Sunta grabbed her hand before she could get to it.

"Before you do that, let me show you something."

She took the phone from Medallion and placed it on the nightstand as they exited the room. She led Medallion to the kitchen where the aroma engulfed her. Medallion took in a deep breath and became intoxicated with the wonderful smell.

"What have you been down here cooking? It smells so good?"

"Just a little something I put together. Taste it" Sunta dipped a spoon into the warm pot and bought it to Medallion lips.

Medallion sipped the soup in the spoon and instantly fell in love with the taste.

"Sunta, this is so good. What is it?"

"Oh… it's just a little old family recipe." She put the spoon back into the pot and stirred the soup with it.

"Well, can I have some more? It's really good."

"Oh… not right now. It's got to stew a little bit more. Besides it's for sleeping. Have a bowl before you go to sleep every night."

"I don't know if I can wait until then to have some more."

Sunta laughed as she continued to stir the pot.

"I'm sure you can. Just have a little bit every night and you'll start to see a difference. I see you always worried. Figured you probably need a good night's rest."

"Well thank you. I'll do that." Medallion looked around the room in curiosity.

"What you looking for?"

"Where is the baby?"

"Oh, he upstairs resting."

"I'm going to go check on him and then I'm going to call my husband."

"Okay. I'm going to go and find some wood for the fireplace."

Medallion began to walk away and felt a little dizzy.

"You were right about the soup. I think I'm a bit woozy just from that little bit."

"Yes, it can knock you out if you aren't careful."

Chapter 33

Making her way through the bare trees which bordered the edge of the property, the crisp leaves under her feet crackled and crunched. As she walked, she collected bark from the trees she passed, and cold fresh water from the stream nearby. Continuing through the woods, she finally came across a clearing where six cabins came into view.

"I'm home." Sunta said as she continued to the last cabin in the row.

She walked to the door allowing her hands to slide down the weathered and splintered wooden slats that made up the cabin's entryway; remembering the last time it shut leaving her there on one side and her sisters on the other.

She pushed open the rickety old door to the dark cabin. The boards on the floor were worn. The tin roof was riddled with holes. The window panes were gone. She walked slowly through the cabin remembering the good times.

Looking at the place where the table once sat by the pane-less window was a lonely chair. Sunta sat in it looking around the room, and breathing in the stale air, triggering memories of years gone past. Sunta began to hear the echo of long ago conversations.

"Jendi… My belly growing."

"I seen it been getting bigger."

"I think he fixed me this time."

"Yeah… I guess he did. How it make you feel?"

"I guess I'm okay. This the third one so I'm use to feeling it inside me. You think Bettye going to let me keep this one?"

"You know how she is when it comes to new babies. She don't want no more born on this plantation so they be sold off and no telling where they be."

Jendi thought about her twins she never got to see. The thickness of their shiny silky black hair and the crinkles in their lighter-than-hers newborn skin. They were sold as soon as they left her womb. Never being granted the opportunity to know the color of their eyes.

"You right Jendi, but she said she dreamt of the fish. You know the one fish with all the colors. She ain't never had a dream about a colored fish before. This may be the sign that this one be born free."

Jendi nodded in agreement "We gotta tell her the babe here. If that colorful fish a sign, she got to know the baby here so she'll know freedom coming soon."

"If that's the sign for sure, then she gotta let me keep it."

They hugged each other as their excitement grew about the good news.

Sunta rubbed her small bump as she allowed her mind to wonder about her future.

"There's something about this baby that feel different inside me."

"Like how? What make it so different this time?"

"I don't know for sure, but maybe because I'm different now. I know more. I seen more."

"You think you gonna ask Bettye to bless this one?"

"I am."

Sunta beamed at the thought of Bettye welcoming her first birth by anointing her belly with oils, seasonal flowers in bloom, and fresh water.

"Well when you gonna tell her?"

"Tonight. Now that harvest season over and we doing the big dinner, I'll tell her while we eating and laughing. She'll be in a good mood after eating so much."

"That's a good idea, Sunta."

"I think I'm goin' to tell Mary before dinner so she can be on my side. You know… in case Bettye choosing to end this one as well."

Jendi giggled with excitement as she imagined how dinner would go with the impending announcement.

"Well I ain't going to say nothing to Alice, Lily, or Gloria about it. You know they can't hold no secret."

They both laughed knowing how true the statement was about the other three sisters.

"But I'm going to go and get them to help me make sure dinner is extra special."

Sunta gave Jendi a hug before she left Sunta sitting at the table by the window.

Allowing the memory to fade, she said to herself, *"I remember…"*

Sunta looked down at the floor beneath her. She stomped her foot listening for the hollow sound of the loose floor board. She stood and walked around the cabin, stomping to find it in order to uncover the secret that lay beneath.

"I know it's around here somewhere."

Finally, in the corner of the room, she heard the hollowed sound of empty space beneath the floor. She kneeled and used her hands to pry three slats away from the others surrounding them. Sticking her hand in the deep hole, she pulled out a narrow cedar box. Sitting with crossed legs on the floor, she opened it; relieved its contents were still there. *I almost thought it won't going to be here…*

Resting in the narrow cedar box was a small aged-stained satchel and wrapped in a brown and dingy rag, the knife used in all sacrificial ceremonies her mother would perform in secret.

"Now I know me and my baby going to be together after the good death. This knife is going to make sure of it."

She wrapped it back in its cloth and put it back in the box. She then pulled out the small satchel which sat beside the sacred knife within the narrow container. Carefully she opened it pouring the soil held within it out and into her hand.

She pinched a small clump of the earth between two of her fingers which was still buoyant and moist.

"After all these years, I can still feel the power."

The satchel carried the most important element of any ceremony the sisters and their mother ever performed. It was the dirt from their grandparent's homeland, Africa.

Sunta remembered how her mother told tales of how the makeshift satchel was carried over the big water covered by their hair's plats and braids her mother's mother wore in her head. The pouch was small and only held a little soil so it was only used for special occasions allowing it to last as long as it did. Hidden in the floor of the slave quarters, it was the only symbol left of who they were before coming to Glory Hill.

"On my mother and all who have gone before me, I'm going to use this last bit of earth to send me and my son home. Mo si ilẹ iya mi ni Mo dupẹ lọwọ."

Chapter 34

Sunta pulled the cabin's door closed with her one free hand and looked up at the day's cloudy blue sky spotting the hint of a full moon in the distance.

"When day meets night…"

Smiling at the thought of the time growing near, she stepped off of the cabin's porch, placing the contents of her other hands down and picking out the bark, winter berries, and fresh water she'd gathered on her way to the last home she'd known. With string from her garment and strands of Medallion's hair she pulled from her brush in the bathroom, she intertwined them and placed it all on the ground. With the knife, she dug through the hardened ground to dig a hole. She crushed the berries and smeared them on the dried bark. The intertwined hair and string were placed on the smeared bark and then put inside the hole. She covered the hole with the hardened earth before putting fresh spring water over it.

"Now she will come and see. She will be able to know what sacrifice is. The love from a mother to their child".

***

Too warm to be winter and hair damp from the humidity in the air, sweat beads dripped from her forehead and swelled on her upper lips. Medallion found herself walking in the dark of night with only the brightness of the moon as her only source of light. She felt her way through the darkness of the dense woods with only instinct as her compass. She came across a clearing where a row of small cabins watching over a lake beside the great willow tree. She continued to walk to them.

Lightning flashed, and the low roll of thunder rumbled in the distance. As she got closer, there were six vacant cabins standing side-by-side. The last cabin on the end with a light shining through its window caught her attention. Medallion found herself drawn to it, allowing herself to continue the walk to the cabin's door.

Stepping onto the porch, she noticed the light from the window flickered and danced because the people inside the cabin were moving around. Getting closer to the cabin's door, a woman's head peeked out to look around and then the door shut after she'd pulled her head back in. Finally, at the cabin's window, Medallion looked through it and saw more women gathering things in a rush as if they were preparing to escape. She turned her head towards the sky in time to see lightening skid across the sky. She twisted her head back to the window and found herself in the cabin— right in the midst of the women as they scurried in their preparation. She walked around the small cabin seemingly unnoticed.

A loud scream of agony could be heard coming from behind the closed door on the other side of the kitchen. The women stopped what they were doing and they all went to the room. Medallion followed and pushed her way through the group to find a young woman shrieking in agony and curled on the wood splintered floor with blood all around.

Medallion reached down and towards the woman to help while she lay screaming in pain. She felt the tug on her arm from one of the other women standing beside her and without looking her way, she said with an echo to her voice, "Do not interfere. This is what has to be."

Medallion looked at the young woman on the floor once again, her face covered by the darkness in the room.

"What can I do to help you?"

The woman let out another scream and then grabbed Medallion's wrist.

"SAVE HIM!!"

Chapter 35

Medallion awoke from her restless sleep. The light of the moon shone in her bedroom mirror. The ticking noise of the clock was the only sound. She could feel the sheets underneath her were damp from her sweat as she rose from the bed. She made her way to the bathroom where she flicked on the light.

"These dreams are getting worse." Medallion mused out loud.

Slightly disoriented, she turned on the sink and cupped her hands to catch the luke-warm water flowing from the faucet. Splashing the water on her face to look at herself in the mirror, she was puzzled by the fact she'd fallen asleep for such a long time and by her dream being so vivid. The last thing she remembered was taking a sip of the soup and heading upstairs to check on the baby.

She turned the faucet off and left the bathroom, hitting the light switch as she left. She headed for the clock sitting on the nightstand to check the time. *11:45… I guess I'll check on the kid since I'm up.*

She opened the door to the room. The hall was dark- darker than Medallion had ever experienced. Walking cautiously down the hallway, she peeked into the baby's room where she heard the solemn voice of a woman humming. Medallion opened the door wider and walked in.

"Sunta… is that you?" Medallion whispered into the darkness. "Why is the room so dark, Sunta? Sunta are you in here?"

The melodic humming continued without regard to Medallion's question. She tried to turn the light on by flicking the light switch by the door, but it was no use. In the corner, the nightlight began to glow brightly and cast a faint illumination on the rocking chair by the window. It moved rhythmically back and forth with the melodic hum. And suddenly before Medallion's eyes, the ghostly shape of a woman materialized in the rocking chair and aimlessly gazed out of the window into the darkness. The humming also appeared to belong to her as she began to sing a sweet lullaby.

How did she do that? Medallion knew her eyes were playing tricks on her. She was sure there wasn't anyone sitting in that chair a moment before. She walked over to the woman. There was a glow all over her. The woman was singing to a baby wrapped in stained and torn cloths in her arms.

"My beautiful baby, my beautiful child," the woman sang in a sweet low voice.

Medallion's heart swelled with an overwhelming yearning for her own son as she watched the bond grow between the baby and the mother who lovingly caressed the precious bundle with care. Suddenly the woman began to scream in agonizing pain. She dropped her hands lifelessly and from them, the bundle tumbled from her lap. Medallion screamed in horror as she tried to catch it before it hit the floor. But when the bundle landed, there was nothing in the cloth. Medallion was confused. *Where is the baby?* She looked up at the screaming woman as she grabbed her own hair while looking around in a mask of fiery rage.

Medallion braced herself with her hands planted on the floor and underneath her fingertips she felt a sticky ooze. She looked at her finger tips and saw the blood drip from them and onto the floor. She gasped in horror and followed the trail of blood to its origin. She saw the stream of blood flowing from the woman's legs. Her gown saturated with her own blood as she held her stomach.

Medallion grabbed the woman's arm which pulled the woman's hand away from her womb exposing its blood-filled abyss that oozed from her and onto her bare feet seeping into the floor beneath them. The frightened woman let out a shrill scream of agony forcing Medallion to cover her ears and close her eyes pleading with herself to remove the horrid image from her memory. A finger on her chin forcing her to look up, her eyes meeting the woman's mournful stare. For the first time, Medallion saw her solemn eyes filled with tears. Her mouth was contorted as if she wanted to say something but when she opened it to speak, all she could do was scream the high-pitched shriek Medallion had tried to escape. This time the ear-piercing sound filled Medallion with the barren woman's pain and she began to scream in agony with her. Her own tears began to flow as heavy as the woman's knowing she was feeling the same loss as the woman.

"Why!" Medallion screamed as she sat up in her bed. Her chest heaved rapidly up and down. She looked at the clock on the nightstand just as it read 11:45. *It was a dream.*

She pulled herself out of the bed and opened the door to the bedroom. Where there was darkness before, the moon now shown through the Palladian window above the door and into the widow's walk hallway. She went to the baby's room and opened the door. The room was filled with the moonlight unlike the blackness before. The rocking chair by the window was still, and the baby laid silently in the crib as he slept. Medallion sighed with relief and closed the door. *It was only dream. But why was the woman from it Sunta?*

Chapter 36

The next morning, Medallion awoke and looked over and out of her bedroom window. The branches from the tree right outside of it that stretched and reached across the window were bare of their leaves. The ice that glazed the branches weighed them down forcing them to bow heavily from the weight. *It's morning... What was that last night?*

She rubbed her temples. The lingering grogginess left her head swimming. Slowly, she made her way out of the bed grabbing a robe to cover herself as she headed down the steps to the main floor of the house.

"Mor'nan ma'am."

Sunta pleasantly smiled as she greeted Medallion from the kitchen.

"Baby all fed and dressed for the day. Want something to eat?"

Sunta continued stirring the pot heating on the stove as Medallion passed by her on the way to the coffee pot.

"What happened last night? I only remember going to check on the baby."

Sunta laughed before she responded.

"Chile, you went upstairs to check on your babe and then fell asleep quicker than you could shake a finger."

"What was in that soup I sipped? I've never been that unconscious in my life?"

"I forgot to tell you, that soup is a dreamcatcher. It reveals your deep thoughts and connects them to what's troubling you most so you can solve your problems. I been seeing you running round here worried 'bout your husband so I thought I give you a little bit of help fixing what's broken 'tween you two."

Sunta looked Medallion over; seeing the anguish from her tumultuous night's rest and satisfied at her work.

"Won't nothing in that soup but some berries and herbs I picked out in the woods over yonder. T'wont nothing you ain't never tasted before. I'm sure of it. Being your aunt does what she does and all."

"What do you know about Aunt Mary and what she does?"

Medallion grabbed her mug full of fresh warm brew as soon as she heard the ding from the coffee maker.

"Looking through the cabinets and seeing all the herbs. Plus, she got candles and little dolls decorating the house. It ain't that hard to tell."

Sunta continued to stir the pot. Medallion looked considering Sunta was right. The décor did have hints of a witches touch.

"I don't think that soup worked like you thought."

"Oh? How so?"

"I didn't dream about my husband I dreamed about a woman dying."

"Well that soup don't lie. You dreamed about that woman for some reason. You might got to go rest yourself and think on that dream and how it can help you fix your problem."

"Felt more like a nightmare than a lesson." Medallion shook her head to remove the remnants of the bad encounter out of her thoughts. "I ain't no dream reader and I'm not trying to think about that mess no more than I have to. It creeped me out."

Sunta shrugged her shoulders and poured a glass full of what she'd made in the pot.

"Where's the baby?"

"Oh He's resting in the family room over there. He likes the smells from the kitchen. Would you like me to go get him for you?"

Medallion scrunched up her face and then took a gulp of her coffee.

"No. I'm fine. I've got to make a call to my husband. You can watch him while I do that can't you?"

"I sure can. He's such a good baby."

Medallion took her mug and headed back up the stairs, but before she hit the first step she stopped and hollered back into the kitchen.

"I don't know what you put in that soup or how much I was supposed to drink but I will never have anymore. Last night's dream had me all messed up."

Sunta shouted back. "I'm sure it wasn't the soup. Never heard anyone say anything bad about it before."

Chapter 37

Back in her room, Medallion found her phone and began to call Waymen just when the phone indicated there was an incoming call from Aunt Mary.

"Hey Auntie. How is everything?"

"All is fine here, Medallion. I'm just checking up on you. How are you, Mrs. Jackie, and the baby? Is Waymen on his way?"

"Well, you heard Mrs. Jackie had that nasty fall. We sent her to the hospital, and then she was going to be on her way back to Richmond after that. I hope she made it before the snow hit."

"Oh… there was a storm?"

"Yeah. Real bad one. Came through last night. Woke up, and there was snow on the ground and ice everywhere. I'm not here by myself though."

"So Waymen made it down there before the snow hit?"

"Um… no. Me and him not really on speaking terms yet."

"Speaking terms? What do you mean?"

"Well… He thinks I was trying to hide the fact about who the baby's father was. See… he found the results, and confronted me over the phone. Now he wants a divorce and won't take my calls."

Aunt Mary sucked her teeth and sighed heavily before she began her chastising.

"Really Medallion? You are still playing games with this man. How could you have not told him about the baby before you left for the house? I don't even blame him for not wanting to be with you anymore. You really have gone too far this time."

"Oh, Auntie. You know Waymen and I go through this all the time. It's no big deal that he's calling for a divorce and not speaking to me at this exact moment. He just needs time to cool down and when he does, he'll be here, and we'll make up."

"What you don't understand, Medallion is that you can't fix this one. This man is hurt, and you did this to him, and to top it off, you bought a baby into this bad situation and you don't even care. Medallion… I really need you to focus on your priorities and own up to the mess you've made. You can't go through life hurting people and thinking they are going to be okay later."

Medallion listened with a heavy heart. Deep down she knew she'd really hurt Waymen, but she wasn't ready to accept the fact that this time was the last straw.

"Auntie… You know and I know you are right. Hell… I know I fucked up with him, but I'm really trying to be optimistic about it. I don't want to be without him."

"Well, what do you plan on doing about it?"

"I was going to head back to Richmond and really prove to him that I want to keep the relationship, but this snow is really bad up here, and I can't leave the house. In a couple of days, when the roads are clear, I'll head back and Waymen and I will figure things out."

"You shouldn't be traveling with the baby all by yourself. Just stay down there, and I'll see if I can get Waymen to come see you."

"No. It's okay. I'll probably just leave the baby here. I have a girl staying with me."

"A what? Who is sh—"

"Never mind that. I have a question to ask you. I found a very old picture in the memory box stashed in your closet. I wanted to ask you who the ladies are."

"What picture? What do you mean you found the memory box?"

"Auntie, don't be coy. I know you know what I'm talking about. I finally snagged a glimpse of D.W. after all these years."

"Oh Medallion." Aunt Mary chuckled. "I wasn't being coy. I'm just surprised you bought up the memory box. I haven't thought about that thing in so long.

"Well, there were a lot of interesting pictures and news clippings in it. I saw the article of when you bought the family home. That was a big deal back then."

"Yes it was. Things like that didn't happen then. I'm sure there were others who've done it, but around here… as small as these counties in Virginia are, it was a huge deal."

"Well, I'm proud of you that you did it. But that's not what I'm talking about. I'm talking about the picture of the seven enslaved women who were owned by Master Johnson."

My sisters. Aunt Mary grew silent at the thought of the picture. She swallowed her panic before she spoke.

"Well, what do you want to know about the picture?"

"I mean, who are they? Why do you have a picture of them? Are they family? What do you know about them? One of the girl's kind of looks like you and one looks a lot like mom."

"Medallion, you're talking too fast for me to keep up with this conversation. How about we talk about it another time. Maybe over tea when you get back."

"Yeah, yeah, Auntie. You just trying to skirt the issue like you always do about the past."

"I have my reasons Medallion. You'll know once I've left here."

"Don't start with that talk Aunt Mary. You'll be here long enough to see me be a grandma."

Aunt Mary laughed knowing that Medallion's words were half true.

"Maybe. If God allows it."

"The funniest thing though about this picture."

"Yes?"

"Well, one of the girls in the picture?"

"Yes, what about her?"

"Well, she kind of looks like the girl that's staying with me."

Chapter 38

"Rock a bye baby, on the tree top. When the wind blows, the cradle will rock. When the bow breaks, the cradle will fall, and down will come baby. Cradle and all."

Sunta sang the words as she prepared Isaiah for the ceremony.

"'Lijah, my sweet. We gonna be together real soon."

Sunta poured a little of the powder that was in the satchel around her neck into the palm of her hand. She then placed the powder on a small saucer and drizzled oil onto it and stirred the mixture with her finger until it had the consistency of mud.

"We only have a few more days until you ready for the good death, and then we can go back together. I won't be alone, and you can be with someone who loves you."

Sunta walked over to Isaiah who was sitting in the little rocker that was placed on the counter. She placed the tip of her nose on the tip of his and nuzzled them together.

"'Lijah, you smell just like I dreamed you would."

She gave him a kiss on the cheek and then opened his shirt. Looking for his pulse, she placed a finger over his heart. Sunta's lip quivered with pride and joy as his heartbeat thumped in his chest with a quick rhythm.

"Yes baby. I know. You heart beats for your mama— me. Not that monster upstairs but for me… your true mama.

She picked up the saucer. Twisting her mouth, she spit into the bowl.

"And now for you my baby."

Sunta reached out and put the tip of her pointer finger into Isaiah's mouth to collect some of his drool. His eyes lit up as he smiled at the tickling feeling of her finger grazing the inside of his cheek and lip. Sunta smiled at his delight and used her middle finger to tickle his nose in response.

She mixed Isaiah's saliva into the paste. She then opened her blouse and covered the flesh where her heart was with the paste and then did the same for Isaiah. Finally, she closed her eyes and stood very still. The room was quiet. She took slow deep breaths as she absorbed the energy of life within the walls of the house. As she opened her eyes, she inhaled and then exhaled her enchantment.

"Ori mo pe o. Omọ mi lati inu mi ni mo di ọkan li ọkan lati lù kan bi ọkan. Ase! Ase! Ase O!" She whispered her words and paused. Feeling the energy beginning to gather around her. "Ori mo pe o. Omọ mi lati inu mi ni mo di ọkan li ọkan lati lù kan bi ọkan. Ashe! Ashe! Ashe O!"

Sunta spoke the words louder as she breathed in and exhaled. She felt stronger. More powerful. Her strength was growing. She felt full of life as she remembered how warmth felt when it was cold, how electrifying it felt when her heart fluttered with excitement, and how her blood would rush inside her body when she was furious.

"Ori mo pe o. Omọ mi lati inu mi ni mo di ọkan li ọkan lati lù kan bi ọkan. Ashe! Ashe! Ashe O!"

She spoke again with the conviction to evoke all the elements around her knowing the energy contained within everything from life to death was at her will. She felt the intensity of that energy fill her up. "The time to connect our souls is here." She began to glow a radiant color of gold. Her skin illuminated as her strength continued to gather. The feeling within her was so strong, Sunta began to vibrate and levitated slightly above the ceramic kitchen floor. Her eyes rolled until the whites of her eyes shown.

"Ori mo pe o. Omọ mi lati inu mi ni mo di ọkan li ọkan lati lù kan bi ọkan. Gba agbara ni ayika wa lati di wa."

Sunta's voice grew louder and louder as she repeated the words faster and faster. Her body continued to vibrate as it became stiff and erect— hands straight by her side; fingers splayed apart and rigid and elongated. Her feet were arched to where her toes pointed straight down; the tips barely grazing the floor.

What in the world is going on downstairs? Medallion could hear the mumbling from the kitchen. The voice sounded unfamiliar. *Sunta must have turned the television on.* Needing to take a break from scrolling through her social media pages, she decided to walk downstairs and tell Sunta to 'turn it down' instead of yelling through the home's intercom.

As she made her way down the steps, she could see a faint shimmer coming from the kitchen. *What is going on in there?* As she tiptoed to the kitchen, the mumblings she heard were more distinct, but the words didn't make any sense. *What is she saying? Who is she talking to? She may have gone crazy.*

She crept slowly to the kitchen entrance where she saw Sunta repeating the unfamiliar words over and over again. The baby sat in front of Sunta watching, and it appeared as if the glow was coming from the both of them. *What in the world is going on?!* Not knowing what to do, Medallion backed away from the kitchen and hurriedly went back upstairs. She grabbed her phone and began to dial.

"Hello?"

"Oh my God! Waymen! Something crazy is going on! You have to come down. Waymen… the girl! There's something w—"

"Medallion. I am so tired of you and these games. I don't even know why I answered the phone. I told you we are through. Please, stop calling me."

The line went dead before Medallion could explain anything further. *Aunt Mary… I need to call her*. Medallion's hands shook as she dialed the number.

"Hello?"

"Auntie! Something's wrong! The girl! I think she's lost it! One minute she's hanging out with me and watching the baby, and the next minute, she's having a seizure and glowing! She even has the baby glowing! I don't know what to do! I need you t—"

"Wait a minute. Slow down. What are talking about?"

"The girl! She came a couple of days ago, and I asked her to stay after Nurse Jackie left. Now she's here and I think something is wrong with her."

"Why are you so scared of her Medda? What's going on up there?"

"It's hard to explain Auntie..."

"Well then slow down and take a breath and tell me everything."

Medallion paused before she began to recant the events of the last few days. "Okay... so it's like... Things. Things have been happening..." She shook her head in frustration as Nurse Jackie's warning began ringing in her head. "I should have listened to Nurse Jackie. I should have called her like I said I would so she could tell me what she knew. She kept trying to tell me..."

"What? What did Mrs. Jackie have to tell you about the girl?"

"Auntie... there's this girl... Wait. Let me start from the beginning."

"Medda you are confusing me."

"Okay... so remember when I told you about how the baby almost died but Mrs. Jackie saved him?"

"Yes... I remember. I don't want to think about that, but what does that have to do with the girl?"

"I don't know but that night he almost died... the walls they were like breathing or something. And the paintings of all those old people... the Elders? It was like they were watching the whole thing.

It was creepy but I wasn't scared because I felt like they were there to assist. I— I thanked them for helping save Isaiah." Medallion paused as she continued to remember the past few days. "And then... the next day..."

"Medallion, that house should be clear of any spirit trying to do harm. It's not a portal for nothing bad to fear. What you experienced was real. The spirits that belong there are there for a reason. It's family and love you felt from them."

"I get that part Auntie. But it's some more stuff. See... this girl. She came out the woods, but she didn't have a coat on or shoes... Mrs. Jackie didn't like her from the start but I didn't listen, so I let her stay after Mrs. Jackie left and ever since she been here, I been having dreams of bloody woman and ghost babies."

"Ghost babies?"

"Yeah! I had a crazy dream about a woman given birth on a dirt floor. She was crying and screaming and there was blood everywhere but there wasn't a baby."

"Medallion..."

"And now her and Isaiah are downstairs glowing. Like I said it's just been crazy, and I should have been called you. I don't know how to handle stuff like this."

Aunt Mary began to shake in terror. She knew from what Medallion spoke of the girl was not of this realm. *She must have come when the baby crossed back over.*

"Medallion. You have to listen to me. I have a spell book. I need you to find it. I keep it in the attic. When you have it, I need you to call me back. We have to figure out who she is and what she wants. I feel you and Isaiah's life may be in danger if you don't."

"Where in the attic should I look for the book, Auntie?"

"I have kept the book in the attic, but with all the renovations, it may have been moved. You'll have to start there, and you'll have to hurry. Find the book. Figure out what she wants but be discrete. We can't let her know what is going on."

Medallion nodded her head with determination, and then responded, "Yes. I'll find the book, and I'll call you back."

Medallion hung up the phone, and as she headed out of the room, Sunta stood before her holding the baby. The glow she and Isaiah emanated while in the kitchen was gone, but there was a look of suspicion Sunta could not hide. Her glaring eyes made Medallion feel uncomfortable.

"What you doing in here?" Sunta said.

"Oh nothing. I was talking to my aunt on the phone." Medallion held the phone up so that Sunta could see it.

"What y'all was talking 'bout?"

"Oh… just the weather. I was telling her about the snow, and how we may be stuck here for a while."

Isaiah let out an irritable pout. Sunta patted him on the bottom to settle him; never taking her eyes off Medallion.

"Shush now, babe. Everything is all right."

"Here, let me take him."

Medallion sensed the animosity from Sunta. She didn't know what the young girl had planned for them, but the sooner she could get them away from her, the better.

"No, he's fine with me." Sunta stepped away from Medallion as she grabbed for her son. "It's time for his bath anyway. Maybe you want to go and find your husband or something. I'll take good care of 'Lijah."

"You mean Isaiah. His name is Isaiah."

Sunta stared at Medallion with discontent a few moments longer and then made her way back down the steps as Medallion followed her with her eyes.

"I've got to find that book before it's too late."

Chapter 39

After her phone call with Medallion, Mary headed for the room behind the stairs. The plain white door with a wreath made of twigs and ordinary garden flowers was placed top center of it. The door blended in well with the rest of the room's décor being in an inconspicuous spot. Because of that, no one really noticed it, and was never curious enough to ask where it led. She pulled out the skeleton key she kept in her pocket and put it in the door's keyhole to unlock it. The dainty door was actually quite heavy and creaked when opened. The light from outside of the room sliced the darkness within it. The floating dust particles danced in the light as the door opened wider. It had been a while since she'd been in her special room, but the time had come for her to mix one of her stronger spells to help save her niece and nephew.

Turning on the light in the dark room, Mary viewed the shelves filled with jars and stacks of books. The room was not much bigger than a parlor bathroom but it held all the things that she needed. She reached for a few jars filled with different colored liquids and one jar holding a big root soaking in black water. She placed them on the empty counter.

She grabbed an old clay bowl and placed it on the counter next to her ingredients. Once she had all of her materials, she slowly bent over and rolled the rug away that was under her feet. Underneath the rug was a circle carved into the wood floor and retraced in white chalk. The carved circle was rigid with several etched in lines that made up its composition. She lit four candles and placed one on each of the four arrows etched into the floor outside of the circle.

Mary gathered her ingredients and sat in the middle of the circle. She closed her eyes and thought of images of her niece. She needed to see her clearly so the ancestors and the spirits could see her too. Memories of her as a young girl flashed through Mary's mind.

She remembered Medallion's fifth birthday party and how they had a big celebration in the backyard to include clowns and a petting zoo. Then, she remembered Medallion when she got her driver's license, and how happy she was to finally have more independence. She'd worn her favorite pink top for good luck, and when she got her license, she jumped up and down with excitement. Mary surprised her with a red convertible Mercedes- the exact one she'd displayed prominently on her vision board. Mary remembered how her hair bounced as she landed after each hop.

The wedding... She remembered Medallion in all white at the alter when she said 'I do'. Jumping the broom... Waving goodbye to go on her honeymoon... And then she remembered Medallion when she came over to tell her the good news about her pregnancy. She held her tummy in excitement. They cried tears of joy together both knowing how blessed she was.

All good moments in Medallion's life... Mary needed the ancestors to see a descendant worth saving; that her life was not in vain. A woman of virtue and honor... Mary wanted the ancestors to see Medallion's true spirit because that's what mattered to them; not the physical form and actions of selfishness and greed Medallion insisted on portraying.

"Gods from above. Gods from below. I evoke the powers of strength and protection. Come forth to set the tortured spirit free that dwells amongst us!"

The candles that surrounded the circle began to shake and then toppled over causing the flame from each one to sleek around the circle. Each flame connected to the other until it made a perimeter around her.

"Gods from above, and gods from below, I submit to you a sacrifice. I call upon my ancestors to stand with the present to protect our future!"

Mary quickly grabbed the knife that lay beside her. She took it in one hand holding it tightly while gripping the sharp edge with her other and slowly slid the knife down her palm. The thickly rich blood from her hand oozed between her fingers and dripped into the carved niche on the floor where Mary sat.

Chapter 40

The branches brushed and scratched their arms and faces as they made their way through the brush. With only the starry night as their light and their guide, they stumbled over sticks, and rocks during their secret journey to the rendezvous point. Bettye led the group and the women followed. None spoke of the death of their baby sister, Sunta even though the loss was devastating. Of them all, Bettye took the loss the hardest because she was like Sunta's mother; their own being lost to them many years before.

But Bettye knew she could not grieve for Sunta. Not tonight. Her charge was to get the rest of the sisters to freedom, and she could not do that if her eyes were filled with tears and her heart singing a song of regret. Instead, she chose to wear Sunta's blood. The blood she spilled while trying to bear her child... It was Sunta's blood that had dried on her clothes as she labored in that back room to keep her and Elijah living during the time when the line between life and death was blurred.

Back when they were in the cabin, when Mary offered her the washbowl after Sunta took her last breath, Bettye turned her nose up to it and pushed it away.

"No. As long as I'm covered in her blood, she is with us, and we will carry her blood to freedom if not her body."

Mary nodded her head understanding the importance of them all making it and not leaving one behind. She put the basin of water back in the corner and grabbed the baby from Bettye's arms.

"Well, you carry Sunta. I'll carry her son."

Still torn from the loss of Sunta, Bettye willingly gave up the baby. She walked out of the room where Sunta laid lifeless and met the others in the shadows of the wood's edge. Bettye hugged each sister before she began to speak.

"Sisters," Bettye began. Her head lowered in grief. She took a deep breath and let her eyes guide her head up and steady. "Our sister is gone. Her body is here, but her soul is free. She is at peace, and we shall find ours once we leave here. Gather your things 'fore the time has come for us to go."

Bettye looked at Sunta's baby boy gathered in Mary's hand. He rested silently, and Bettye was grateful to him that he stayed peaceful enough to come.

"We taking Sunta's boy with us. We will not leave our family behind."

Bettye raised her arms up high to show her blood stained skin. The women nodded in agreement. One by one, they turned towards the woods; each cautious step taken, they checked for signs of Master Johnson or his overseer. Lily, the last in line, looked back at the cabin they once called home and whispered a farewell to Sunta.

"Rest in peace sistah 'cause you is loved."

Chapter 41

Medallion left the bedroom and heard Sunta in the baby's room singing and humming nursey rhymes. She crept to the nursery door and saw them there. Sunta sat in the rocking chair while coddling Isaiah. As she sang, Medallion saw the way Isaiah looked at her. He was mesmerized and appeared to look at her in awe. For the first time, she saw the image of a mother she wanted to be for him. Sunta looked nurturing. She looked like she loved and protected him. *Maybe he's better off with her. I for sure haven't shown him any love. It wasn't but a day ago that I was thinking about giving him away.*

She turned away from the scene. *I may not have seen what I saw downstairs. I have been feeling a little strange. It could have been the coffee… or the lack of it that made me think I saw something.* She scratched her head in wonderment and then walked back towards her room. Medallion chuckled at how absurd she reacted. *And to think I told my aunt that crazy mess. I wonder if she believed me. I should call her back and tell her never mind and there isn't a problem.*

Just before she made it to her bedroom, she looked to her left and saw the narrow brown door leading to the attic. Remembering her aunt told her the book of spells would be up in the attic, she decided it would be better to get the book than calling her aunt. *If that book is there and it holds spells like Auntie said, there will probably be a spell in to get Waymen back.*

Medallion smiled devilishly at her idea. *Waymen is my first priority. If I can't have Waymen, I don't want anyone else.* Medallion opened the door with the antique glass knob and began her journey to the attic to find the book.

Chapter 42

Each narrow stair leading into the attic creaked deeply as if bracing for each step upward into the deep, dusty, dry-aired attic. Once she reached the top, she flicked on the lights and saw a sea of boxes stacked high. There was old furniture covered in white cloths and a layer of dust over all of it. There were forgotten toys placed on flat surfaces, and older clothing hung on the rafters. Huge paintings were wedged in between piles of covered objects. A few bikes hung from the ceiling and old rugs were rolled up and leaning against bookcases. Medallion couldn't believe how packed the attic was. *How am I supposed to find that book in all of this mess?*

Cautiously stepping through the maze of things crammed into the space, Medallion played the guessing game as she peered and peeked into boxes she thought the book would be in. As she made her way from one stack of boxes to the other, she lifted the white coverings over the furniture in hopes the book would be underneath. *Auntie knows she needs to get rid of some of this stuff.*

Making it to the other side of the attic, Medallion stumbled over a covered pile of things. Grabbing her ankle in pain, she lost her balance and fell into an overstuffed couch. A puff of dust rushed up to the ceiling of the attic.

"This attic is too much of a mess. How am I supposed to find anything in here?"

Medallion's voice was weary. Her aunt told her the book was in the attic, but there was no end to the clutter, and the probability of finding the book was becoming less and less.

As she stabled herself on the couch to begin her search again, her fingertips hit a box that laid beside her on the couch. She looked over her shoulder to identify the object. It was an old tattered 8x8 wooden brown box. *This looks like the box in Auntie's room downstairs in the closet.*

Each of the corners on the box was covered by a worn leather patch. The box had a gold hinge on the back of it and on the front, was a closed lock. She pulled on the lock but it would not pull apart. Curious, she shook the box and there was a muffled sound in return. *This can't possibly be the book. If it's so special, why would it be in this old raggedy box?* As she was about to put the box back on the couch and continue her search, she accidently grazed the bottom of it, and felt an object attached to it. She turned the box over and saw a key taped to the bottom.

"Voila!"

Medallion pulled the key away from the box and used it to open it. There inside, lay a book. There wasn't any writing or descriptive markings to help decipher if this was the book she was told to look for. *It's got to be. What else kind of book would be in a locked box in a cluttered attic?*

Medallion opened the book revealing its old weathered pages. There, on the first page was an inscription: *To the one who is chosen to lead. I give you this gift.* The print was almost illegible as it had faded over time, but when Medallion touched the page, the letters became luminescent as she glided her fingers across them. Chills went up her spine as she knew this was the book her aunt told her to find.

She carefully opened the book to page one. There, she saw the drawing of a huge tree, and on the tree were branches, and on each branch were names. *Presla, Hailey, Ember, Bettye, Mary, Medallion. Medallion? Why is my name on here?*

She looked at the names once more. *These must have been the women who passed the book down, but why is my name here? Aunt Mary hasn't given me this book?* The thought of the book being in her ownership was unsettling. *Why hasn't she given me the book yet if I'm supposed to have it? Had she given this book to me before now, I know I could have used it to keep Waymen and get rid of my little problem the right way.*

Medallion walked towards the steps as she thought of her baby with the strange woman, Sunta and how in the last couple of days, Sunta was closer to her son than she'd ever been. *Never mind that. I have to find the spell. I need Waymen more than he knows.*

Eager to get started on her new plan, she put the book back in its box, before tucking the box under her arm and heading down the stairs.

Chapter 43

Ooooh… this looks cool. A binding spell. I can use it on that low-life, Rodney. He really needs to learn his lesson. For what seemed like hours, Medallion read the ingredients of spells, read aloud and to herself words and phrases for rituals in a language she was never taught. She took mental notes of the things referenced that caught her interest as her mind raced with possibilities of what she could do with the book if she could convince her aunt to give it to her.

She flipped the page once more. Her eyes widened with delight.

"Ifẹ si ifẹ kan… A Love Spell."

Medallion ran her fingers slowly down the page wanting the words to absorb into the tips of her fingers and infuse the knowledge.

As she read the words aloud, her delight became disappointment.

"Love is an emotion that comes from within. It cannot be created. Love between two people grows like a seed to a mighty tree. Love cannot be manipulated. Instead, a prayer for happiness, trust, and honor can be said for a more powerful love that no spell can create."

She closed the book and set it beside her on the bed in frustration.

"What good is this stuff if I can't get the one thing I want?"

In a huff, she flopped back on the bed when she heard a buzz come from the lamp on the nightstand before it went out. The room was as dark as the night outside without the lamp's light.

"Not this again…" Medallion reached over and pulled the lamp's switch a few times but still there was darkness.

The room then became cold. Chill bumps perforated her skin. She got off the bed and made her way through the dark room to hit the light switch on the wall but the lights in the ceiling failed to come on. She flicked the switch once more but the room stayed dark.

"Ugh! I hate this old electrical system. You'd think with all the money she put in this place, she would have at least had the electrical system upgraded too." Medallion voiced her irritation through clinched teeth and underneath her breath.

Walking out of the room, she tried the light switch in the hall. *Figures. No light in my room. No light in the hall. These lights must all run on the same circuit.* Continuing cautiously down the hall, she came across Isaiah's room. The door was closed to the nursery. She tapped on it quietly thinking Sunta would be in there sleeping, but she didn't respond. Medallion turned the door knob and the door opened freely. The nursery showed no light as well. *Guess it was a waste to invest in those silly night lights.* Medallion strained her eyes to see if Sunta was sleep in the twin sized bed that ran parallel to one of the walls, but the room was too dark too see anything within it.

Knowing her way around the room, she stepped in further; making her way to the baby's crib. She couldn't see him but laid her hand into the crib and felt around for his chest. She felt his heart beat and the rise and fall of his chest as he breathed. He was sleeping soundly in the crib. She slightly reached up and stroked the curvature of his fat cheek. The action almost felt motherly to her, and at that moment, she regretted more and more her actions towards her little one.

"MMMMiiiinnnneeee" A slow whispered voice spoke in the darkest corner of the nursery. Startled, Medallion pulled her hand away from Isaiah.

"Sunta? Are you in here," Medallion whispered not wanting to wake her son.

There was no answer. She waited by the crib not wanting to take a step further in the room. For the first time, she felt a fear. There was a presence in the room. Not a person. Not Sunta. Medallion knew she was not alone.

"MMMMiiiinnnneeee," The whispered voice said once more.

The hair on Medallion's arms slowly began to rise and she felt her skin become riddled with bumps. "Who is in here?"

Medallion looked down at Isaiah, hearing his breath. The room was too dark to see. She tried to reach out and grab him, but her arms were locked by her sides. Panicking, she began to look about the room for anything that could help her and Isaiah, but the room was black and full of darkness and nothing more.

The voice rose in volume as it said the word, "MMMMMMiiiiiiiinnnneeeee" in a raspy and harsh tone; almost a shrill.

Something was there and was ready to take what was theirs. Medallion feared it was her life.

The darkness of the room began to shift. Medallion became dizzy, and the feeling was growing stronger. She began to feel the air in the room around her. It was almost like something touching her skin; crawling up and down it— prickly but smooth.

Out of the corner of her eye. She saw it. Something moved. She waited to see if it would move again, but the darkness became still once more. She blinked her eyes while trying to adjust her vision to the shifting blackness around her. Finally, she saw Isaiah's crib and was relieved he still rested soundly, unbothered by the voice staking claim on what is theirs.

Medallion held her breath as she saw something shift in the darkest corner of the room— where the darkness hadn't changed. She needed more light— more light to see what was haunting the dark corner. She looked over at the heavily curtained window, and made the decision to open it, but her arms and legs would not move. An unseen force kept her planted where she stood. *I'm stronger than this. I cannot let it beat me. I need to save me and my baby.* With all her strength, she pulled her arms away from her body, and then struggled to make her feet move one by one towards the window. Determined to fight through the darkness and its hold on her, she was able to fling the curtains open; flooding the room with the moonlight.

Outside of the window stood a garden light high above on its wooden pole. A few feet in the yard was the weeping willow with its limbs bowed in its umbrella like shape; each branch covered in snow. The snow covered the lawn in a white unbothered sheet of powder and it glistened with speckles of ice mixed within. All was peaceful outside of the window… quiet and still. She then looked around the dark room now brighter with the help of the moonlight. Medallion's eyes frantically darted back and forth looking for any clues that someone was in there with her, but her son was her only company.

Once again, Medallion's eyes settled on the dark corner fearful of what could lurk in its shadows. Unlike its surroundings, the corner still felt like an abyss and void of light, but there was something there hiding and waiting. She could almost see it. She heard the slow croaking groan coming from the dark corner as it slowly started to brighten up. The croaking groan grew louder as a hint of white... stark white... in the shape of a face appeared from the darkness staring at her. Medallion's body trembled with fear as a red thin smile curled upwards on the stark white face floating slowly out of the dark corner.

She caught her breath and shut her mouth in fear as the face materialized. She breathed fast and heavy out of her nose unable to escape the room and the trance the face held her in. The eyes of the white face were only pitch-black holes holding nothing inside, but Medallion felt the darkness of the eyes watching her every move. The sight of it made her breath lock in her throat. The room grew colder, and Medallion's tremble became a shiver. As the face moved out of the corner, the darkness began to expand and engulf the room. The light from outside the window was no longer Medallion's savior.

The darkness began to swiftly surround her. It appeared to crawl up the walls and across the floor until it began to suffocate her.

She opened her mouth to scream out if only to gain control of whatever it is that wanted what was theirs. But there was no sound. Her voice was stifled. *The baby...* She thought as she looked over at the crib. Medallion quickly made it to the crib and wrapped Isaiah in her arms before the darkness came down over him like a blanket.

The croaking moan stopped and there was nothing but silence. Medallion held Isaiah tightly in her arms as she tried to leave the room. She heard the nursery door slam shut before she could reach it, and then she felt the warm breath on her shoulder breathing slowly. Medallion began to tremble. The thing in the corner was near. Something touched the back of her shoulder. She turned to look, and outside of the window she saw it. There stood the elongated white face with the thin red smile looking at her through the window and standing by the light post with a long, thin, translucent body.

Medallion heard the slow croaking moan once again, and this time it wasn't coming from the room, but from the figure standing by the post outside.

"MMMMMMMIIIIIINNNNNNNNEEEEEEE!!!!" The figure said in a hollowed echo that sent more chills up Medallion's body.

As the figure continued to shout, it began to move towards the window with its long awkward arms stretched and reaching for what it wanted. Medallion watched in fear, and finally understood what the scary figured desired. She gripped Isaiah tightly as her body was finally released from the grip of fear. Medallion's throat let go, and she let out a blood curdling shrill which startled Isaiah, making him cry. With no hesitation, she pulled the nursery door open and ran out of the room as the door slammed shut behind her.

Chapter 44

Mary laid in the middle of the circle of protection she'd created praying to the ancestors for sight. She needed to know what kind of spirit Medallion was dealing with to help her in the battle she would surely have to face. On her back and with the palms of her hands facing up, her fingers were stretched and rigid.

"Speak to me sisters. Whisper to me the spirit that dwells with our daughter. Make it known that it is not welcomed among the living. Cast the haunt from this place and return it to the depths from which it has arisen."

For hours Mary repeated the same request over and over hoping for a glimpse of what Medallion would need to fight but was only met with stillness around her. Suddenly, as if the last time she spoke the words were like the first request, Mary could begin to feel the fog lifting from her inner eye exposing the unwelcomed spirit walking amongst the living.

Chapter 45

Medallion ran down the hall shrieking as the voice from the nursey bellowed. The croaking moan vibrated through the home making the walls shake. Medallion ran into her room with Isaiah tucked between her arm and her body. He cried uncontrollably from being startled out of his sleep.

Before she could close the door, she glimpsed the ghostly figure standing in the middle of the hall ricket with its limbs bent crooked and inward. Its head was tilted and askew. It began to morph by twisting and contorting its body while staring back at Medallion.

"MMMMMMMMMIIIIIIIIINNNNNNNEEEEE!!!!!" It yelled and began its crooked walk to Medallion.

"NO! STAY AWAY FROM ME!" Medallion screamed at it in fear and tried to slam the door shut.

She yelled out in despair not knowing what to do. *The alarm!* Medallion went hurriedly out of the room barely escaping the grasp of the spirit slowly making its way to her. Skipping most of the steps and holding Isaiah as safely as she could, she traveled down the stairs and darted to the home alarm keypad and pushed the big red panic button. The house lights lit up and began to sound in sync with the rhythmic wail. Ready to make her escape, she turned around to head for the front door when she saw the thing standing in her path.

"NOOOOO!" Medallion screamed while trying to run off in the opposite direction.

The ghostly spirit screeched as it began to dissipate becoming a mist. As Medallion screamed, the ghost forced its way inside her body. She grabbed her own neck in panic not knowing how to stop what was happening. Finally she stopped screaming. Her eyes rolled to the back of her head as it tilted back. Her chin pointed to the sky, and then back down slowly. Her eyes slid open hiding a sinister satisfaction that wasn't her own.

Hitting the passcode on the alarm, the house fell silent while the lights that blinked in sequence with the alert stopped flashing. Medallion looked down at the screaming baby she held. She rocked him back and forth and smiled in a satisfied manner.

"Be calm now my baby. Mama's here."

Isaiah quieted and listened to the voice knowing that his mama was now here for him.

Chapter 46

Sitting curled up in the center of her circle, Mary wept. *I'm too late. Medallion is lost to me. I'm too late.* Mary's inner vision could only allow her to see but not intervene. What she saw was something she never thought she'd witness. There in her foyer at the big family home, stood her niece fighting the spirit of her sister Sunta. The sister she saw die so many years ago... The pain of watching Sunta die was only surpassed by her sister possessing the child she raised. Over the many decades Mary had lived, she attempted to reach Sunta and let her know Elijah was okay, that she could rest in peace, but Sunta refused to respond.

From her visions, Mary knew why Sunta came back and how she did it. From Isaiah's brush with death where Sunta latched onto him in The White, to her finally being able to possess Medallion... Tears for the peril both souls were in flowed from Mary. *The baby is in danger. My niece is in danger, and Sunta has to go.*

"I have to go to them and fix this."

Mary helped herself up from the circle and blew out the candles. She left the little room underneath the steps and picked up her phone to dial the only person who would be able to help her and her family. After the third ring, Waymen answered.

"Hey, Aunt Mary," Waymen said wearily.

He loved Medallion's aunt, and usually didn't mind her meddling in their issues, but this time, he didn't need her trying to convince him to make up with his wife. As far as he was concerned the marriage was over.

"Waymen. I need your help," Mary said with angst and a tremble in her voice.

"Aunt Mary, what's up? You sound scared. Is everything okay?"

"Waymen. Something is terribly wrong at the big house. You have to take me to Medallion."

He sucked his teeth and sighed at the thought of seeing Medallion and the baby.

"Waymen, I know you don't want to take me, and I don't blame you, but I don't have anyone else to call— I can't call anyone else. It's got to be you. Medallion's in trouble. You might be the only thing that can save her."

Thinking on her words and the panic in her voice, Waymen rethought his initial reaction to stay away and knew he had to do something.

"Aunt Mary, I'm on my way. I'll help in any way I can."

"Bless you, Waymen, because it's a matter of life and death for both her and the baby."

Back in the nursery, Sunta paid no attention to the sound of Medallion's voice echoing inside of the stolen physique. Her determination to take her baby with her was her sole purpose. With the potion from that morning and the ritual in the kitchen, the transition had already started for Isaiah. She looked at him feeling the same emotions on the day she met her Elijah. Those were the eyes staring back at her before her soul left her body and were burned into her memory.

"'Lijah, our time is coming real soon."

Sunta put her hand to her chest and a finger to his finding their heartbeats were in sync even though hers was an echo of what was once there. As she whispered softly to Isaiah in a sing-song voice, she became excited for the beginning of his transformation. As their heartbeats thumped in the same rhythm a tear fell out of her eye.

"He's falling in love with his true mother."

She stroked his hair and he smiled and cooed as if longing for her touch.

"Baby of mine. Baby of mine. How I love this baby of mine."

Chapter 47

"There, there babe."

Sunta placed Isaiah in his crib and patted his little round belly. He tilted his lip upwards into a crooked smile. Sunta smiled back adoringly. She kissed her first two fingers and then placed the fingers on his cheeks. Isaiah cooed at her touch making Sunta smile too.

"Finally I can be the mother to my son. I knew we would be together one day. Now our time together begins."

Sunta placed a blanket over Isaiah and headed for the door of the nursery.

"'Night sweet baby. Come mornin' time we begin our journey."

Sunta turned the light off in the nursery and headed for the stairs. Making her way towards the steps, she stood in front of the ornate hanging mirror in the hallway for a glimpse of the reflection staring back at her. Almost stunned to not see herself staring back, she approached the mirror cautious but surprised.

Everything about the face staring back at her was foreign. The hair cascaded slightly past her shoulders instead of it being in coils or under a scarf. *So soft…* Sunta touched the strands delicately as not to disturb them. She pressed her hand against the cheek. The flesh— supple and smooth. The lips—full and pouty. Even though the face was not Sunta's the soul never lied, and the eyes staring back in the reflection were definitely hers.

Chapter 48

"Aunt Mary, look, you have to tell me what's going on. Now, I know I agreed to take you to Medallion, but why is it so important that we get there at this late hour? What's going on out there?"

In the dark of night, Waymen and Mary rode through the snow covered roads trying to make it to Medallion. Driving had not been easy as they left the city. The roads had not been cleared by the big snowplows, and the fear of sliding on the ice was real, but Mary was determined to get to Medallion and Isaiah before it was too late. After she got Waymen to agree to take her, she began packing all the items she would need to capture Sunta and send her back with a possibility of delivering her to the ancestors— the sisters.

"Waymen, it's hard to explain what's going on. Let's just please get there." Mary was tense as she thought of all the conceivable things Sunta could plan to do.

"When we arrive, just be prepared to call out for Medallion. Right now, she's not the woman you married... she's someone else."

Waymen shook his head sarcastically.

"With all due respect Aunt Mary, the girl I married is long gone. Been gone when she started messing around with Rodney."

Mary put her hand on his lap and patted it understandingly.

"Waymen, I know. I told her to stop messing around with your heart. I warned her it was no good to be carrying on such a torrid affair, but she didn't listen. I know you had big plans for you and her to live out your lives together and have a great big family. I had my plans for her too. I was preparing her to do great things to benefit our family but for the both of us, she just wasn't ready."

"What do you mean you were preparing her? Preparing her for what?"

Waymen kept his eyes on the dangerous roads while listening intently. Mary let out a deep breath not wanting to go into the discussion any further, but knowing she had to if she wanted Waymen's help.

"Waymen, I know you know about what I do."

"Yes, I know you're an herbalist and you help people when they are sick. What? You were preparing her to be an herbalist like you?"

"Yes, something like that." Mary nodded slowly.

"But what does that have to do with right now? If Medallion and the baby are in danger, how is preparing to be an herbalist going to save her?"

"Because being an herbalist is not all that there is. Waymen, Medallion is a direct descendent of a very powerful line of divine women."

"Huh? A what?"

"An Amosu... an Aje, Or the more Americanized term... a witch. Medallion has been blessed with magic."

"Medallion's a witch?"

Waymen's voice trailed off as he thought about the revelation, and then instantly began thinking back on if she ever casted any spells on him. All the times he'd taken her back began to resurface. All the times he appeared as the butt of a demented joke when Rodney would boast around the office about his affair with Medallion came to the forefront of his memories. The whispers from his peers and co-workers began to resonate within him. How he desperately tried to ignore the affair wanting to believe that Medallion was either going to change or the rumors were false. His body began to tense up, and his teeth were clenched to grit. His temper began to fume, and his eyesight began to blur. His rage was so big about the thought of being manipulated for so long, he pulled over on the side of the road trying to regain his composure.

"Waymen, don't stop driving. We can't waste any time. We have to get there before it's too late."

"I'm sorry Aunt Mary, but no. I can't help her. I can't help you. No offense, but this woman— this *witch* has made me look like a fool all these years for sport. It's her fault I acted this way. I see now. I see what she did. If she's a witch like you said she is, she put a spell on me long ago to make me be her love slave! No. I'm not helping this woman."

"Waymen, calm down—"

"And you! You know what she was capable of and you allowed her to bewitch me! Why would you let her do something like this to someone?!"

"Waymen, you have it all wron—"

"No! You come off so sweet and caring, but all the time, you allowed her to entrap me! I can't believe I didn't see it! I can't believe—"

Mary raised her hand and slapped Waymen across his cheek.

"Will you just calm down! She did not cast a spell on you!"

Mary huffed out loud placing her clasped hands in her lap as she stared straight forward out onto the dark and snowy road.

Waymen held his cheek in astonishment. The pain of Mary's hand stinging his cheek pulsated and radiated with heat. He realized he'd lost control and took the time they sat in silence to calm down.

After a few minutes, Mary noticed Waymen's breathing had slowed to a more even pace and his shoulders were not as tense as they were before.

"You ready to listen and understand?"

Waymen nodded in silence.

"Medallion didn't cast a spell on you."

Waymen turned to Mary to protest, but she held her one finger up signaling him to hold his words.

"She didn't put a spell on you because she doesn't know what she is. Like I said, I was preparing her to be an Amosu, but I could tell by the way she treated you that she was not ready. I was hoping the baby would have healed your marriage and make her settle down and focus so that I could pass on our heritage to her, but I was wrong."

Waymen sat still not knowing what to say, but he knew Mary was being truthful. Mary had always regarded him as her family, and for all that she's done for him, allowing Medallion to cast a spell on him would be out of her character.

"Waymen, everything you went through with Medallion was out of the love you had for her. You believed in who she really is and took all the embarrassment and stress from her because you loved her. She didn't put a spell on you. You could have walked away from her anytime you wanted to— like you did a couple of days ago. It was a choice you made to stick it out with her. And that's why I need you to come with me to help save her. Because I know you still love her and love is going to be what saves her."

"I love her... that's true, but do you see my side of this? It's frustrating trying to love this girl and be the perfect husband... forgiving her every time SHE does wrong."

"But who said you had to try and be the 'perfect husband'?" Mary retorted. "You put yourself in that stressful place trying to prove something to the world... or— how do y'all say it now-a-days... 'The Haters'? Ain't no one tell you to be perfect. What it looks like to me is that you like your position in this marriage. You like looking like 'Boo-Boo The Fool'. If you didn't you would do something about it— like giving ultimatums for cheating that you really could enforce. You yourself couldn't even stick to staying away from her. Admit it... you came back on your own several times. Rarely did she even have to do anything to make you come back around."

Waymen allowed Aunt Mary's words to sink in to really process what she was saying, and she was right. Only he could change

Medallion's treatment of him. What he understood in that moment was she was not all to blame for her bad behavior.

"Waymen... you are the best man I could have ever prayed for to take care of my most precious possession. Yes, she loves you. However, you have to be strong enough to tell her how you expect to be loved so she can take care of you the right way." Mary stroked the side of his face in a comforting gesture.

"Help me save Medallion. Be valiant and strong like you've always been because those are your greatest qualities. With all that's going on right now, we need that type of force to win against what we're up against. When tonight's all done, make your final decision on if you want to stay married to her or not. If you decide to stay married, have a long talk with her about what you require as her husband. Let her know those boundaries... those healthy boundaries to be a happy and healthy husband for her are nonnegotiable.

"As usual you make good sense. I should have come to you before I made the harsh decision to leave her and the baby. And as much as I want to say I wasn't weak for her, I was. I was weak by allowing her to cheat, and even though I love her with every breath in me, I used it as an excuse to stay in this toxic cycle with her. I know she didn't put a spell on me. I just didn't want to admit it."

"I'm glad you know she didn't put a spell on you, Waymen. I've watched you two together, and believe me, the love you have for that wife of yours is too strong by itself and doesn't need anything—especially magic for it to be as powerful as it is." Mary pulled his chin close to her with the tip of her finger until his glance met hers.

Listen to me when I tell you this... Love can't be manipulated and there is no spell that will ever make you fall in love. You either are or you not." She then smiled delicately and patted his cheek where she struck it; planting her lips on his cheek to kiss the sting of the unpleasant moment away.

Mary's words rejuvenated him; igniting the desire to be with his wife as his wedding vows instructed. "Alright Auntie." Waymen chuckled. "I'll admit I was and probably still am a fool for her."

Mary chuckled as well admiring his willingness to keep his marriage the only way he knew how. "Not a fool at all. Just a boy trying to love a girl."

Waymen gave Mary a hug and put the car in drive and got back on the road.

She pointed her finger in the direction of the dark snow-covered road ahead of them more determined than ever to bring order to this world and the other. "Now let's get down there and save our family."

Chapter 49

"Are you sho you want to do this Mary?"

"Yes, Bettye. We can't go no further wit you. Po lil' babe is tired. He fussy, and y'all just can't risk it wit him."

Weary, Mary patted the new born on his back while slightly bouncing him to help keep him from crying any louder.

"He wants his mama, Bettye. I can feel it with every whimper, every squirm."

"Mary, it just don't seem right to leave you. We already lost one sister, and I promised to get you all to freedom no matter what."

"I know Bettye, but he can't go on. Leave us behind. I'll lay low and figure out a way to keep us safe."

She looked at the bundle in her arms. His eyes shimmered underneath the dark sky. His skin still new and fresh with the shade of the darkest coal. He was beautiful.

"What's going on here? Bettye, we have to get going if we plan to make it over the state line."

The young white woman who Bettye and her sisters met up with to help them cross to freedom joined Bettye at her side. She could see the sisters were in the midst of a dilemma. She looked from Bettye to Mary and then at the fussy child and could tell they were making a hard decision about him.

"We can't just leave them Mrs. Sarah, but Mary thinks we ought to." Bettye's voice quivered as she spoke. "I promised I'd get them to freedom and that's what I plan to do."

She straightened her stance as her mind was made up.

"Mary and the baby are coming with us."

Sarah placed a hand on Bettye's arm.

"Patience Bettye, but Mary's right. We can't keep them with us. He could jeopardize everything if he continues."

Bettye began to protest but Sarah held her hand up to stop her.

"Hear me out. They can't go with us, but I have a place where she and the baby will be safe. She can raise the boy until he is old enough to travel. Until he can, they will live like they are free. They will be safe."

Bettye stiffened her body at the thought of being separated from her sister. They'd never been apart. Even when the Master threatened to do so, Bettye always found a way to keep them together.

"No… no. We can all stay then. Me and my sisters. We can all go with Mary and the boy and live like we are free until he's old enough to travel."

"No Bettye. You must go. It's a risk just for Mary to stay back. You have to get the others across the border. If you don't, all that you are doing will be in vain." Sarah pleaded hoping Bettye would make the right choice.

"Yes, Bettye. Get the others to freedom. I can come later, and we can be a family— a whole family once again." Mary desperately hugged Bettye as a plea for her to make the right choice. "Go, Bettye. I'm begging you… *PLEASE!*" Mary whispered into Bettye's ear.

Bettye pulled away from their embrace taking a long look at Mary's petitioning eyes waiting for her stubborn stare to concede but also knowing it wouldn't. She held her hands out towards the baby, and Mary handed him over. Bettye hugged him tightly.

"Boy… you done took two of my sisters from me in one night. You a powerful force. You stay like that, son. Until we meet again."

Bettye kissed his forehead and handed him to Sarah.

"Ma'am… hold onto him for a bit. My sisters and I have to prepare."

Bettye walked over to the other sisters and told them the plan. A few of them gasped and a few cried. Once Bettye finished talking to them, they walked over to Mary; all were sorrowful with tear stained eyes.

Gloria, the fourth sister, the one that Mary helped raise as her own, was the first to hug her. She embraced her as hard as she could. She held her tightly, wanting to keep her essence with her always. She begrudgingly pulled herself away, and then reached in her bag pulling out a cedar box.

"Here's the book, Mary. You've always been the keeper. Bring it when we see you again."

Mary nodded and tucked the book in her bag. Bettye approached Mary grabbing both of her hands and looking into her eyes.

"Until we meet again, you hold the key. Keep him and the book safe.

"I will. I vow they will always be safe with me."

"Sisters, gather around," Bettye said as she let go of Mary's hands and backed away.

The sisters formed a circle around Mary. They closed their eyes and began to pray their individual prayers of safety, and love. Bettye's prayer turned into a low hum that the sisters began to mimic. Eventually, their individual prayers became a chant as they swayed in spiritual rhythm. Mary felt the energy from the circle fill her soul. Her body began to warm, and her head became dizzy. Her legs grew weak, but she still stood strong to receive the blessings her sisters bestowed. Her arms were heavy from the weight of the power growing in her, but she still reached her limbs high as she felt the ancestors and the energy of the circle run through her body.

"Mary, the second Amosu born from the strongest, Makeda, our mother." Bettye's voice rose and rumbled as she passed the energy of the circle to Mary. "Mary, our sister, we protect you in this circle. We keep you safe in this circle. We gift life that will last until we meet again."

The sisters clutched each other's hands tighter as they forced as much of the energy towards Mary. They continued to hum and chant almost unconsciously, but still focused.

"As we let go of our hands, we will not let go of each other. Let this circle be unbroken 'til we meet again."

As Bettye spoke the last words, an invisible powerful force went through Mary and wrapped around her. The wind from the force pushed past the women as it rushed to be with Mary and absorb into her soul.

The women let go of each other's hands as the wind calmed. The dark woods were quiet out of respect as the sister's controlled nature's energy to empower theirs. One by one, the night chirpers began their calls once again as if knowing what needed to be done was now done. Bettye opened her eyes and the other sisters did the same. She looked around and saw the other escaped slaves looked on in quiet amazement. They began to whisper amongst each other about the mystery they'd just witnessed. Sarah stood furthest away from the miracle, holding the baby and waiting patiently, knowing it best not to interfere.

Mary walked over to Bettye with tears of joy filling her eyes. She placed her hands over her heart.

"I feel you. I feel all of you here."

She patted her chest as her heart beat strong. She wrapped Bettye into her arms; holding her tightly.

"Never let me go 'cause I ain't letting you go."

Filled with all the emotion the day brought, Bettye burst into tears not able to hold in anything any longer.

"Mary, we gon' miss you. I'm gon' miss you. Find us when its time, but if we never meet again, we are with you. Take care of that boy. Keep the book safe."

"I will Bettye, and we'll be together soon."

Chapter 50

Only two counties away... Mary's phone vibrated in her pocketbook as she and Waymen entered Melville County. *She* pulled the phone out and looked at the number flashing across it. *I don't know who this is.* Mary hit the ignore button not wanting to be distracted from the task at hand. As she put the phone back, it began to buzz once more. She looked at the number that flashed across the screen and it was the same number from before. Now curious, she hit the "Accept" button to take the call.

"Hello, Mary?"

"Yes? Who is this?"

"This is Nurse Jackie. I need to talk with you."

"Jackie! Are you okay? Something terrible has happened."

"Yes. I know. I felt something strong come through me not too long ago. I think Medallion might be in trouble."

"She is, Jackie. I'm on my way to her now. I've got Waymen with me too."

"Waymen? How'd you get him to come?"

"Long story, but he is on board. We're passing through Melville right now. I should be at the house in an hour."

"Mary, I'm so glad you are coming but you must know something. It's a spirit there, and it's powerful. You may need some help."

"Jackie, I saw, and I know. She's my sister Sunta, and she wants that baby. I have to stop her before she takes the life of Isaiah and Medallion."

"It makes sense now. But Mary, you can't stop her by yourself."

"I have to try Jackie."

"Well, I can come with you."

"But your leg…"

"I'm fine. It's wrapped up. It ain't nothing but a sprang. I'm movable. I'm supposed to be discharged tomorrow anyway. Come swing by the hospital. I'll be waiting outside for you."

"Are you sure?"

"Yes, I'm sure. I owe you so much. I'll be waiting for you when you get here."

Nurse Jackie hung up the phone before Mary could protest any further.

"Waymen, we need to make a stop at the hospital before we go to the house."

He looked at Mary with apprehension.

"What's going on at the house? I mean you told me Medallion is a witch and all but what else am I going up against."

"It's hard to explain, but just do as I say and everything will be just fine."

Chapter 51

Preparing the brew for the ceremony, the knock at the front door startled Sunta. She peeked from the kitchen and looked at the locked door. *I wonder who that is.* Putting her ladle back in the simmering pot, she curiously headed to the entryway. Two more knocks resonated from the door as Sunta approached it.

"Who is it?"

"Police ma'am. We got an alarm from this number…"

"Just following up to make sure everything was alright," the other cop stated finishing the first cop's sentence.

Sunta opened the door to see two smiling officers. Both were bundled in coat scarves, and hats.

"Good evening, sirs. I didn't catch all you said from behind the door."

"Well good evening, Mrs. Medallion. Glad to see you don't have that candle holder this time," Officer Richardson said with a laugh while extending his hand to greet her.

She shook it politely and then stood at the door waiting for them to continue.

"Well, like I said, we got notification that your alarm was going off so we decided to come check it out."

Officer Frazier shivered from the cold weather as he stood in front of Sunta trying to explain why they'd come.

"Mrs. Medallion, uh… do you mind if we can come in? It's a might cold out here. It'd be nice to come in and warm up before we have to get back in the truck and head on back to the station."

Sunta smiled at the request, and at the fact they couldn't tell it wasn't Medallion they were talking to.

"Well, where are my manners?" Sunta stepped aside so that they could enter. "Do come in and get warm."

"Thank you so much, Mrs. Medallion. We do apologize for taking so long in getting out here. The roads are so bad from all this snow."

"Yeah, they weren't playing when they said this was going to be one of the worst storms this year."

The three of them chuckled at how true the meteorologist was.

"Well, as you can see, everything is fine."

"Yup, things look great, but you know we have to do our part and come out and check on you like we did the first night you were here... it's all a part of the job." Officer Frazier pulled out his pad and pencil to take notes for his report. "So if you don't mind telling me, what tripped the alarm?"

"I don't know. Maybe an animal?" Sunta shrugged her shoulders in bewilderment.

"Mmm… something smells really good. What do you have cooking?"

Oh! I almost forgot the brew! Sunta took off for the kitchen where she saw her pot bubbling over the top.

"Oh! It's ruined!" Sunta turned the stove off and took the pot off the hot eye. "I'm going to have to start over now."

"Well, it sure doesn't smell ruined. Want me to test it out for you?" The officer grabbed a bowl and spoon from the drying dishes on the counter near the sink to help himself. He grabbed the ladle and proceeded to dip it in for a serving from the aroma filled pot. "What is that rosemary in there?"

He took a whiff of the air above the stove as he started to dip his spoon into the bowl.

Sunta pulled the bowl and the spoon out of the officer's hand dumping its contents in the trash.

"Sir, I did not make this for you."

"Whoa, my apologies. It just smelled so good, and I was so cold."

"Maybe we should go…"

"Yes, please," Sunta stated, irritated by their intrusion.

"Well, like we said, it looks like there's nothing wrong here."

The two police headed for the front door. The latter of the two turned back at Sunta as a question popped into his head.

"Hey… are you here by yourself?"

"No. The baby is here."

"No. I mean what happened to the old lady that was here with you the other day."

"Oh. She left. She couldn't stay."

Chapter 52

Waymen crept his car cautiously through the parking lot until he could pull up to the hospital. As she promised, Nurse Jackie was waiting for them, sitting in a wheelchair. A young petite nurse was also there waiting with her. Waymen put the car in park and got out to help Nurse Jackie. He stuck his hand out to greet the nurse.

"Thank you for sitting with her."

The nurse handed Waymen the crutches and then proceeded to help Nurse Jackie out of the wheelchair.

"Oh, no problem at all, but her release date is not until tomorrow. Ms. Jackie insisted that she be absolved from the hospital's care right this moment. She told me you guys were coming tonight and wouldn't be able to come tomorrow. This is against our policy. I hope I don't get in trouble with this."

"Oh nonsense." Nurse Jackie said as she hobbled to the car.

"Don't worry. We'll take good care of her."

Waymen smiled politely turning his attention back to Mrs. Jackie. The young nurse watched as he helped Nurse Jackie into the car. After he closed her door, he hurried back to the driver's side and got back into the car.

"You ladies all strapped in and ready to go?"

"Yes Waymen, let's get on the road." Waymen started the car and began his slow trek to the house.

Nurse Jackie settled into the back as Mary began.

"Jackie, Thank you for coming. I thought I could do this by myself, but I don't think I can. I honestly don't know if she remembers me. If she's angry at me... I just want her to let Medallion go and leave the baby. She has to go back. This is not her world any longer."

"I don't know, Mary. When I first met her, she looked and felt real. She wasn't just a spirit, but almost living. I think her will to take this baby back with her is driving her strength."

"I'm sure of it. Her son meant the world to her, and her last words were about him. We will have to use a lot of our power to send her back. And the bad part about it is that we don't have a lot of time to do it. Through my visions, I saw she wants to perform the good death on Isaiah which will take her and him to the afterlife. If she succeeds, Medallion will be left without her son. We must hurry before we are too late."

Chapter 53

Sunta watched the snow glisten and fall under the moon through the windows that made up the Four Seasons room. She was finally appeased- finally at one with her baby. She'd waited for this moment for such a long time. Sitting in The White for so very long was all she knew, and all she thought about was reuniting with the child she had to leave behind.

The storm that left several feet of snow was finally gone, and the world outside of the big home was quiet. The few snowflakes that fell, staggered in pace compared to earlier in the night. Sunta smiled at the moment. She looked around realizing she was real. *I can walk around and be here in this life with my son.* She let the fingers of the body she inhabited graze down the other arm. She felt the tingle of her own touch. *I am here. I can stay here. Maybe I don't have to go back to The White. I can stay here and watch my son grow up in this world instead of crossing over into the other.*

The whistle from the tea kettle pulled her out of her thoughts, and as she walked over to the stove, her body became hot. She began convulsing. Her body pumped rapidly as she fell to the ground. Sunta let out a loud scream as she gathered her arms around herself; holding onto her torso. She felt as if she were filling up from the inside and bursting from her seams. She broke into a cold sweat, and her eyes rolled back into her head.

"SUNTA!!!"

"NOOOOO!" Sunta cried out to the echoing voice within her.

"SUNTA LET ME OUT!!!"

"NOOOOO!!!! HE'S MINE NOW! I BELONG WITH HIM!!"

The pain Sunta felt all over was agonizing. Medallion's soul was fighting to regain control of her body, but Sunta was fighting harder to keep it. Sunta writhed around on the floor trying to keep Medallion suppressed.

"You can't have him, Sunta! He's my son!"

Medallion's voice rattled around Sunta's head. The voice was loud and overpowering and the words struck one by one.

"I will not let him go! I will have him and he WILL. BE. MINE!" Sunta screamed the words as she struggled with her internal tormentor.

Soon after, the battle within Medallion's body calmed leaving Sunta exhausted. She breathed heavily in and out as she slowly picked herself up from the floor. She dragged her aching body upwards and heaved herself onto the counter. Her face rested on the counter's cold granite slab as she took the aftermath of the violent fight with Medallion. *For a moment, I thought I could stay here with my son and live in this body, but I can't. I know now that I have to go back, and he will have to come with me.*

Sunta rose from the counter and looked around the kitchen. *I have everything here. I just need one more thing.* She began rummaging the cabinets. She looked at the clock noting that it was getting close to the appointed hour. Looking over at her simmering pot. With not enough to make a new batch, she resolved to settle for the burnt contents. She picked up her ladle and reached into the tall silver stew pot to swirl the mixture within it. With her ladle, she scooped a bowl full to examine the broth. She frowned at the scorched smell and its brownish color. However, she was relieved that it had sat undisturbed after going through her ordeal so close to the stove top. She put the label and the mixture back in the pot to continue her search for the last element of the ceremony.

Where can it be? It can't be far from here... it's got to be here. Close by... Sunta continued pulling and clanging pots and pans as she searched and searched. *The book. I can't finish until I have the book.* She soon realized that it was not close. She left the kitchen and headed back upstairs remembering how suspicious Medallion looked earlier. *What were you doing when I wasn't looking?* With a sly grin Sunta scurried to the master bedroom. She flung the double doors open and quickly scanned the room. *Nothing yet, but I know it's here. It's got to be.*

Sunta swiftly began checking the drawers of the dressers and the nightstands, making her way to look under the bed and thumbing through the small bookcase underneath the window holding Mary's intimate books. While looking at the titles, she paused when she saw the family bible- tattered from many years of use.

Sunta touched the spine of it softly, and then picked it up from the shelf. She thumbed through the pages breathing in a whiff of its dusty, moldy fragrance. Memories of her sisters came back to her. Too young to remember her true mother, she clung to the endearment she had for a sister who raised her as her own- Bettye. *Love is what my momma taught us. I remember. Right from this book, she taught us about all the love Jesus had and sacrificed for us. Jesus sacrificed his life for love. I sacrificed mine for love too.*

Closing the pages of the Bible, a folded piece of paper fell out landing in her lap. She tucked the book under her arm and opened the worn down and yellowed piece of paper: "Medallion, This Bible will guide you through this life, but our book will guide you through your other. Guard both with your heart and use their teachings to carry on what has been passed down. Love, Mary."

Sunta remembered how important it was to pass the family traditions on. When she was younger, Bettye would walk her through the woods looking for fresh berries to eat and pretty flowers to pick. She would tell Sunta the stories their mama passed to her about lands full of people like them running free, laughing, playing, and singing.

Before they would return to their quarters, Bettye would hug her and let her know she was next in line. She would be the keeper of the stories, the family, and the magic. Those moments with Bettye were so special to her and knowing she was the keeper kept her close to her eldest sister. Sunta longed for the day when it would be her turn, but that day never came. The night she gave birth to her son, they left her in their cabin taking the family, her precious boy, and the book. She ran her hand over the Bible's smooth surface and bowed her head in sorrow as she looked at the letter once again. Bitterness and anger began to fuel her and she felt her strength grow. She began to tingle all over from the feeling of her sister's betrayal and the glow she tried to hide over the last few days began to shine bright. "That girl thinks she can take everything from me. Bettye told me I'm the keeper. She can't have my baby and my family." Sunta shoved the paper back in the Bible and headed for the next closet determined to find the book Bettye meant for her to have.

Chapter 54

The space where she was trapped was dark and cold. The air surrounding her seemed to be made of melted ice. Wet. However, her body felt warm, but still she shivered. Not because of the cold, but because of fear for what the future would bring.

Where am I? Medallion lifted her hands in front of her but was not able to see her fingers. She was in the darkest space she could ever imagine. Then she heard the humming again. It was the same kind of hum from the nursery- same melody. The humming voice was all around her and she didn't know where to run… or even if she should run. But as she tried to make up her mind on whether to stay or to go, a calm settled over her soul as the humming voice grew near.

Medallion listened, and realized the humming was actually not the same from the nursery. The voice was deeper and more soothing than the one that she feared. As she listened, a light in the dark space began to grow. And as it grew, it began to take on a shape… the soft silhouette shape of a woman. She looked at the tall woman who appeared powerful and mighty. Her shoulders were stern and her chin was strong. The glance in her eyes was all-knowing but there was also a tenderness of a welcomed familiarity. Gradually, the darkness all around the woman faded. And where there was darkness, there was now light, and the light morphed the darkness into a place more inviting.

No longer in the empty darkness, Medallion stood in a place full of trees, and flowers in bloom, and feet tickling green grass. The songs the birds chirped came from the trees that shaded her. People began to appear; walking past her never noticing her or the woman she instinctively began to follow. Then Medallion saw it. In front of them both, stood the home- the Glory Hill Plantation in all its splendor. The woman looked back at Medallion smiling and both stared at each other for a moment as if old friends. The woman held out her hand for Medallion to grab it.

Medallion rested her hand into the woman's and they both began to walk to Glory.

"Bettye…" Medallion said knowing who she was the moment their hands connected.

"Yes, child. I'm here."

"Sunta… she has my baby."

"I knew she would come for him. She wants to bring him back with her."

Bettye led Medallion behind Glory Hill and down the path to the slave quarters. Six of them were standing in a row. As they approached, Medallion could smell the fragrant blooms and hear the brook babbling in the distance. Once they reached them, Bettye walked over to the most run-down shack on the end. As they entered the cabin, the light from the day was no longer. It was now night, and the ghostly women in the little cabin were scurrying around gathering things preparing to go. Without hesitation, Bettye joined them. She smiled no longer but hurried herself to the back room in a panic. Bettye looked over her shoulder towards the other women in the room.

"How far 'long is she?"

"She too early, Bettye. This not the time fo' dis to happen."

Bettye grabbed a cloth before she entered the room. Curious and confused, Medallion walked into the room behind Bettye. There, on the floor, she saw Sunta writhing in pain.

"Bettye, what's going on? What's wrong with her?"

Without taking her eyes from Sunta, Bettye spoke with urgency.

"Don't ask no questions right now. Get the circle started. We have to get her ready to pass."

Medallion looked around and saw the women forming the circle. She pulled herself from the floor and stood between two of the women and grabbed a hand on each side of her. *Sunta is giving birth.* Medallion listened to Bettye guide the woman in their chant and then she saw the baby boy appear as Sunta's life slowly slipped away. Medallion caught a glimpse of the baby with the bluest eyes and coal dark skin wrapped in a bundle.

"Isaiah? Her baby looks like mine..."

"Mary, take dis hea babe and let's get ready to go."

Bettye handed the baby to Mary as the other ladies continued to prepare for the journey. Medallion's eyes darted to the woman holding the baby boy, shocked to see her Aunt standing with them.

"Auntie… Aunt Mary?"

The woman she thought was her aunt swiftly brushed past her with the baby in her arms. Medallion began to follow but Bettye held her back.

"But that's my Aunt Mary. Why is she here?"

"Mary's part of the memory." Bettye stood beside Medallion as the scene grew dark, and now stood under a single light from above.

"But why is she part of Sunta's memory? Why are we back on the plantation? What is this place?"

"Medallion, Sunta is my sister. Mary is our sister. You are a descendent of all of us."

Medallion listened to Bettye confused.

"But why am I looking at Sunta give birth in the slave quarters behind Glory Hill to my baby?"

"Medallion, you know the answer to your own questions. You know there is something special about Mary… That there is something special about Sunta… There is even something special about your son, Isaiah."

Medallion closed her eyes and thought about the picture she saw in the memory box, and the family bible her Aunt always brought out at the family reunions with the names of the women, and Bettye's name was there. And then the spell book... The logic of what Bettye was trying to explain to Medallion suddenly overwhelmed her and she began to cry. The tears rolled down her face as she nodded her head in agreement.

"Yes, I do know. Aunt Mary, she's your sister… Sunta's sister. But how? Why is she *still* here? Why is she still living? How can that be?"

"She's the carrier. She had to protect what's ours that's why. She knew what had to be done to keep our line alive." Bettye raised her hand and pointed a finger at Medallion while she continued. "You were to be next… to take over for Mary because her time to rest will come. But you— you are no longer the one who will do it. You have been passed over."

Medallion began to cry harder remembering all the times her aunt tried to teach her all that she knew. She lowered her head in shame while her shoulders shook while she cried harder.

"She tried to teach me, but I wouldn't let her. I turned what she meant for good into something bad. She warned me. But Sunta… Is she here to take my place?"

"No. Sunta wants the baby who has become a reminder of the child she left behind so long ago. She's ready to take Isaiah back with her as Elijah. But you have to stop her. If she takes him with her, there won't be no one here to carry us on."

"My baby… she can't have him," Medallion said with fire and determination.

"But she will if you don't stop her. He's next in line. He's the one who will keep us among the living. Save him for the sake of our family."

"But how? How am I supposed to do that? I've screwed everything else up."

Medallion went silent as she lamented over her last statement. Bettye quietly watched as Medallion looked towards the ground.

"Look where I am. I'm here… somewhere. Sunta is out there… in my body with my son. She deserves him more than I do." She looked up at Bettye who had a solemn expression of pity on her face. "Can't she just be with him? Let her stay amongst the living and raise Isaiah. I'll just stay here. It's better off like this. I haven't been the best person."

Bettye walked over to Medallion and put her hand on her shoulder.

"It's not supposed to be this way, that's why. Everything has their place in this world. Sunta's time has come and gone. It's your time to live… with your son… to protect him. When your time is up, you will know, and will go peacefully. Sunta has refused. She needs to come back, and this time, she will not have the choice to wait. She will come and take her place with the rest of her sisters."

"I understand, but how do I do that? How do I leave this place so that I can protect him?"

"I'm here to help you do that but promise that you will stop her. If you don't, she will take your son with her back to this place."

Medallion nodded her head in understanding as Bettye placed Medallion's hands into hers. Bettye closed her eyes and bowed her head, and as she did, Medallion felt a transference of warmth growing within her. As she became warmer, Bettye became colder.

Chapter 55

Waymen pulled up to the entrance of Glory Hill as the clock on the car's dashboard digitally blinked *10:00*. The impacted snow covering the roads made the trip to the plantation hard. He hesitantly looked up the driveway knowing under all the snow there were deep ditches that he could potentially slide into. Not only were there ditches to think about, but the long driveway had not yet been shoveled.

Waymen pushed down on the brake stopping the car to think of a way to get them closer to the house without having to get out and walk the long driveway to the front door. Mary saw on Waymen's face that he was trying to figure out the best way to get them there.

"Waymen, we'll have to walk it if we want to make it there in time."

He looked at Aunt Mary, and then at Nurse Jackie in bewilderment.

"How are you two going to make it and Ms. Jackie can barely walk?"

"My bones are old but my will is strong," Nurse Jackie spoke with a determined look on her face as she stared up the snow-filled driveway. "I'll make it up there if it's the last thing I do."

Realizing that he wasn't going to be able to talk them out of walking, he put the car in park and turned the ignition off.

"Alright ladies… I hope you have on your heaviest coats because it's cold out there, and we have a long way to walk."

"Don't worry about us. We are going to be fine. Let's just hurry. We don't have any more time to waste if we want to save Isaiah and Medda."

Waymen nodded in agreement as the three of them opened the car door. He looked up the driveway's path one more time; estimating the distance from the car to the house. *This is going to take about 20 minutes to make it to the front door. I could make it there faster if I were by myself…* Waymen helped the women out of the car while trying to figure out the most efficient way for them all to make it to the house.

"Waymen, you need to get there before we do. We've already wasted too much time and waiting on two old ladies is just going to make it worse. Hurry up the way, and we'll meet you there."

"Are you sure about this? I mean, I don't think it would take us that long to get up there if I help you."

He watched as Nurse Jackie steadied herself on Mary. The two woman positioned themselves so that Mary supported most of Nurse Jackie's weight while both stood upright.

"We are going to be fine. Now, hurry along. We'll meet you there soon."

He nodded his head in obligement and with a swift pace, began his way up the path. Aunt Mary and Nurse Jackie slowly began their trek up the driveway as well.

"Mary, do you think we will be there in time?"

"I sure hope we do. We've come this far. It'd be a shame if we didn't."

The two ladies walked a bit in silence with only the crunch sound of the fallen snow under their feet before the nurse spoke again.

"So, Sunta's your sister?"

"Yes… the baby of us seven."

"But why? Why is she back?"

"She never left." Mary reflected quietly on her words and finally admitted what she'd known all along. "We never knew if that Chant of Forever would work just right or not but we had to try. We had to save the baby or they both would have been lost to us. The only thing we could do was take a chance."

Chapter 56

Sunta continued to prepare the room for Isaiah's final ceremony. There wasn't much time before the appointed hour, but not only that, Medallion's body didn't feel as she expected. Two souls could never occupy a human vessel, and Medallion was still there within. Soon, Sunta wouldn't be strong enough to keep her restrained and she would lose her opportunity to take Isaiah with her.

Sunta stepped out of the dining room which was filled with lit candles. For the ritual, she had removed all the chairs around the table and decorated the top of it with straw she'd broken from the broom, and a white cloth dipped and dried in a white chalky paste she made sat on top of the straw. Hung from the chandelier were bags of sage and peppermint to ward off any spirits that may try to enter as they left the living. The pot of broth they would both drink right before the good death sat across from where the cloth and straw were. And as she walked out of the room, on the floor by the door, Sunta drew the chalked line that served as the boundary that death could not cross.

In the distance, she heard Isaiah coo from his upstairs bedroom. As she turned towards the staircase, her vision blurred and the feeling of nausea overcame her; bringing her to her knees. The room began to spin, and the flesh she inhabited began to burn as if a fire was ignited from within. Sunta let out a screech that burned her throat, and as she opened her mouth in pain, her soul was set free.

Medallion opened her eyes to see Sunta in front of her. Exhausted, she picked herself up from the floor and was now standing in front of Sunta.

"You will not have my baby. He is mine to protect. He will not go with you. He will stay with me on this earth to be the keeper of our family."

"You don't love him. I'm his mama. He belong wit' me and only me! I let him go once, but not never again!"

With her hands stretched in front of her, Sunta lunged for Medallion and grabbed her around the neck.

"If I got ta kill you for my baby I will!"

Medallion moved out of the way as Sunta lunged; giving her an opportunity to head for the staircase. Medallion heard Sunta thump to the ground having missed her opportunity to apprehend her.

Running towards the baby's room, Medallion could hear Sunta running up the stairways behind her. *I need to reach Isaiah before she stops me. If she gets him before I do, I won't have a chance.*

As Medallion was about to rush into the nursery, Sunta grabbed her by the length of her ponytail and yanked her back out. Medallion let out a loud scream as she fell backwards onto the floor.

Sunta leaped over Medallion and hurriedly made her way to Isaiah now screaming loudly in his crib. She picked him up, prepared to run back into the hall, but Medallion stood in front of her; blocking Sunta's way out.

"You'll have to go through me to get out of this room with my child."

"Well if that's what I have to do…"

Sunta reached out her arm with the palm of her hand facing Medallion. A shot of forceful light appeared from it and headed directly to Medallion.

Medallion's eyes widened as the beam of light hit her right in her chest; knocking her into the hallway and over the banister. Sunta rushed out of the room and saw Medallion dangling from the railing for dear life. Sunta quickly ran down the stairway and back into the dining room. She placed Isaiah on the white cloth laying on the dining room table that covered the straw underneath it.

Out of breath, she looked out the window in a panic in hopes that the moon was aligned just right to begin the ceremony. *Almost time.* She went back to the staircase to see if Medallion was still there, but to her surprise she wasn't. Worried, she went back to the dining room, and there stood Medallion with Isaiah in her arms.

"You will not take him!"

Medallion braced Isaiah closer to her chest as she glared at Sunta; determined to win against her.

Angered, Sunta charged the room but was slammed backwards into the hall. She writhed to the floor in agony and shock.

"You have some magic, well so do I!" Medallion yelled from the candle lit dining room. "You will not have my baby!"

When Medallion was trapped inside of herself, Bettye engraved the knowledge of the ancestors on her knowing Medallion would need more than just physical strength to defeat her sister. Looking around the dining room, Medallion quickly found the sage brush and the bowl of broth that Sunta planned to use when performing the good death on Isaiah.

Waymen looked up at Glory and noticed how dark and cold it appeared. As he continued up the path, in a window on the east wing, he saw a flicker of light and a shadow of someone walk past. *I pray that it's Medallion and she's okay. Even though she was wrong, neither she nor the baby deserve this. She is still my wife, and I took vows to love, respect, honor, and protect her until death do us part. I have to do my best to do that.* Reaching the front door of Glory, he slowly turned the knob finding it unlocked, and Waymen stepped in.

***

Glory didn't feel as welcoming to Waymen as he was use to. The cold weather outside, and the unknown within its walls removed the happy feeling he always felt when entering the corridor. The dark of the room along with the remodeling made it difficult for Waymen to maneuver his way through the house. He tried his best to quiet himself as he walked slowly from room to room; peeking through doors and around corners.

"You will not take him!"

Waymen went into alert when hearing Medallion yell out from the east wing of the house. Then, he heard the thud of someone hit the floor. Without hesitation, he made his way to where he heard Medallion hoping he wasn't too late.

Chapter 57

Medallion!" Waymen breathily said seeing her standing in the dining room with the baby in her arms.

"Waymen!" She put Isaiah down and made her way over to him. She placed her arms around his neck as he pulled her into his embrace.

"I heard the noise and thought something had happened to you. Are you okay? Where is she? Did she hurt you?"

"Oh my God. Waymen!" She peered around him to the wall she struck Sunta against and was shocked to see she'd vanished. "Sunta! She's not there."

He looked behind him seeing the empty wall.

"Where could she have gone? I came as soon as I heard."

They both looked around panicked neither seeing a trace of her.

"Medallion, go get Isaiah. We have to get out of here and fast."

Medallion agreed then rushed to gather up Isaiah. When she turned back around to head out of the dining room, there stood Sunta with Waymen under a serious trance. His eyes were in the back of his head with the whites of them shining bright.

"Waymen..." Medallion spoke under her breath. "Let him go! He's not yours!"

"I don't want him. You have what's mine and I'm ready to trade."

She clutched Isaiah tightly knowing she could only make one choice.

She frantically shook her head in defiance while stifling her tears.

"No. You cannot have Isaiah. He has to stay here... with me... with his family... our family. *OUR* family." Medallion began to walk slowly towards Sunta while she continued to plead with her.

"Sunta... you and I... We are family. We... Isaiah and I, are direct descendants of you. He has to stay here so that our family can continue to grow."

Standing face to face with Medallion, Sunta looked from her to Isaiah. Her baby's face, but it wasn't him. It wasn't her sweet baby boy she held before she took her last breath.

"I just want my baby. I've waited for him for so long, and he's not here," She said in a whimpered tone.

"Let Waymen go. Let us go. Let Bettye help you pass through so you can finally rest."

"Bettye... My sister..." Sunta looked up from Isaiah and then at Medallion.

"She's waiting for you."

Sunta smiled remembering her family.

"I thought they forgot about me. Did she have my baby boy?"

Medallion shook her head, "No".

"She didn't say. But she's waiting on you, and she can help you fi—"

Sunta grew angry listening to Medallion's excuse about the baby the sisters swore to protect.

"I told her to watch over him, and don't let nothing happen to him! He's not with them?! I can't leave here without him!"

Sunta glanced at the clock on the wall, and then snatched Isaiah from Medallion's arms. Before Medallion could realize what happened, Sunta and the baby disappeared. The spell Waymen was under let him go and he fell to the floor unconscious.

Medallion looked all around but couldn't see where Sunta had gone. *Where did she go? She* ran towards the dining room hoping to see them there, but the room was empty.

"Medallion!" Aunt Mary said in exhausted relief. "I thought I'd never see you again!"

Medallion ran towards Mary surprised to see her there. She wrapped her arms around her; relieved that help had come.

"Aunt Mary... I'm so glad to see you. Sunta... she has Isaiah, but I don't know where."

Medallion began to sob. Aunt Mary rubbed her back to console her.

"There, there child. All is not lost. There's still hope and there's still time."

"It's all my fault, Auntie. I should have listened to you. All those times you warned me I should have listened!"

Mary pulled Medallion away from her; holding Medallion's shoulder's as she spoke.

"No need to cry about those things now. What's done is done, and all we can do is right the wrongs. Stay focused now. We have to get Isaiah and send Sunta back."

Mary looked over her shoulder at Nurse Jackie who sat on the bench by the front door.

"Look over there." Aunt Mary smiled at Nurse Jackie. "I bought us some extra help. I knew we couldn't do this without her."

Nurse Jackie smiled and nodded a greeting towards Medallion. Medallion smiled back and mouthed "thank you" as her eyes showed her gratefulness.

Chapter 58

"Waymen. Wake up, Waymen." Medallion lightly tapped him on his cheek as he began to arouse. "Waymen. Wake up, baby. You've got to get out of here. It's not safe for you to be here."

"Wha— where am I?" Waymen slowly opened his eyes and slid himself up from lying on the floor to a seated position. "What happened?"

"Waymen, I need you to leave. It's not safe. Sunta might try to harm you again, so I need you to go."

"Sunta? Who is Sun—" Waymen finally realized what happened. His expression grew angry; thinking of how Sunta had terrorized his family. "Sunta. Where is she?"

"We don't know. Aunt Mary's here and we're trying to figure it out, but you have to go."

"No. I'm not leaving here without you and Isaiah."

He stood up and then helped Medallion from the floor.

"You have to, Waymen. She's strong, and she's getting stronger as it grows time for her to leave. We can protect ourselves from her because of our craft, but you'll be vulnerable. We need all our energy and skill to get Isaiah. We can't afford to keep you both safe. It'll be better if you leave now."

"But Medallion, I want to help."

"I know you do." She smiled at him. At that moment she felt so grateful that even after all she'd done to him, he still wanted to protect her. "But you have to go."

"But I—"

"No, Waymen. Go. For once, let me do right by you. Let me protect you. I can't do that if you're here."

Medallion pulled him in for a kiss. He accepted and they held each other in a tender embrace; both remembering how much they truly loved each other.

"Waymen, leave out the back door and go to the barn and wait for me there."

Waymen made his way to the front door but with the door knob in his hand he hesitated to leave. Slowly, he looked back at Medallion and smiled at her proudly.

"I love you, Medallion."

She took in his words and let a tear roll from her eye. She blew him a kiss and fluttered her fingers in a goodbye.

"I love you too. Way-Bae"

He closed the door behind him as he walked out of the house. The room fell quiet once Waymen left. Medallion looked towards her Aunt and Nurse Jackie. Neither looked weary. Instead, they were ready for a fight. Nurse Jackie stood up from the chair and without a word, slowly began to make her way to the dining room. Mary turned and followed. She looked over her shoulder at Medallion and said, "Now, my sweet girl. It's time to get your baby back."

Chapter 59

The three ladies gathered in the dining room. Mary picked up the ornate knife that was prepared and blessed for Isaiah's sacrifice. The blade was shiny and plain to the normal eye, but the eye of an Aje like her could see the blessing had already been inscribed when she rotated it in her hand. Mary closed her eyes and waved her hovered hand over the knife. The heat that expelled from it warmed her palm indicating it was almost time for the ritual.

"Jackie, erase the chalk-line from the room's entry. Sunta will need to return to this place soon and this is where we shall capture her. The knife is ready for Isaiah. This sacrifice is the only way she can take him back with her."

Nurse Jackie walked back to the door and erased the line of protection with her hand.

"But where is she now?" Medallion's eyes darted all over the room wondering where Sunta would appear.

"She's near. She can't hide in her spirit form for long. She'll need that energy to pass through. But we are not going to wait for her. We are going to bring her to us."

"What was that? Did you hear that?" Medallion jumped in surprise and rushed out of the dining room."

"Hear what Medallion?" Mary hurried to the dining room entrance to see where Medallion ran off to.

"The baby's cry! I just heard Isaiah! He's upstairs!" Medallion ran down the hall towards the back stairs.

"Medallion! He's not there! Come back in here!"

"Auntie! He is! I can hear him!"

Mary made her way to Medallion who stood at the bottom of the steps straining to hear the faint cry once more.

"He's not there, Medallion. He's not upstairs. He's with Sunta. She hasn't let him go. What you are hearing are his echoes while in cosmic space parallel to us. Come back to the dining room. He'll be here soon."

Mary gently took Medallion by the shoulders and led her back to the ritual area.

"I've prepared the table. It's very close to the hour." Nurse Jackie said when she saw them both enter.

"Medallion," Mary used her index finger to guide Medallion's chin up to where their eyes could meet. "This is going to be a hard task. We have to get Sunta here so we can send her back. You'll need to concentrate on helping us send her away. You've never used the little bit of skills I taught you. Tonight is your test. Do exactly as I say and you will have your son."

"Auntie... I'm scared. Can't you and Nurse Jackie handle this by yourself? Up until this moment, I've only screwed things up."

"Don't think about what you should have done. Think about what you need to do." Mary said in a stern voice. "You have got to make it right and bring this baby back. Jackie and I are powerful together. And we could probably do this ourselves, but it will be a struggle, and we are too old to fight Sunta. We need your love for your baby— for Waymen and Isaiah to help us drive her from this place."

With Mary's words of encouragement, she dried her tears with the back of her hand ready for the task at hand.

"Okay. I'm ready. Tell me what I need to do."

Chapter 60

Mary finished making a triangle on the floor around the table out of the ashes that the ceremonial candle had burned. She then took her place in the corner part of the triangle she just created.

"Alright ladies, please stand in the corners of this triangle. Medallion, you stand at the top of it. He will need to see you so he'll know he is loved by you. Jackie, you take the other corner across from me. We will send our energy to Medallion when the time is needed."

Both ladies got in position in their corners of the triangle.

"Now, kneel to your knees and raise your hands high to the sky. Breathe in deeply and let's quiet our hearts as we summon the ancestors and spirits that still dwell on this land."

Both Medallion and Jackie did as instructed while Mary continued her directive.

"Think only of the sweet baby, Isaiah. He will carry on our legacy. He will grow to be a strong man. Stronger than any of his forefathers!"

Medallion envisioned her son in her arms being cradled by him. Then flashes of his future began to come. She saw him… there at Glory. Tall. Handsome. His children... there were four... all girls, and his wife was by his side. Medallion smiled at the thought. *The strongest of us all. Bettye was right.* She began to feel the strength of his inherited powers, and she knew he would use them for good— unlike she'd done.

The curtains rustled and danced as the air in the room began to move. The flames on the candles swayed slowly following the direction of the breeze.

"They are coming. The ancestors are gathering. Let us give thanks to them for carrying the burden so that we did not have to."

With her hands still high, Mary began a slow chant that Jackie and Medallion both joined in on.

The candle lights dimmed as the room began to vibrate. Isaiah's sweet cry became louder as a bright light pierced the atmosphere in the room. Medallion gasped as she saw Sunta step through the lighted opening with Isaiah in her hands.

"My baby!" Medallion gasped, and without hesitation she leaped at Sunta grabbing the sacred knife while charging her.

"Medallion, wait! No!"

Mary reached out to pull Medallion back from Sunta. The energy the summons caused was very strong. As Mary watched Medallion lunge for Sunta, she feared what could possibly go wrong.

"Mary! The energy! It's too powerful!" Jackie looked on as she saw Medallion make a desperate attempt for her child.

Medallion reached into the glowing energy emitting from Sunta and Isaiah. She wrapped her arms around both and they all crashed into the dining room wall and then fell to the floor, breaking the stream of light they had created to bring Sunta into their space. Mary quickly acted by grabbing Isaiah out of harm's way.

"Jackie, take him away from here. There is much more that needs to be done. He can't be a part of this." Jackie nodded in agreement and hobbled her way out of the room and out of sight.

Mary turned around and looked on as Medallion struggled with Sunta. The energy that was used to make Sunta reappear with Isaiah made the spirit even stronger. Mary saw that she had mortal and immortal powers, but to her surprise, so did Medallion.

Anger fueled Medallion's advance on Sunta. With the sacred knife in her hand she knew it would be the perfect opportunity to send Sunta back from whence she came. Medallion's attack landed her directly on Sunta where she straddled her waist. She held the knife above her head and pointed it down and directly at Sunta's heart.

"This time when you die, you will not be coming back!"

Guided by Medallion's hand, the knife swiftly came down headed for Sunta's chest, but Sunta raised her hands in enough time creating a light that was so bright, it blinded Medallion; knocking her off balance. Medallion shielded her eyes. Sunta used that opportunity to knock the knife from her hand and then pushed Medallion off her.

"I'm not going back without my baby!"

Sunta hurried towards Medallion with the knife in her hand.

"Sunta! No!" Mary screamed out as she watched Sunta plunge the knife into her beloved niece. Mary ran over to them and fell to her knees as Medallion's blood poured out of her chest. Medallion's eyes staring blankly at Mary went lifeless as she began to slip away.

Chapter 61

Sunta turned away from Medallion slowly and looked at Mary inquisitively.

"Sissy... how did you... I mean, what you doin' hea?" Overjoyed to see Mary, Sunta tried to hug her but Mary pushes her away and begins crying

Sunta's lip quivered and her eyes filled with tears. She saw Mary bent over Medallion trying to push the blood back into her body.

"Why you crying for dis woman? Why you sad fha huh?"

"Because... I love her. And I tried so hard to help her see what she had was worth cherishing. But it's too late."

Sunta shook her head in denial.

"Nah-ah sissy. We can save her. You got the power. You saved me that time... remember? Remember... Elijah? Me and him here together now."

"No, Sunta. Not Elijah. Isaiah. Your baby is Elijah, and he's not here."

"No. My baby IS Isaiah. My baby alive!"

Mary turned her head sharply and looked at her sister with anger and fire in her eyes.

"Listen to me. Your baby is gone. Elijah is gone! Isaiah is here! He's not your son! He belonged with her! With Medallion! She was to teach him! She was to pass to him our story... our heritage... our legacy!"

Sunta looked at her astonished. "But he look like my baby! He look like me!"

"Because in some ways he is you, Sunta, but in most ways he is not."

"But—"

"I raised your boy many, many moons ago. He was the best out of all. He grew into a handsome young man and raised a family of his own, who had children of their own..."

Mary looked over at Medallion. Her body was still. No life. She touched her softly, and felt how the heat from it was slowly leaving her. *Her spirit will be here soon. Time to prepare...*

"Which gave birth to her."

Mary raised herself from the floor and made her way to the table to clear it off. Sunta did not move from beside Medallion. She continued to look at her curiously at first but then with recognition.

"Sissy... she belong to me too? She kin?"

"Yes, Sunta. She is Elijah's great, great granddaughter. Bring her to the table. We have to get her ready. My weary old bones can't carry them like I use to."

"Whatchu mean? Dis here child is mine?" Sunta looked from Medallion's body and back at Mary in shock.

"Yes. She's a part of you… and so is Isaiah. That's probably what you've been seeing in him all this time... you. Now, bring her over here and place her on this table. It's getting late."

Sunta took one more long stare at Medallion. With the peace of death on Medallion's face, Sunta began to see her for who she truly was. The softness around her lips was that of her beloved Bettye. The shape of her closed eyes were Jendi's.

"I didn't see it before... She is all of us." Sunta bent down and kissed Medallion on the cheek. "I'm so sorry I did this to you daughter."

Tears of regret swelled in her eyes.

"Please forgive me for hurting you."

She lifted Medallion from the floor and gently placed her on the table.

"Go on and get ready. They coming for you too."

"Who coming?"

"The sisters. They coming to guide you back and take Medallion on."

"No. I'm not going back there."

"Sunta, you can't stay here. Your powers are almost gone. If you don't go back with our sisters, you'll be stuck in this world only to haunt it… never to return to the afterworld."

"No, Mary. I can't go back to The White Place. You can't make me. I'll stay here and haunt it if I have to, but I don't want to go back there!"

Sympathetic, Mary patted Sunta's hand as she watched her weep with fear of returning.

"Sunta, you were only there because you didn't know how to let go. This time, when the sisters come, let go of this place. Leave with them and never want to return. On the other side, everything you seek will be there."

"But why didn't they come for me the last time? Why didn't the ancestors meet me?"

"I don't know, Sunta. We were young. We were inexperienced. We were on the run. We may not have performed the ceremony correctly. But this time, we will not let that happen."

"My word... what has happened?" Nurse Jackie peeked her head into the dining room and saw Medallion laid out on the table. "Is she...dead?"

"Sadly, yes. You're just in time to help us prepare her for her departure. Sunta's leaving too."

Sunta nodded her head slowly in agreement.

"I believe I'm ready. There's nothing for me here. What I want is long gone."

Sunta looked over at Isaiah sleep in Nurse Jackie's arms.

"I wanted Isaiah to be Elijah so bad. I never saw that he wasn't. He don't belong to me, and now I must go and meet my son on the other side." The room fell quiet as the all wept in mourning for the loss of Medallion when a small creak of the floorboard made them all turn their attention to the dining room's entrance.

"Medallion..."

Waymen walked slowly into the room astonished to see his wife. Her body lifeless. Eyes closed. Hands clasped together over her abdomen.

As soon as she heard him utter Medallion's name, Mary bowed her head in sorrow.

"Waymen, I didn't want you to find out this way."

"I went to the barn like she told me. I saw a flash of a bright light come from the house and knew something was wrong. I came as fast as I could. Am I too late? Is she going to be okay?"

"She's gone, Waymen. But I can say she finally figured out how to put someone else first. She fought for the both of you."

The impact of Mary's words brought tears to his eyes. Waymen walked over to Medallion and laid a hand on hers.

"I can't believe she's gone. She told me she loved me and that everything was going to be alright. I— can't... I can't go on if she's not with me."

Waymen's tears began to flow freely; landing on Medallion's forehead as he delicately kissed her cheek.

"It'll be okay, Waymen." Mary patted him on the back while guiding him away from the body. "She'll need you one more time. You'll have to help her transition— help her let go of this world and pass to the other without any feelings of unfinished business. When her spiritual body awakens and it sees you, she will know it's okay to go."

"Why did this have to happen?"

Waymen pondered his question, and then out of the corner of his eye, he caught a glimpse of Sunta.

"It was you." The anger within him began to build as Sunta came into full view. "You came here and ruined everything! You took her away from me! You took her away from her son!"

"Now Waymen… she didn't know. What's done has been done. We can only prepare for the passing."

With his fist balled, he quickly turned away from Sunta; hiding the anger that began to spill out.

Chapter 62

"Let us all quiet our hearts as the hour is now upon us." The room was quiet as they all stood around the table holding Medallion's body. "Jackie, place Isaiah by his mother."

Jackie carefully laid the sleeping Isaiah by Medallion, and then stepped back to her spot around the table.

"Now, Waymen, place your hand over her heart. She loved you with all of it even though she didn't always show it. Jackie and I will hold one of her hands as we were her counsel and guided her as best we could."

"What you want me to do, Sissy?"

"Her spirit will soon come. You will be able to welcome her when it appears."

"And little Isaiah. He lays beside her, as she will be his protector as he journeys through this life. When her spirit comes, she will see him and know she will guard him because he belongs to her." Mary bowed her head. "Now we call the ancestors. They will usher both Medallion and Sunta to the afterlife never to return to this world because they are both at peace."

Mary fell silent. She raced through her memories and found her sisters. It was their last happy time together. It was a warm summer evening. They sat on the porch of the cabin at the end of the work day imagining what it would be like to be free and off of the plantation.

Chapter 63

"We gon' be free come soon. Just 'nother couple of days and our days on Glory Hill will be just a memory."

"You right, Gloria. And my baby gone be born free. He ain't gone never know what it feels like to be a slave. He only gon' know what it feels like to be a free man!" Sunta proudly rubbed her belly at the thought of freedom for her child.

"How you so sure it's a boy?"

"I don't know fo' sho. But every time I call 'em a boy my feet tingle so I think he trying to tell me he a boy."

The sisters continued to watch the fireflies flicker over the lake while the cicadas' song filled the air. The warm summer breeze was comforting. Bettye finally came out of the house and joined the five younger sisters on the porch.

"Bettye, where is Sissy? I haven't seen her all day."

"She been busy, Sunta."

"Doing what? Master ain't give her a day off from the fields. She not in trouble is she?"

"Nah… she been busy but look over yonder. She coming on up the path now."

Mary approached the cabin and smiled fondly at her sisters.

"Mary, you just in time. I was just asking about you. Come here and lay your hand on my belly. The baby kicking. Must know you here."

Mary gladly placed her palm on Sunta's stomach and felt the little flutter of the baby's kick.

"That feel beautiful, Sunta. That's a strong one. Won't be long before we get to see his little face."

"Yes ma'am. Won't be long at all."

Mary removed her hand and stood in front of her sisters once more.

"My sisters. I have gone on a journey and I need your help."

"What journey you been on all day?"

"Hush, Alice. Let Mary finish fo' you go asking questions."

"I done crossed over to help out some of our own kin. This been a tough one, but we have to help their spirit pass on."

"I know all about it, Mary. I guided Medda back to save Isaiah."

"Yes. And she did a good job. But with all that went on, she was able to help Isaiah but she wasn't able to save herself. So now, she coming over to sit on this porch with us so she needs our help crossing."

"We have to go meet her?"

"Yes, Jendi. Listen closely. You can hear them calling for us now."

The sisters could faintly hear the sound of the prayers Waymen, Jackie, and Mary recited requesting they come. One by one, they got up from the porch and made their way to the big willow tree at the back of the cabin by the lake.

Sunta was the last to get up. As she began to pass her, Mary grabbed her hand and squeezed it.

"Sunta, you stay here and rest. You already doing your part."

"You sure? I may be carrying this baby, but I'm strong enough to help."

"Yes. I'm sure. You already doing your part. You stay here and enjoy watching them lightening bugs scoot 'cross the sky. We'll be back real soon."

"Alright now. I'll sit here if that's what you want."

Chapter 64

She laid on the table in silence. She saw them all standing over her as if watching for something to happen to her. She felt them touching her affectionately. Waymen's hand was on her heart. Aunt Mary and Nurse Jackie were each holding one of her hands. Isaiah was laying by her side. Each one was there because they loved her. Their touch reminded her of their love. She wanted to reach out and touch them back, but she was trapped inside of herself.

"Medallion… it's time to go," She heard her Aunt Mary say.

"Leave this body and join with the others who have crossed before you."

Instinctively, Medallion raised her arms with her hands high making her way out of her physical self.

***

"Join your Egungun. You have transcended as designed." As Mary spoke the words, she saw Medallion's spirit rise from her body. A yellow glow surrounded her essence. The glow finally dimmed, and her soul came into view. Medallion pleasantly looked down on them.

"Medallion..." Waymen looked up and said through tears. Medallion looked at him as he spoke. "It's okay for you to go. I forgive you. I will take care of Isaiah. He is our son."

Medallion listened without saying a word allowing her warm smile to confirm his guardianship.

"Be at peace, Medallion. I will teach him our history. He has been chosen to take your place in line to carry our legacy. He will be strong and can carry on our family. He will inherit all that is ours. He will be great."

Medallion slowly turned to her Aunt; acknowledging her words of confirmation.

"Medallion, it is time for you to leave this place. Sunta, your great, great, great grandmother will go with you. You will take your place with my sisters. You will protect Isaiah... watch over him as he grows. Your earthly job is done, and your spiritual job has just begun."

"Look..."

Nurse Jackie called their attention to the window looking out to the great willow tree. Walking across the snow-covered grass, the sisters made their way to the house.

"They're here," Mary said to both Sunta and Medallion.

They all watched the sisters walk up to the window where they stopped and waited patiently.

"My sisters. They here. They finally came fo' me. I nevah thought I see the day they would come."

"Sunta, take Medallion with you to join them. They will lead you to your baby. It's time."

"Okay Sissy. I'm ready."

Sunta closed her eyes and began to fade away, and then reappeared beside Medallion. She took Medallion's hand; both women joining the sisters outside of the window. Reunited, they walked back to the great willow disappearing in a mist.

Chapter 65

Mary sat on the porch swing of her small cottage tucked away in a quiet neighborhood in the city of Richmond. The spring air was full of the smell of blooming flowers and the sounds of chirping birds. It was a quiet afternoon which had become a part of her peaceful day. Closing her eyes as the spring breeze brushed across her face, the faint aroma of lavender wisped like a blessing being kissed on her cheek as a thank you for a job well done for all that she'd endured. *Medallion…* She thought to herself. A slight smile curled her lips reminding her Medallion was gone but not forgotten. Hearing a car door slam, Mary opened her eyes once again ready to greet her company.

"Hey Auntie!" Waymen waved to Mary as he opened the back door to his car. "We're here for lunch and a lesson."

Mary smiled brightly when Waymen opened the back door and Isaiah popped out.

"Isaiah, my dear! You made it!"

"Hi, Auntie!"

Isaiah ran up the sidewalk and onto the porch. He stretched his arms out wide and then wrapping them around her neck. He gave her a big kiss and then sat on the porch beside her.

"Why, Isaiah! It's so good to see you. It's been such a long time. Stand up. Let me look at you"

Isaiah jumped off the porch and proudly stood in front of Mary showcasing how big he'd gotten.

"Auntie, look how tall I am!"

"Yes, Isaiah. For a four year old, you are a big boy. Auntie is so proud of how much you've grown since the last time I saw you. Now, help your dear old Auntie off this porch and let's go make lunch."

Mary grabbed his hand as she stood from the porch.

"It's good to see you Aunt Mary. You are looking well as always." Waymen gave Mary a hug as they all made their way into the house.

"It's been a long time. How are you two doing? Here, have a seat at the counter. I've made your favorite today."

"We've been doing great. The new job in California has been a challenge but being the President of a new division is never dull. Always something going on. We would have visited earlier this year, but work has kept me very busy. However, we would never miss today."

"I knew you wouldn't. After all, it is her birthday."

"Yes, it's been four years since that night. So much has changed— like me starting to feel my age." Mary rubbed the back of her neck in between preparing lunch.

"Are you okay, Auntie?"

"Yes, baby. Auntie's fine. Just getting a little tired these days. I truly believe a part of me left with Medallion and Sunta that night. The time is finally going to come when it's time for me to move on."

"Auntie, don't talk like that. You're going to be with us for a long time."

"Chile, I've already been here for a long while now." Mary let out a little chuckle slightly elated that the day would finally come for her to rest. "I've seen a lot, Waymen. I don't know when I'll go, but when I do, I'll be ready."

"I understand, Auntie. You have done a great job keeping the traditions and the family alive. When the time comes, I know you'll be ready."

"But not before I teach this young man everything I know."

Mary looked over at Isaiah who was sitting on the floor across the room coloring.

"He's so special. And he picks up the lessons so fast. With the FaceTime and Skype sessions in between our visits he's moving right along."

"He has been moving quickly through your lessons. He loves the little things you teach him, and he's taken up an interest in nature— bugs, insects, all those things. I know little boys are supposed to love that stuff, but he just has a true bond with the outside."

"Well he should. The natural energy that connects us to nature... the air... the ground... the sea is within us all. We have the power to change and manipulate everything around us. The average person doesn't understand it and can't harness their own power let alone connect it to the power of the natural elements. But Isaiah... He understands without understanding. He will always be in tune and it's going to be amazing to see." Mary let out another chuckle. "What he's learning now, he's going to need when he grows up. I've already seen what the world is going to look like when he's of age and I'm no longer here but that's another conversation for another time."

With understanding that the future was not for Aunt Mary to tell, he didn't ask follow-up questions of what's in store for his son. What he already knew was Isaiah's future was bright and there was no need to worry. He followed Mary out the kitchen to help her set the table.

"Medallion would have loved to see him growing up. I'm sure she would have been an excellent mother." Waymen lamented as he placed the plates and the utensils onto the table.

"Maybe, but that wasn't her charge. She is going to keep him safe from above with a little help from my sisters."

Pouring the last cup of juice, Waymen and Mary sat at the table.

"Isaiah, come join us for lunch."

"Okay Auntie!" Isaiah put his crayons away and made his way to the table for his favorite meal.

Acknowledgements

I started writing the concept of this story in 2013. In the middle of 2016, I assumed I'd written my last word on this project but it felt incomplete... like there was a story element lacking. What I didn't know then but know now is that 2013 to 2020 were my years of transition and growth. This novel went through those changes with me. As I come to the close of this exciting story of heritage and love… which had me searching for answers to unresolved story plots within this book and my life, I am settled and ready for my next chapter… and a new story to write.

A special shout out goes to my mom. Since this story's inception, mommy has believed in this book and has repeatedly called it "her story". Not because there is any resemblance of her life, but it reminds her of a story she would read. I've run every idea in this novel by her and if it didn't have her approval, it didn't make it in the book. Thanks Ma. Thank you, thank you.

To Ari, my writing partner, the homegirl, the sister, the cousin, the motivation. You have and will always be a great source for everything. Thank you for keeping me focused.

Thank you to my husband. 20 plus years of love and friendship is something I cherish. Our bond and your insight will forever be my muse. We make a great team. I love you.

To the rest of my family and friends who supported me through the writing of this novel, I thank you.

With love,

Adenike.

ade_b_lu@outlook.com

ade_b_lu

CPSIA information can be obtained
at www.ICGtesting.com
Printed in the USA
LVHW030157090620
657618LV00014B/1266

9 780989 522335